Other books of fiction by William Cobb

A Walk Through Fire (novel)
Somewhere in All This Green (story collection)
Coming of Age at the Y (novel)
A Spring of Souls (novel)
Wings of Morning (novel)
Harry Reunited (novel)

The Hermit King
and
Other Stories

by
William Cobb

Livingston Press
at
The University of West Alabama

Copyright © 2005 William Cobb
All rights reserved, including electronic text
ISBN 1-931982-65-1, library binding
ISBN 1-931982-66-X, trade paper
isbn 13 978-1931982-66-5 trade paper
isbn 13 978-1931982-65-8, lib. bind.
Library of Congress Control Number 2005904657
Printed on acid-free paper.
Printed in the United States of America,
Publishers Graphics
Hardcover binding by: Heckman Bindery

Acknowledgments
The Best of It....*Thicket*
Brother Bobby's Eye....*Shenandoah*
Passin Side/Suicide....*Alabama Literary Review*
Walking Strawberry....*Southern Humanities Review*
Birmingham: Mother's Day 1961, appears here for the first time.

Typing: Jason Blackmon, Larry Cowan, Chris Hawkins,
Pat Burchfield
Typesetting and page layout: David E. Smith
Proofreading: Margaret Walburn, Chris Hawkins

Cover design: Jennifer Brown
Cover Layout: Jennifer Brown
Cover photo: Pat Burchfield

This is a work of fiction.
Surely you know the rest: any resemblance
to persons living or dead is coincidental.

Livingston Press is part of The University of West Alabama,
and thereby has non-profit status.
Donations are tax-deductible:
brothers and sisters, we need 'em.

first edition
6 5 4 3 3 2 1

Table of Contents

Foreword, Bert Hitchcock   *vi*

The Hermit King   *1*

The Best of It   *131*

Birmingham: Mother's Day 1961   *145*

Brother Bobby's Eye   *156*

Passin Side/ Suicide   *168*

Walking Strawberrry   *179*

Foreword

Once upon a past time, when I was a new parent and long before I got to be grandparental age, a cross-stitch pillow propped on the bed of my parents-in-law fixed itself in my memory. "Grandchildren," said its yellow letters on a green background, "are the treasures of a long life."

Anyone who has heard William Cobb talk about these particular living treasures in his life cannot doubt the pride and joy of his experience along this line. Now, with the reissuing of his novel The Hermit King (slightly revised) along with the publication of five new short stories of his in a single volume, I find myself (as may he) thinking literary grandparentage. I muse the joys and satisfactions of creativeness, reflect on the relentless passage of time, consider the facts of "age" and "generation" for all us living creatures, including writers.

As we all get old[er], there is bad news and there is good news. The ample not-good I will leave for delivery by physicians and pharmacists, ophth-almologists, audiologists, and other like tribes, and instead, for you and me, now, concentrate on good news. Actually there is a good bit of good news—for some writers, a great bit. Skill and craftsmanship are, in fact, likely to grow over a growing number of years and practice. And, not unrelated perhaps but more essential, the experiencing of more and more life offers promising potential if not sure prospect of increased insight into the human condition, maybe even some understanding or comprehension of it. Maybe even—who knows ?—wisdom?

William Cobb has authored seven books of fiction, not counting this present volume or his writings for the stage. His first novel, Coming of Age at the Y (remember this title), appeared in 1984 and was followed two years later by The Hermit King. The next decade saw publication of A Walk Through Fire (1992), Harry Reunited (1995), and Spring of Souls (1999). His single twenty-first century novel (so far) is Wings of Morning (2001). A collection of short fiction, Somewhere in All This Green: New and Collected Stories (1998), is retrospective of a talent in this form that was first evidenced when Cobb's "The Stone Soldier" was the Reader's Digest Foundation's first-prize winner and supplied the title for Prize College Stories of 1964 published by the editors of Story magazine.

Although the author's preceding novel expressly employed the phrase for its title, The Hermit King is a classic American coming-of-age book. Arguably even more classic because its title does not advertise the type, Cobb's second, 1986, novel features, traditionally, the youthful adolescent. Hallie Fisque and Billy Malone, who are at the beginning edge of teenagedness and the seventh grade, are not already high school graduates (and do not possess a name) like Delores Lovelady, the central character of Coming of Age at the Y. The Hermit King is set not in a city and a Young Women's Christian Association residence but in a small town and family homes. And unlike its predecessor, it is not a comic novel but a poignant and bittersweet one.

Back outside the context of Cobb's own early output of fiction—this novel indeed displays most of the definitive features of coming-of-age literature, especially the American variety. Susan Ashley Gohlman's characterization of the type as fiction "about enrolling in, attending, and graduating from the school of life" is memorable, though we may want to specify youth, non-deliberateness, and informality as being involved in the educational process she outlines. One textbook enumeration of fictional themes pairs "Coming-of Age" with "Initiation," and states this educational or developmental journey in the pre-/post-terms of "Innocence v. Experience." George W.S. Trow, Jr.'s 1970s' analysis of "the adolescent mode" hits most of the bases: "the mode of exploration, becoming, growth, and pain."

If The Hermit King is in some ways representative or typical, it is so positively. It is among those illustrative exemplars that make a particular kind of writing reputable and appealing in the first place. Being this does not mean that it can't also be distinctive, however, and The Hermit King is—beginning with its old, striking title figure, a.k.a. Joe Bynymo a.k.a. Armistead King, and not ending with its dual and differently-gendered young protagonists.

The ending of this novel, its final two-sentence paragraph, focuses on the two young persons. Simply, movingly it both closes out the book's dramatic action and opens up the future worlds that these individuals, and we, and our progeny, will know: "'Don't cry, Hallie,'" he said, and he put his hand on her arm and squeezed it gently. And they both knew what a futile and useless gesture it was."

The future.

When I first read The Hermit King, which is set in Hammond, Alabama, in the summer of 1944, I wondered what might lie ahead for Billy and Hallie, and for their creator William Cobb, also to his old acquaintances a Billy. Now, sixty years after the novel's setting and twenty since its publication, I am introduced to five new short stories by William Cobb, and I fancifully indulge the notion that in their older characters I am seeing Billy Malone and Hallie Fisque again, and/or their children, whatever any of their names may presently be. They have different identities, different from the youthful characters of The Hermit King, and differing now from respective story to respective story. My own projection for Billy tallies most closely with Harry Whitaker in this volume's final story, "Walking Strawberry" (an inspired title, by the way). An elderly famous artist, Harry faces a crisis just as Billy once did, but a crisis quintessentially of age, of long life, and not of youth. "Walking Strawberry" ends differently than The Hermit King does—more conclusively, and more salutarily. In response to his wife's question about a painting, "Did you finish it?", Harry's answer is "Yes. Yes. I did."

Let us hope that William Cobb is not finished.

There are great-grandchildren, too.

Bert Hitchcock
Auburn, Alabama. May 2005

The Hermit King

for Meredith

Hammond, Alabama
Summer, 1944

THERE WAS A LEGEND, told over old, dying fires in grates, or maybe swapped back and forth over sandwiches being consumed at noon, of the deer hunts that touched the edge of the swamp, the type of legend that a boy of twelve would never tire of listening to; and afterwards, after the sandwiches, during the long, dripping, slate-gray November afternoon on the stand, listening to the dogs, far off in the otherwise quiet woods, he would peer back into the gloom, into the tangle of vines gray and stiff with winter, as if straining to get a glimpse of the hermit, watching for any movement in the still gloom that might indicate his presence, the old Negro who had been walking along the river bank one spring day when the high wind came up and blew him against a white oak tree so that now his eye, one eye, looked off into space and his cheeks were scarred, and he had his seasons turned around so that he wore a heavy, black overcoat in the summer and went around half naked in the winter, back in the swamp so deep that only a few men had ever seen him since, and they came back saying that he had come up, loomed up, out of the swamp like a huge brown apparition, calling himself Joe Bynymo, and waving his arms around like a madman. That was the legend of the long fall and winter, the legend with which he, with which many in the town grew up.

And the rest: always told with laughter at Mr. Sam Golson's store, how, years ago, on those rare occasions when the hermit would come to town, to walk the streets and sidewalks, in the long black overcoat touching the ground, he'd had, slung over his shoulder and trailing behind him like a dusty snake, a long black bull-whip. He was never known to say a word. And the little children, black and white, would hide in the bushes when they'd see him coming, and then jump out and dance around, chanting, chanting "Bynymo, Bynymo, Hit im in the belly with a fawty-foe!" And the old Hermit would loose the whip with its slick wooden handle and circle it slowly over his head, while the children scattered squealing in mock terror in all directions. There were times when a slow child would get popped on the rump.

> "Bynymo, Bynymo,
> Hit im in the belly
> With a fawty-foe!"

One

He would be much older before he would forget the sounds of his grandmother's old house: the hum and rattle of the pump outside the window (his grand-mother's house sat just outside the city limits, so that they had to have a well), the creaking tinkle of the dishes and glasses in the cabinets when somebody heavy strolled across the linoleum floor, the birds, sparrows and blue jays and redbirds, chattering in the privet hedge across the front yard, loud through the opened windows, his grandmother and his mother fussing at Ned Clay, the yard man; he would tense, listening, and a sudden thrill would pass down his spine, like when a rabbit runs across your grave, a thrill at hearing them talking, at being hidden and their not knowing he was listening.

"Ned Clay!" his grandmother would say; she never called him just Ned. "You come here, Ned Clay!"

"He ain't comin. He actin like he don't hear you," Hess, his grandmother's cook would say, disgust in her voice, pleased to be on his grandmother's side. "He lazy, he ain't worth nothing."

"You shut up, Hess, you hear me?" his grandmother would say. "Ned Clay!"

"What in the world are they shouting about?" his mother would say, passing through the room, her hand over her forehead, her eyes squinted.

"My head is splittin, Lord." She always had headaches now, ever since his father had been gone for good; she would pass on out into the kitchen, and soon the house would be quiet again, and he would be once more aware of the birds, and suddenly the pump would rattle and begin to hum.

During the long afternoons, sometimes there was Miss Lillian Fisque, his grandmother's best friend, who would come for a visit; she would come up the walk, slowly, inspecting his grandmother's verbena, her head bobbing as she looked at the condition of the crepe myrtle bushes and the smilax and wisteria growing over the porch. She always stopped at the steps. "Yoohoo, Eva, anybody to home?" she'd call out. He was sitting in the swing, behind the smilax; "Ma-Ma's in the kitchen," he said, and Miss Lillian jumped and craned her neck around at him; she always had little round red spots, about the size of a quarter, on each cheek, and her hair was colored bright red and stuck out from under her hat in tight little ringlets. She always carried a lace handkerchief, clutched at her throat, and in the summertime she carried a Japanese fan that her first cousin had sent her from the Orient during the first world war.

"Billy! Don't startle me like that, son. Eva's in the kitchen?"

"Yessum," he said.

"Hallie couldn't come," she said. "It was much too hot." Hallie was her niece, who was spending the summer with her and her sister, another old maid, in their big old house.

"Yessum," he said. He watched Miss Lillian come slowly up the steps and go through the screen door, letting the door thump behind her. And he sat, thinking of Hallie and Miss Lillian and Miss Julia:

They lived in a big two-story house just about a mile down the highway from his grandmother's house; the most striking thing about it, aside from its total lack of paint, was the fact that it sat right up against the highway. When the engineers, years before, had laid out the road, for some reason they had let it run right through the front yard, so that now the cars whizzed by within spitting distance of the front steps. When he thought of the house, he thought of it as being "straight up." It was only one room deep, four main rooms, two sitting on top of two, like blocks, with a kitchen tacked on to the back on the left hand side; it had a porch all across the front, with six narrow columns rising to the second floor roof. What whiteness it once had was now long since gone, and the house was a drab gray, with heavy shutters over most of the windows; in some of the windows could be seen flimsy, yellowish white drapes, and the light behind the windows at night was flickery and orange. Many people expressed surprise when they found out for the first time that the house was occupied; he liked it. He and Hallie had explored every inch of it, the damp, silent and dark front hall, with the faded wallpaper showing naked little cupids flying around, the high ceilinged rooms with their walls crammed with pictures, paintings of the two old women's mother and father, Hallie's grandparents, whose eyes followed you wherever you went in the room, next to pictures torn at random from magazines and stuck on the wall with yellowed, see-through tape, the parlor with all of its furniture and its four potted palm trees, one in each corner, and its cold fireplaces. The upstairs bedrooms were lined around the walls with locked trunks, which they looked at longingly, and the sunlight filtered through the dusty windows in shafts, and little stars of dust danced in it in the musty cool rooms. It was usually a quiet house; Hallie's Aunt Julia went about the house silently, dressed always in a plain, gray dress, her brown and gray hair pulled back in a loose bun at the back of her neck; she was short and heavy, and she wore men's bedroom slippers that flip-flapped on the stairs as she panted up and down. She always seemed to carry a dust rag around with her, and she looked suspiciously at them whenever they passed through a room as she was cleaning; rarely did she ever say anything.

"She won't eat nothing that doesn't come out of a can," Hallie told him.

"Why don't she talk more?"

"Aunt Lil says it's cause she ain't got anything to say," Hallie said.

They could hear, anywhere in the house, Miss Lillian fussing at Miss Julia, and they would look at each other and giggle; Miss Julia would just stand there and look at the floor, and Miss Lillian would stomp her foot and make her head shake and jiggle. In the mornings she sat in the darkened parlor, narrow slits of light coming through the closed blinds, closed up against the heat, and sipped her coffee out of a little, delicate cup. "Hallie, dear," she'd say, "don't walk so heavy. Your Aunt Lillian is irregular this moanin." They would look at each other and tiptoe by the door and giggle silently. And Miss Julia would glare at them, without a word, when they passed through the kitchen on the way outside.

He liked to watch her as they walked: she was already taller than him, and her legs seemed thin and awkward sticking out of the shorts, and her arms seemed to flop around when she walked. Her blond hair was streaked brown, and in the sunlight it had a strange, greenish tint to it that came from swimming in the swimming pool; her face was brown, flecked with freckles, and her green eyes seemed very light-colored in her face. At first, he hadn't trusted her: Miss Lillian had come up the walk one afternoon in the late spring, and he had heard her through the screen of the open window, "Yahoo, anybody to home?" and had heard her mumbling something to somebody, and he had looked out to see who it was; she was standing, in a green dress, with a little lace cap over her neatly combed curls, shifting from one foot to the other, looking around nervously. As he watched, he saw that she was clutching a lace handkerchief like Miss Lillian's; it made her awkward, as though she didn't quite know what to do with it. "Eva," Miss Lillian said to his grandmother, "I want to present my niece, Hallie Fisque, who'll be spending the summer with me and Julia." She was being very formal and proper.

"Well, how nice," his grandmother said. She was looking at Hallie, who was looking off down at the barn. "What a pretty dress," his grandmother said. And then, after a minute, "Well, won't yall come on in and have some iced tea," and he heard them enter the house and after a minute his grandmother coming down the hall. "Billy!" she said, "Billy, come on out here and meet Miss Lillian's niece."

And so they sat, he and Hallie having Coke in tall glasses, Miss Lillian and his grandmother having iced tea; she didn't look at him. Later, at his grandmother's suggestion, they walked down the road toward the river; the grass was new and smelled fresh and damp, and the sunlight was warm on their thin, spring clothes. They neared the river, and a slight breeze picked up gently and caused the streaming branches of the willows along the road to drift slowly back and forth; the sour, muddy smell of the river drifted to them on the breeze. She told him about herself; she lived in Prichard, outside Mobile, with her father; her mother was dead and she would be in the seventh grade when school started back.

"My daddy's dead, too," he said, quickly, and when she didn't say anything, he said, "He died in the war, in Germany. They didn't ever find him or anything."

"In the army?" she said. And he nodded. He looked at her; she seemed sad, and she wouldn't look back at him. They sat on the limerock ledge, near the edge of the bluff, looking out over the river that curved gently far below them, at the new, light green of the swamps on the other side, colored brightly in the late spring sunlight. He sat back and plucked a sprig of new grass and chewed it, and she twisted the lace handkerchief around her hand; he could see the skin turning red where the tightness of the handkerchief bound it, and he saw the awkwardness of her legs and the uncomfortable angle at which the loose-fitting skirt fell away from them.

"Listen," she said, after a minute, "you want a cigarette?"

"Sure," he said, looking sideways at her, "you got some?"

She unbuttoned her blouse and fished around inside; in a minute she came up with two cigarettes, mashed and misshapen, with shreds of tobacco coming from the ends, and she brought out two matches, heavy, awkward kitchen matches, and they lit up and sat there and smoked the cigarettes looking out over the river.

HIS GRANDMOTHER'S HOUSE: his grandmother's house was a big, rambling yellow house with a porch around three sides; most of the floors, and especially the halls, were covered with worn, creaky linoleum, and the walls were made with wide planks with cracks between them. The linoleum was cool to bare feet in the summertime, and the main hall, always dark, was quiet and smelled musty and closed off, especially if the glass doors, covered with dust-acrid chintz curtains, which opened into the living room, were closed. The hallway was one of his favorite rooms; it was wide, and lining one side were several old wardrobes whose metal hangers tinkled together when someone heavy-footed walked by them. The wardrobes, there were three, were never locked, and he knew their contents; in one were two of his father's old suits, dark and heavy and coarse wool, and there were some old dresses, smelling faintly of lilac soap and powder. He had also found two old bonnets, like the women in the western picture shows wore; and there were odds and ends, including, in the bottom of one, a tall stack of the Saturday Evening Post, which didn't interest him except for the little cartoons in the back, and a stack of National Geographics, some of which were worn at the sections showing bare-breasted native girls in the jungles of Africa and the South Pacific. The other favorite room was the front bedroom, or what his mother and grandmother referred to as the sun porch.

The sun porch had windows around two sides; it stuck out from the corner of the house as though it had been added as an afterthought, which it had, and there were two doors leading to it, one from the living room and one from the porch. And its floor slanted away from the house and shook when you walked on it, and there was one huge old iron bed in the middle of the room with an old, stuffed down mattress on it so that, on those occasions when they had enough company, which rarely happened any more, when he would sleep on the bed with someone, his mother or one of his cousins, he would wake up during the night and find himself and his bed partner jammed together in the middle of the bed, deep in a cavern formed by the high edges of the mattress. The sun porch was always flooded with light, much brighter than the rest of the house, and it always seemed neat and unlived in; it was, he supposed, their guest room. There was a dresser that didn't match the bed, a set of odds and ends: a heavy hand mirror that his grandmother had once gotten for a present and had never liked, so had never used, lying on a yellowed, knitted doily; a powder music box that had belonged to his mother when she was a little girl, black with delicate, creamy line drawings of Chinese ladies in long dresses on the top; a heavy, hefty bronze statue of Vulcan, in Birmingham, with SOUVENIR OF THE MAGIC CITY written around the base, and a cut glass perfume bottle, empty. And there was a huge wardrobe in here, too, but it was uninteresting, because in it his grandmother kept all the winter blankets and quilts, folded and sprinkled with moth balls and crystals, so that the slight, sharp smell of the camphor permeated the entire room, even when the wardrobe doors were closed. The most interesting thing about the room, and the thing that drew him to it, was the closet: it was a big, walk-in closet, and because no one slept on the sun porch regularly, there were no clothes in it; it was a storage closet. He discovered that he could go into the closet and close the door and turn on the overhead light and sit on the cool floor, cool because there was no insulation under the rough planks of the sun porch floor, and surrounded by the musty, dust smell of old things, look for hours. There was even an old mandolin, with most of the strings gone, in a rotted, cardboard case, which he remembered, as a small child, seeing his grandmother bring out and strum on, until she gave it up to him to play with; he didn't think it had ever had all its strings, even when his grandmother strummed on it. And there were several cardboard boxes (he was at first shocked, then later amused, when he realized that his grandmother never threw anything away); one box contained some old letters and postcards. He had gone through them carefully, opening the stiff and crinkly envelopes, pulling out old Christmas cards signed "Bessie Ruth and Earl," and "The Hills," and "Hope to see you all sometime around Christmas, Edward and Mary Ann"; and high school graduation invitations (a stack of thirteen, all alike, turned out to be some of his mother's); there was a picture, yellowed and with rounded corners and a black and white checked border, a snapshot of a soldier in a World War One uniform, standing in full field dress with a pack on his back and a rifle on his shoulder, grinning widely, that, when he turned over, turned out to be a postcard, addressed to Eva Malone, his grandmother; it was written in a scrawl, with lots of curlicues and fancy swirls: "how are you all there in Hammond fine I hope kiss them all for me love to everyone from George Allen Malone," who, his grandmother had said, was his great Uncle George, who had been killed in Germany just as his father had been. The picture fascinated him.

Two

It was in the timeless, twilit evenings that he looked at Hallie; when the red sun would sit, poised for what seemed at least an hour just over the river, when they would sit on his grandmother's porch, in the swing, or on her aunt's porch, in the creaky old rocker. She always now wore green or khaki shorts, with a wrinkled shirt hanging out; he hadn't, in fact, seen her in a dress since that first day in late spring. He had decided that she was pretty, and when she wasn't looking, he stole glimpses of her little, bubble-like breasts under the loose fitting shirt. Her blonde hair seemed to grow more sun-bleached, and it fell, straight, past her ears and almost to her shoulders, the curls and waves of an early visit permanent wave now long since gone. (She had a habit of quickly pushing it behind her left ear, but she would toss her head when she did it and it would usually fall right back.) She had one line of freckles that ran across her nose and ended in two clusters, one under each pale green eye, and her lips were full and sort of pouty, like some of the women he'd seen in the picture shows, and her legs, sticking out of the shorts, were long and sunbrowned and lightly dappled with short white hairs. When they walked she would usually walk faster than he would; she had a loping awkward way of walking, and he would never tell her to slow down.

And that summer, they walked a lot, after they grew to trust each other, after the first awkwardness.

He had been walking down the road, his rolled jeans flapping around his bare feet (rolled because his grandmother refused to hem them: "I ain't letting em out ever two months," she said), the dust rising in little puffs behind him as he strode, when he passed her aunts' house, and saw her sitting on the front steps; she was leaning forward, her chin on her bare knees, her legs still winter-white, staring straight ahead. She seemed to be concentrating on a clump of dusty Cherokee roses across the road. He stopped and watched her a minute, then he walked across the sandy yard, a yard littered with bottle caps and bits of paper; his feet were soundless in the sand, and just as he came up to her, from the side, he saw that she was mumbling to herself.

"Son-of-a-bitch," she said. He stopped.

"Who?" he said, and she jumped and jerked toward him.

Her green eyes glared at him for a moment. Then she said,

"It's you."

"Me?" he said.

"No, I mean it's you walked up here and yelled at me."

"I ain't yelled at you," he said.

She had resumed her position and was staring at the clump of roses again; he eased himself down on the steps beside her. They sat in silence for a minute.

"Daddy," she said, suddenly.

"What?" he said.

"Daddy is a son-of-a-bitch. That's what I was mumblin about when you walked up on me." He sat looking at her; the sky was gray and overcast, and there was a distant roll of thunder in the west. "He's really not bad, you know? He's just stupid."

"Yeah," was all he said.

"I mean, here I am, sent off to live with Aunt Lil and Aunt Julia, all summer, to learn to act like a lady. Now that's stupid, if you know what I mean."

"Yeah, I know what you mean," he said.

She stared glumly ahead. "Look," he said, "I'm on my way to Mr.

Sam's store for Ma-Ma, come on and go with me and we'll get us a couple of Luckies."

Mr. Sam Golson's store was just on the edge of town, sitting facing the main highway with a two-story false front. There were two gas pumps and a little shed in front, and there were two smooth, well worn wooden benches, one on either side of the front door, and the hardpacked ground between the door and the two gas pumps was paved with cold-drink caps that had been tracked and stomped into an even, mosaic-like pattern. There were always one or two Negroes sitting on the benches out front in the patch of shade, drinking tall, sweating, orange or red or cola-brown drinks; today there were several, as the thunder rolled close and the heavy sky threatened. The first big drops had started to fall as they arrived at the store, the drops pelting the earth and making little round beads of water in the dust beside the pavement on the road. They ran under the shed, hearing drops thumping on the corrugated tin roof; the Negroes all nodded to them, and they entered the cool gloom of the store.

Mr. Sam came scurrying up from whatever he was doing in the back of the store, his glasses perched on his forehead, leaning forward to peer at them. "Git wet?" was his greeting.

"Nossir, we made it," the boy said. The myriad smells of the store were even heavier with the dampness outside, and the flies seemed thicker and the gloom deeper because of the lack of sunlight.

"What you need this morning?" Mr. Sam said.

"Got any Double Bubble?" the boy said, and Mr. Sam nodded his head sadly.

"Can't hardly ever git it, and can't keep it when I do. The war is hard on old and young alike, ain't it." He was now shaking his head. "Nope, fore you ask, ain't got no Tootsie Rolls, either."

"Ma-Ma needs a sack o corn meal," the boy said. "And two Lucky Strikes." Mr. Sam kept an open pack of cigarettes behind the counter, from which he sold them, one by one, mostly to Negroes, for two cents apiece. He went behind the counter and took down a sack of corn meal, then reached over and shook out two cigarettes and looked at them shrewdly.

"Now the young lady there," he said, nodding to Hallie, "Looks like she might prefer a dip of snuff to a nasty old cigarette."

"She's Miss Lillian Fisque's niece, come to stay the summer," the boy said.

"Pleased to meet you, Miss Fisque," Mr. Sam said.

"Hallie," the girl said.

"Hallie," Mr. Sam said. He was still holding the cigarettes. "Now you want the meal put on Miss Eva's bill, but you want to pay cash for the cigarettes, right?"

"Yessir," the boy said, and he put a nickel on the counter and Mr. Sam gave him the cigarettes.

"Don't want no Sen-Sen today?" Mr. Sam asked. He pulled open the cash drawer and laid a penny on the counter by the cigarettes, and the boy put them into his shirt pocket.

"Nossir," he said. They could hear the rain lashing outside now, and a sudden loud clap of thunder rocked the store, and the dark atmosphere seemed to grow muggier. Some of the Negroes were coming in the front door to get away from the blowing rain. The two of them wandered toward the back of the store; there was nobody around the cold stove, and the bottle caps were scattered over the checker board in disarray. They sat there for a long moment, neither speaking; he looked over at her, and she was staring at the stove, her arms crossed across her chest.

"It'll stop directly," he said, and she just brushed, with irritation, at a fly that flitted about her head. "You want a Coke?"

"I like fountain Cokes," she said, "with a squirt o cherry in em."

"You can get em downtown. Cherry Cokes," he said.

There was laughter coming form the front of the store as Mr. Sam dispensed the cold drinks and, now as noon approached, the cans of sardines and boxes of crackers and half-pound wedges of cheese. The Negroes squatted around on their haunches, eating the sardines, pulling them out of the can whole and tilting their heads back and dropping them in, then turning up the bubbly cold drinks to wash them down. One old Negro woman sat in a chair by the door, eating from a whole loaf of cinnamon rolls, the cellophane neatly folded back, fanning slowly with a cardboard fan with her free hand.

"I believe it's slackin up," he said. Just then there was another burst of thunder and the wind lashed a sheet of rain across the front of the store.

"Do tell," she said.

"You want to smoke these cigarettes?" he said.

"In here?"

"Sure, why not?"

"Won't that old bastard tell on us?" she said. He was looking at her, his hand poised at his shirt pocket.

"Boy, they sure learn you to cuss in Prichard, don't they?"

She looked at him, her face irritated; then she almost smiled. He got the cigarettes out and gave her one, then lit it for her from a box of waterproof matches that he carried; they sat and puffed in silence for a moment, the thick smoke rising in clouds over their heads to disappear up among the harness and rubber boots hanging from the rafters. She looked at him out of the corners of her eyes. She said, quietly:

"Shit."

He looked at her; she looked back challengingly.

"Goddam," he said.

"Pussy."

"Screwin," he said.

"Son-of-a-bitch."

"Shit," he said.

"That's mine," she said.

"All right, fuck, then," he said, and he whispered it.

"What are yall carryin on about back here?" Mr. Sam said, and both of them sat upright quickly; he was walking briskly, in his way, back to where they were sitting. He eyed their cigarettes, but he said nothing, "Storm's letting up."

"We got to go, then," the boy said, "I got to get this meal home to Ma-Ma."

"Yall come back," Mr. Sam said.

THE WORLD HAD been washed clean by the storm; the sun streamed through the clouds in long, slanted rays, and the now dustless treeleaves gleamed green in the sunlight. The smell of the rain lingered in the air, and on the moisture came the smell of honeysuckle along the fences and the minty scent of the grass in the pastures. There was a stillness, and they walked in silence for a long time, the boy swinging the sack of meal at the end of his arm, the girl plodding along, her sandals making little squishy sounds in the damp sand along the edge of the road. The plums were thick in the bushes along the fences, and every now and then, when the full ditches narrowed enough, the girl would hold the sack of meal while the boy jumped the ditch to gather a handful. They bit into the rich, juicy meat of the plums, the juice escaping to run in two tiny paths from the corners of their mouths down their chins. "Now, that's good. Boy, that's good," the girl said; she bit into another plum the size of a small apple, and the juice leaked over her chin. They walked on, the sun out in full now, and when they reached the place where the road widened, if they had seen from a distance, they would have appeared even smaller than they were.

Three

THE STREET WAS Saturday crowded, and the noon-time shower had driven most of the Negroes into the stores or back to the covered wagons and pickup trucks, and the rain had lashed viciously down the narrow streets between the brickfront stores. But now the streets were crowded again, a colorful patchwork of blues and reds; sounds of laughter and curses, and smells of tobacco, lilac perfume, and cheap whiskey. It was through this crowd that Ted Mack Lowery slowly made his way, moving from one side of the sidewalk to the other, stepping around children who suddenly would dart in front of him, catching him in midstride so that he would have to pause, one foot in the air, to change directions. He was a small man, very thin, and dressed in overalls much like those worn by the Negroes around him, with heavy brogan shoes and a white shirt buttoned at its frayed collar; his skin was burned brown by the sun and his hair lay back from his forehead in a flat, greasy plane that showed clearly the marks left by the comb. When Ted Mack grinned, which he did very often, he revealed a broad expanse of blackness where his upper front teeth should have been; all of them were missing between his two incisors, which showed just in the corners of his mouth under his thin lip, stained brown from the snuff that he dipped out of the little round tin he carried in the zipped pocket on the bib of his overalls. He was a pathetic figure as he moved among the crowd; nobody paid any mind to him, and he muttered under his breath as he turned down Woodfin Street and the crowd thickened and the sun, back out now torrid in the street, beat down on his head. He was headed for A. C. Logan's Photo Shop because, on Saturdays, A. C. sold whiskey in his backroom. (He sometimes went with him, on Friday afternoon, in A. C.'s old Cadillac, over to the state liquor store in Uniontown, where they bought several cases of the cheapest corn liquor, all in half-pints; he would load the cases in the trunk while A. C. talked to the men in the store, who were supposed to make a record of such sales but who never did, probably because there were too many of them.) And A. C. owed him a pint and two dollars, and later he was taking all his children to the curb market for ice cream sandwiches, since it was Saturday.

Ted Mack Lowery was something of an enigma to the town; for one thing, he had a Chinese wife. At least, she was Chinese according to Ted Mack, because nobody else knew where she came from. (Mr. Sam Golson said she was a gypsy, that she had come through with a band who had camped out behind the M & L Café on the highway, on the way to their burial ground over near Meridian, Mississippi, and Ted Mack had been out there fooling around with them and had gotten caught in the back seat of a Pontiac with her and had to marry her in some kind of gypsy ceremony right then and there.) She was about three times as big as he was, tall and very fat, with long hair that hung down her back to where her huge buttocks, like balloons, swelled out; and they had six children, all under ten years old, a stepladder of black-haired, black-eyed, chubby children. He worked, sporadically, at a variety of jobs, the most consistent being as a part-time mechanic at the Pontiac place (which, Mr. Sam Golson pointed out, was simply poetic justice) and sometimes he kept a fruit-stand curb market for a friend. They lived in a two-room shanty, painted a dull maroon, out east of town; the only thing that distinguished it from the shanties that most of the Negroes lived in was its location: it sat alone, under a tall oak tree, with a wide, sandy yard, and always, when you passed by there, one or two of the children would be playing in the sand in the littered yard, usually digging in the sand with a tablespoon.

A. C. Logan was leaning on the glass counter in the dim shop, his belly pressed against it, with a toothpick jutting from the corner of his fleshy mouth, when Ted Mack pushed open the door and heard the little bell overhead tinkle. "Look who's done come to git his beauty struck," A. C. said.

"Niggers git thicker ever Saady," Ted Mack said.

"Don't they, now?" A. C. said. "Good for business, though."

"Speakin o your main business—"

A. C. laughed. "Come on," he said, and the two men went through the little door in the flimsy partition and down a dim hall, lit only by one naked bulb, little doors opening into small studios where Logan took the brownish portraits of smiling Negroes or of new-vain adolescent girls who sat together and smiled like Paulette Goddard on the R. C. Cola "Best by Taste Test" signs. They entered a large back room, littered with cameras and equipment piled on tables and benches, the dust thick in the muggy air, the sunlight dimmed as it filtered through the dusty, barred windows that opened off the alley in back. Logan went into a closet and came back with two half-pints of the cheap corn whiskey, which he sat on the table in front of Ted Mack.

"Less have us a quick one," Ted Mack said, and he took out a pocket knife and cut the seal around the neck of the bottle, then pulled the cork out and raised the bottle to his lips. He took a long swallow, his adam's apple in his skinny neck bobbing once, then twice, then three times before he lowered the bottle and handed it to Logan. "Christamighty!" he said.

Logan wiped the neck carefully on his palm, then he took one sip. "Shit," he said, "I don't usually drink my own product."

"It's all made from the same corn," Ted Mack said. He raised the bottle again; tiny beads of sweat had suddenly broken out across his creased forehead. There was a knock on the back door, which opened onto the alley, and Logan went over and opened it, and a Negro woman, dressed in a green dress with shiny orange and blue spangles and beads all over it, stood there.

"How many?" Logan said, and the Negro woman told him four, so he got a brown paper sack and put four of the half-pints in; she took the sack and passed him a wad of wrinkled and dirty bills and turned to go, and Logan said, "Wait just a minute, Auntie, not so fast. Lemme count this greasy stuff," and she stood, very still, hugging the brown package to her breast, while he counted out the bills one by one. Her eyes followed the bills as they passed from one of Logan's hands to the other. "All right," he said, "all here."

Ted Mack had finished the first of the two bottles of whiskey; he was leaning against the table, a smile on his toothless face. "Ain't two o them mine?" he said, pointing to the bills in Logan's hand. Logan peeled off two and handed them to him. "It's Saady, and I'm white," Ted Mack said.

"Too bad you ain't a nigger, then you could afford four of them instead of two and stay drunk two days instead of one," Logan said.

Later that afternoon, Ted Mack Lowery stood unsteadily in a limerock-strewn, still muddy alley in front of a Negro cabin; he leaned forward and peered intently at the cabin, his body swaying gently back and forth. "Henry!" he called suddenly, "hey, Henry!" There was no answer from the house, so he picked up a palm sized piece of limerock and threw it at the house; it thumped against the front door and broke into several pieces that littered the front stoop. Presently the door opened a crack and a head appeared, a Negro woman with flashy black eyes.

"He ain't here," she said, "Gwan away from here."

"I need a jug o shinny," Ted Mack said.

"Henry gone to town," she said.

Ted Mack hooked his thumbs behind the bib of his overalls. "All I want is one jug, you can sell it to me."

"I don't know you," she said.

"What you got to know me for?" Ted Mack said. He came into the yard and approached the house, and the Negro woman pulled back into the house, the door scraping in its frame until only her eyes were showing against the gloomy interior. "What's wrong with you, girl?" Ted Mack said.

"Ain't nothin wrong with me," she said, "an Henry catch you messin round here he cut you up bad."

"One jug, thass all I want, all right?" She looked at him for a moment, then her eyes disappeared and the door pulled firmly shut; in a minute they reappeared, along with an arm and hand, long-fingered and white-palmed, holding what appeared to be a quart fruit jar wrapped in a wrinkled brown paper sack. Ted Mack took it and pulled the jar out and held it up to the light and shook it, then he unzipped a pocket on his overalls and handed over two dollars to her; she dissolved back inside without a word and the door scraped shut behind her.

"Henry don't do you right, you just call me, hear?" Ted Mack called out. "Mister Lowery." There was no sound, no movement, from the house, so Ted Mack unscrewed the cap from the jar and turned it up; the searing liquid burned at his throat, and the fumes, almost like the fumes of kerosene, heavy and greasy, tingled in his nostrils and made him momentarily retch. "Christamighty!" he said, spitting into the dust, "goddam nigger whiskey!"

THE ENTIRE WESTERN sky was glowing red, and a tiny rim of sun, like the edge of a fingernail, still showed over the thick trees of the swamp across the river. The heat of the afternoon still lingered in the air, and all traces of the noon-time shower were now gone, the roadways once again thick with fine dust. Wagons, one by one, slowly made their way out of town, headed back to the outlying farms, the mules plodding head down, the gaudy dresses and the store-bought shirts now stained and wrinkled, ready to be put into the black iron washpots on Monday and boiled and dried and sprinkled and ironed with the heavy cast iron so that they will be crisp when next Saturday comes.

Billie and Hallie sat on her aunts' front porch, watching the wagons go by; now and then, a hand would be raised in greeting, and they would wave, and then the Negroes in the wagon would wave back, the children staring at them with big, round eyes, the women sitting slumped in straight chairs arranged in a line along the side of the wagon. The dusk was thicker, but it would not be first dark for a while yet, and they sat in the old rockers, watching the wagons and the skinny hounds that would leave the wagons and sniff around in the yard and then suddenly dash to catch up.

"Wonder where they're goin?" the girl said. She was sitting with the heels of her sandals hooked over the top rung of the rocker, her chin on her knees.

"Home I reckon," the boy said, after a minute. Another wagon came by, and he was thinking about the time he'd gone with his grandmother to carry Hess some soup, when she'd been sick, and they had gone through the sagging front gate and through the narrow, sandy yard and up to the cabin that was identical to twenty more along the road, with a high-peaked roof and narrow porch, painted a pallid gray, the air heavy with the smell of slop and slime from the small hog pens in the backyards. The inside of the cabin was dark, and Hess was lying on an old brass bed in the corner, and she had begun to moan and groan when they had entered; "I'se got de miseries, Miz Eva," she said over and over again.

His grandmother had sat by the bed, and he had looked around the cabin, at the walls covered with newspaper; layered it appeared almost half an inch thick, with the outer layer the gaudy, multi-colored Sunday funnies. The air in the cabin was stifling, and the smell of the soup mingled with the thick, quilty Negro smell, and he had moved through it, looking at the calendars on the walls, stuck to the newspaper, calendars that went back several years, advertising Willingham's Drug Store and John O. Rowan and Sons' Gin and Patent Medicines and Seeds. There were pictures, torn from magazines, of Jesus, and several small cards of biblical scenes like children are given in Sunday School; and there above the cold fireplace, was a large framed picture of Jesus kneeling in the Garden of Gethsemane; that had been a gift, he knew, because she had brought it to the house to show them, from the Presbyterian Women of the Church, because for years, every Sunday morning at quarter to eleven, she was there to ring the bell, standing in the little vestibule pulling the bell rope and joking with the children. The cabin was crowded with furniture, small tables and cast off chairs and a set of highbacked straw chairs and a round table that she had gotten somewhere. And the tables were loaded down with odds and ends, mirrors and bottles and cooking utensils, and stacks of old magazines and even some books; and sitting around, here and there, were several brightly painted carnival trophies. On the table next to her bed was a green and orange horse, rared up, his front hooves pawing the air, with a clock in its chest; next to that was a cold, smoke-stained kerosene lamp. The only light in the room came through two small, dusty windows.

He stood near the bed and watched his grandmother spoon soup into Hess's toothless mouth; she made little sucking noises with her lips and rolled her muddy-looking eyes around in their sockets. He looked at her carefully, and their eyes met for a moment; his grandmother had lowered the spoon to the bowl. "He a fine boy, Miz Eva," Hess said. He stood looking down at her, and he didn't smile; the cabin and its gloom depressed him. He had just started to piece together the story of Joe Bynymo, and his loneliness in the swamp, and the old Negress in bed reminded him, somehow, of him, and the thick Negro smell of her seemed to him to smell of sorrow or sadness; and suddenly, standing there, he had known that Hess was going to die, not then, but soon, and he looked at his grandmother, the thin hands holding the thick, brown bowl and the heavy kitchen spoon, the almost shapeless dress on the angular, sharp-boned body, her face wrinkled and drawn and her hair the color of congealed bacon grease, lifting, firmly and in a straight line, the spoon of hot soup to the lips of the old Negress. He had stood there, thinking of a crazy old black man who had chosen to live out his life all alone in the swamps, and he tried to imagine him as he was now, young and alive. But Bynymo was only a legend now; he thought of the laughter of the men at Mr. Sam's store, and he turned quickly and went out onto the little narrow porch, into the sunlight and the sour hog smells, and there had been laughter, rich, creamy Negro laughter coming from the porch of a cabin down the road, and he had sat on the front stoop to wait until his grandmother was finished.

"You want to walk?" Hallie said, standing up and brushing the wrinkles out of her shorts, and he looked at her blankly. He stood up.

"Sure," he said, "but it'll be dark before long."

"Who cares?" she said.

"Maybe you ought to tell your aunts where you're goin."

"They don't care," she said, "to hell with them anyway."

They both laughed then, and started down the steps, and they had gotten to the edge of the yard when they heard her Aunt Lil calling, "Hallie? Hallie, where you goin?" She looked at him her crooked smile on her lips, the smile she used when she cursed. "Run!" she said, and they both broke into a run, laughing and sprinting down the edge of the road. "Haaaaalie!" her Aunt Lil called after them.

It was first dark now, and they sat on a smooth, limerock knoll high over the river, looking westward where there now was only one small strip of rose sky over the tangled, black trees. The water of the river, far below them through the dusky haze, was deep black, and yet they both sensed the movement, the lazy, slow lapping and flow of the current; there was a darkening stillness. Sitting with their backs to the lights of the town, they could see, off to the North, where the river made a wide, curving bend, the few flickering lights of the locks, and to the South, in another bend, the graceful curve of the great white bluffs, so brilliant in the day's sunlight, now muted in the darkening evening. They watched a large bird, an owl, a black silhouette against the purple sky, sail smoothly down and settle, with a sudden flapping of wings, in the top of a tree near the river's edge; and, after a minute, his haunting cry broke the silence.

"What's that?" the girl said.

"Old owl," the boy said.

"He sounds lonely, don't he?"

The boy was silent for a moment, as though he were thinking about the loneliness of the owl. "You know, when I hear one of those owls like that, like when I'm home in bed, I lay there wondering if old Joe Bynymo heard the same one I just heard."

Now the girl was silent. After a minute, she said: "Boy, that gives me goose pimples."

"Yeah, I know. But think of him out there, way back in that black swamp over there, just sittin there in front of a fire, with the firelight flickerin off his old cocked eye."

"Hush, now, Billy," she said, "you gonna make me scared."

"But, you know, I can't help thinkin about him. I can't help wonderin if he's as mean as they all say he is."

"He can't be no meaner'n my Aunt Julia, that's for sure," she said

The stars were out now; it was a perfectly clear night, and the stars were a thick, bright canopy overhead, and they sat in silence once again, the boy looking across at the swamp, the girl, her head back, peering at the sky.

"It's beautiful," she said.

"Yeah," he said, "but just think. Under that same sky, way around the world, there's a war goin on."

"I don't like to think about it," she said

"I don't much," he said, "cept for Daddy sometimes."

"Tell me about your daddy," she said.

He was silent for a moment. "Ain't nothin to tell," he said. He leaned back on his elbows, his legs stretched out in front of him, his bare feet crossed at the ankles. He was thinking as he often did, of the Sunday when it all happened: he had been too little to really know what was going on, but he had known something was wrong. All afternoon, his parents had gone about the house whispering, and his mother had sent him outside to play. And it had been a bitter, cold day, with low, thick gray clouds, and he had been listless and unable to play, so he had ended up in the coal bin, filling a scuttle with coal, and he remembered that he had filled it so full that he couldn't carry it to the back porch, and in a fit of temper, for which he knew that he would be whipped, he had dumped half of it in the back yard, halfway to the house, an act of defiance that he couldn't and didn't understand. And that night, after supper, instead of the usual radio shows they all listened to — Charlie McCarthy and Fred Allen and the others that, each Sunday night, with the fire crackling on the grate, they all sat around the old upright Philco and listened to — instead his parents sat in silence, listening to newscasts, and he had been given a funny-book and sent to his room. And it seemed almost the same day, or at least the next morning, though it couldn't have been that quick, that his father was gone; he had come home one time, in the brown uniform, seeming taller with the army cap he wore, and then he had gone and his mother and grandmother had cried. He couldn't remember them crying when they had learned he had been killed; he only remembered his mother taking him down to the square, shortly after they had moved in with his grandmother, and showing him the little plywood plaque fitted neatly onto the wooden rack painted white with black lettering: LYNWOOD H. MALONE, and under that, in small numbers, 1913-1942.

"What's that?" the girl said, suddenly, sitting up straight.

"What?" the boy said; he sat up, too, startled at the sound of her voice.

"I thought I heard a noise," she said, "in those bushes over there." She edged closer to him. It was very dark now, but the bluff was bathed with the glow of the stars.

"Probably a rabbit," he said.

Just then there was a rustling in the clump of bushes, several willow trees sitting about fifty feet back from the bluff and off to their right. It was light enough for them to see the branches move.

"See, I told you," the girl said.

"Who's there?" the boy called out; the rustling stopped and the willows were very still. "Who is it?" the boy yelled, louder now. They stood up, the girl standing very close to him in the dark; they moved away from the edge of the bluff, and he could hear her breathing in the silence.

"Goddam bushes got me," they heard a voice say. Then after a moment, "Ohhhhhh, Jesus," the voice said, "they got me, they got me. . . ." There was more rustling, then the willows began to shake violently; they jumped back.

"Less go," the girl whispered.

"Wait a minute," the boy said. The bushes stopped their frantic shaking. "Who's that?" the boy called.

"These here aints is crawlin all over me," the voice said. "I'm dyin, oh Jesus, I'm dyin!"

"It sounds like Ted Mack Lowery," the boy said. "That you, Mister Lowery?" he called out.

The bushes started to shake violently again, and suddenly they seemed to explode and a man burst from them; he wheeled, his arms flailing the air, then he fell heavily to the earth and lay still. They heard him moan.

"Come on, less see if he's all right," the boy said; and the girl said, "No, less get outta here," pulling at his arm.

"It's just Ted Mack Lowery," the boy said, "he ain't gone hurt nobody, he's drunk." They stood looking at the heap on the ground; he lay on his back, his arms thrown out wildly to the sides. Billy walked slowly up to him, Hallie holding onto his hand, holding back. "Come on, it's all right," he whispered. They stood over him, looking down at him. His mouth was open, and they could see the absence of teeth, the dark bronze leathery skin, the black, greasy hair all wild and tangled.

"He looks like an Indian," the girl whispered.

"Look a there," the boy said, pointing, "he's done peed all over hisself." One of the legs of his overalls showed a wide, fanlike area of darker blue dampness spreading down it. "Mister Lowery," he said, "wake up."

The eyes opened in the head. They rolled around in their sockets, as though unable to focus. He smacked his lips. "Where's my shinny?" he said.

"You musta lost it, Mister Lowery," the boy said.

"Ohhhh, Jesus," he said, "I'm dyin."

"Is he?" the girl said, "is he dyin?"

"Naw," the boy said, "he ain't dyin, he's been drinkin shinny, like niggers drink." He was standing, looking down at Ted Mack; the girl still clung to his hand. "Ned Clay drinks it," he said, "it makes you go crazy."

Ted Mack rolled over and got to his knees, and they backed away from him, and he got slowly to his feet, slipping once back to his knees; he stood before them on wobbly legs, his head nodding forward as though his neck was made of rubber. The bib of his overalls was wet, and they could smell the heavy, sickening odor of vomit and raw whiskey. His eyes were only half open, and he seemed to be trying to open them all the way, his arms hanging loosely at his sides.

"What's he doin now?" the girl whispered.

Ted Mack took a step toward them. He was tilting his head to the side, trying to see them in the darkness. "Woody?" he said. They backed away from him. "Woody, is that you?" His head nodded forward, and he almost slipped to the ground, but he caught himself and somehow balanced on his feet. "I thought you was dead, Woody," he said, "somebody told me long time ago you was dead."

"What's he talkin about?" the girl said.

Just then Ted Mack wheeled and ran and staggered a few steps away from them. "Goddamit, you're dead, Woody!" he screamed, and he turned and tried to run, but fell down and scrambled in the loose limerock; and then he was on his feet again, running toward the road. "Help me, somebody!" he screamed, and he disappeared, and they heard him scrambling in the bushes along the side of the road, and then his brogans hammering in the dust, and then the night was once again quiet.

"He's crazy as hell," the girl said.

The boy stood there, looking off where Ted Mack had disappeared; she had dropped his hand when Ted had left, but now he reached out and took hers for a moment, then he dropped it.

"He thought I was my daddy," he said. "Come on, it's getting late."

And they walked off down the road, side by side, toward home. In the distance, behind them, they could hear the lonely, eerie cry of the owl.

Four

The first thing she was aware of was the sound of the birds outside the open window, chattering and squealing like a bunch of old ladies at a sewing circle meeting. She opened her eyes; the morning sunlight streamed through the windows, and she could see, through the branches of the huge old oak tree in the side yard, patches of clear, light blue June sky; it was already warm in the room and her gown felt clammy and sticky where her body touched the mattress. Her pillow was lumpy and hard, and her left ear hurt where she had rested her head; she lay still for a moment, smelling the smells of the morning, the sharp, Clorox smell of the sheets, changed yesterday and every Saturday, so that the smell faded as the week progressed, the dusty stillness of the room; with its spindly, carved, and curlicued furniture and sun-faded curtains, the delicate smell of coffee and bacon that floated gently up the stairwell. She stretched her legs and rolled over, and the sheets were cool on her bare limbs and her cheeks, and she closed her eyes, not wanting to move; she heard the floor in the hall outside her room creak, and she closed her eyes tighter, and in just a moment she heard her Aunt Lil (she could tell by the footsteps which one it was) come into the room.

"Hallie," she said "Aunt Julia's got breftus ready." She lay very still, pretending to be still asleep. "Wake up, chile," her aunt said. "We don't keep movie star hours in this house." It was the same thing she said every morning that Hallie had been there. "And I want to speak with you this mornin about you runnin off las night, of all things on a Saady night with all those drunk nigras runnin around just lookin for some pure white girl to ruin, why your granddaddy would have whupped me till a fly wouldn't light on me if I'd ever done anythin like that, and your Aunt Julia too, it just wasn't lady-like. Hallie? Hallie, you listenin to me?"

"Yessum," she said, and her voice was muffled against the lumpy pillow, and she still had her eyes closed.

"Well, sit up and look at me, then," Aunt Lil said, and Hallie swung her legs over the side of the bed and sat up; her eyes were still sleep-swollen, and her hair was rumpled and tangled, and her pink gown was bunched in her lap. "Pull your skirt down, Hallie," her aunt said. "I don't know what your daddy's gonna do with you. I declare, runnin off like that, and smokin, too, don't think I haven't smelled it on you, it's enough to make a body faint, that old stale smoke. I hope you don't do it in public."

Hallie was scratching the bottom of her foot, her hair was falling across her face as she intently watched her fingers move back and forth.

"Well have you?" her aunt said.

"What?" she said, looking up.

"Oh my lands," her aunt said, "smoked any o them cigarettes or cigars or whatever it is you smoke, I wouldn't be surprised, in public, where decent folks can see you?"

"Nome," Hallie said.

"Well thank the good Lord for that, anyhow, that's somethin, anyhow. Now you just slip on somethin and come on down to breftus, hear? You can dress after breftus, take you a bath, Lord, I reckon you need one, gallavantin all over town on a Saady night like some little nigra girl." Her aunt was still mumbling as she went out the door, and Hallie frowned after her; then she got up and pulled the gown over her head and stepped into her shorts.

The kitchen was flooded with sunlight, and her Aunt Lil was sitting at the head of the table, sipping delicately at a cup of coffee; she wore a rose-colored dressing gown of some silk-like material, and her face was fully made up, with the little quarter-size spots of rouge on her cheeks and the ringlets of rusty hair neatly in place about her head. Her Aunt Julia was standing at the stove, one hand on the handle of a heavy, cast iron skillet; she wore a drab, gray house dress and the men's slippers that shuffled audibly on the worn linoleum, and she moved back and forth from the stove to the table to spoon out helpings of scrambled eggs and thick grits and bacon.

"What took you so long?" Aunt Lil said when she came into the kitchen.

"I had to pee," Hallie said, sitting at the table and spreading the large, linen napkin across her lap.

"Did you hear that, Julia?" Aunt Lil said. Her Aunt Julia said nothing. "It's number one, Hallie," Aunt Lil said, "at least in this house it's number one."

"I had to do number one, then," Hallie said.

"Well, you still dawdled, you should be prompt when I tell you breftus is ready, your Aunt Julia works very hard to get our meals on the table at regular hours."

Hallie chewed and swallowed a mouthful of scrambled eggs and grits. "I went on and did number two while I was at it," she said.

"Oh," her Aunt Lil said. She patted her mouth with her napkin and picked up her fork and, after a moment, raised a small bit of egg to her mouth. They ate in silence for a while, the only sound the scraping of forks on the plates; her Aunt Julia was eating a bowl of canned peaches for her breakfast, and every now and then she would raise the bowl to her lips and make a little sucking noise as she drank the syrup.

"A delicious breftus, Julia, as always," her Aunt Lil said; and Hallie said, "Why do you say breftus instead of breakfast?"

Her Aunt Lil dabbed at her mouth with the napkin and chuckled. "Your granddaddy always said breftus, chile, and I guess I just picked it up from him; why, you remember, Julia, he used to come bustlin into this very kitchen, rubbin his hands together in the mornins, sayin, 'Ahhhh, I smell me some good breftus cookin!' That was when we still had Punchy, you don't remember Punchy, chile, and he used to love those big ol cathead biscuits she'd cook up, you remember, Julia, and he'd eat enough for three men his size. And, chile, he'd set your daddy on his knee an make him a sanwich, put a big old paddie o sausage in a biscuit and pour syrup over it and you ought to seen your daddy go after it, and your granddaddy used to laugh and laugh and say, "Now any boy that eats like that bound to do big things!" She chuckled, then leaned back into the chair and sighed. "Just thinkin about that sausage makes me sad, chile; now you got to have a little book o stamps to even get a pound o bacon, and you got to make that last you two weeks, why I remember, you do, too, Julia, when the men would kill hogs, your granddaddy and that old nigra man Blount, the first good cold spell we had, and old man Nettles would come out here to help em butcher and we'd have ham and bacon and sausage and the nigras would barbecue pigs' feet and your granddaddy would buy em all a pint o store-bought whiskey and they'd sing all night, and dance and laugh fit to be tied, not like these young ones comin back from the army, they wasn't a sullen one in the bunch. Why, Julia, did I tell you what Miz Watson told me about that girl of hers? She up and married one o those boys come home from the army and come in and told Miz Watson that she wadn't gonna iron no more, she'd cook and wash dishes and sweep and dust and all that, but she wadn't gonna iron no more, thought she was too good to iron, said her husband, if you want to call him that, cause you know they not really married, they never do any more, said he told her she didn't have to iron if she didn't want to. What's it all comin to, Julia?"

"Huh," her Aunt Julia said. She was sitting slumped in the chair, her empty bowl with the spoon propped in it at an angle before her. "If the Lord had meant for niggers to act like white folks, He'd a made em white," she said.

"Amen," her Aunt Lil said. She picked up a bit of bacon and with her little finger crooked delicately out to the side, popped it between her painted red lips. "We got to get ready for church," she said, pushing back from the table.

Hallie frowned, "Do I have to?" she said.

"You promised your daddy, remember?" Aunt Lil said. She was standing up straightening her gown on her thin frame. "Less get started now, or we'll be late," she said, and chuckled, "and Reverend Wallgood always looks at you like you's carryin a road apple in your purse if you come in late."

"Aww, hell," Hallie mumbled, staring at her plate, and her Aunt Lil said, "What? What? None a that, now, hear?" and Hallie looked up at her Aunt Julia across the table, at the fat, dough-like cheeks and the short, peppery hair, and she was startled and somewhat shocked when her Aunt Julia, almost imperceptibly, gave her a quick, short wink.

BILLY SAT FACING his mother across the breakfast table, his grandmother on his right; his mother had complained of a morning headache — "I swear, Martha, somebody'd think you were pregnant!" his grandmother had said — so they had eaten the meal in silence. He was finishing up by running a biscuit around his plate, sopping up the syrup, and he had been stealing glances at his mother; she wore a worn, pink chenille bathrobe, and her hair was tied loosely behind her neck with a black ribbon. She kept her eyes on her plate, and every now and then she would run the palm of her hand across her forehead and sigh.

"Mama," he said suddenly, and she looked up; her eyes seemed watery and faded, and her skin, without any makeup was red-veined and splotchy. "Do I look like Daddy?" She just looked at him. "I mean when he was younger."

"Of course you do," his grandmother said.

"Do you think so, Mama?" he said, not looking at his grandmother.

"Some," she said. "I wouldn't say you's the spittin image of him."

"Ted Mack Lowery, yesterday evenin, saw me and thought I was Daddy," he said. "He was drunk."

"Ted Mack Lowery?" his grandmother said. She had gotten up to clear the table. "Where you been where you'd run into Ted Mack Lowery?"

"Down along the river," he said. "How'd he know Daddy?"

"Everybody knew your daddy," his grandmother said.

"Woody tried to teach him how to fix radios one time," his mother said, "and they used to go cross the river and drink beer together."

"Martha!" his grandmother said, "that ain't anything to be telling him about his daddy."

"He's old enough to know his daddy drank beer sometimes," his mother said. "He knows he wasn't any Ted Mack Lowery."

"All the same . . ." his grandmother said stacking the dishes in the sink. Just then there was a loud, rapid pounding on the back door, and his grandmother wiped her hands on a dish towel and tucked it into the rope belt she was wearing, and she opened the back door and Ned Clay stood there, dressed in a black suit with a white shirt buttoned up at the collar, and he had on an old gray felt hat, sitting squarely on his head.

"Miz Eva . . ." he said, and his grandmother stepped out onto the porch and pulled the door to behind her. They heard muffled voices for a few minutes, then his grandmother reentered the kitchen.

"It's Ned Clay," she said, "he wants to borrow a dollar, and you just stay put, young man, and don't be goin out there cause he's drunk as cooter brown." She took her purse down from the shelf and began to rummage in it. "Been talkin all week about how he was preachin today, out in Shortleaf; I reckon if they want drunk preachin they can get it today, all right," she said. "Crazy niggers," she mumbled, "ain't got sense enough to come in outa the rain, none of em." She shrugged her shoulders in disgust. "Martha, you got a dollar in your purse? I can't find one," she said, and his mother got up and padded out of the room, and he edged away from the table and over to a window that looked out onto the porch.

Ned was standing with his back against the screen, in his black suit, holding his hat with both hands against his belly; his eyes were closed behind his little steel-rimmed glasses that he'd bought at V.J. Elmore's and was very proud of, and his sparse gray hair stuck to his head like little patches of wool. The collar of his shirt, buttoned but without a tie, curled out over lapels of the heavy suit that he wore every Sunday, summer and winter, the shirt that, the boy knew, was the same shirt he wore all week, that he washed and starched and ironed every Friday, that grew increasingly dirtier and more wrinkled as the week wore on, day by day, and became thinner and more frayed week by week until suddenly, one Saturday, he would appear in a brand new one, bought over the counter at Mr. Sam Golson's store. He loved to talk to Ned, but his mother discouraged it. ("Leave him alone," she'd say, "or he won't clip a single blade o grass. I don't know what I put up with him for, anyhow, cept for the fact that I got a grandson big enough but just about lazy enough not to want to work in the yard hisself.") She would yell at them from the kitchen door, when they would be sitting under a tree, Ned sharpening the swing blade, making long, even strokes with the file. "Leave a little blade to cut with Ned Clay!" she would yell, and Ned would say to him, "Always keep your blade sharp, thass one thing you got to learn in life, boy, keep your blade sharp."

Once, after she had yelled at them and gone back inside, Ned had looked at him, his eyes red-rimmed behind the little glasses. "You know somethin, boy?" Ned had said. "Yore grandma ain't got the sense the Lord promised a mule." The boy had sat there, watching the rusty file make the long strokes — a stroke, and then several seconds wait, then another stroke. "Cause she think niggers is gonna stay down." He had put the file down then. "You ain't old enough yet, you ain't white yet, so you don't know; you think you white, but chirren ain't got no color, white or black don't make no difference to chirren."

"Yes it does too," he said, "I'm white and you're black."

"Sho, I'm bigger'n you and blacker'n you, but that don't make no difference to you, only you don't even know it. Maybe you gone take after yore grandma after all." He had resumed the steady stroking with the file. "Yessir, folks, black and white both, that thinks niggers is gonna stay down got another think comin; a man a man, thass all, and you know that, Billy, whether you got sense enough to know you know it or not. But that's cause you ain't got no color." He stopped filing the swing blade and pointed the file at the boy. "Like that nigger over there in the swamp you always axin me about, call hisself Joe Bynymo, got all the white folks round here and half the niggers too thinkin he crazy as a June bug, he ain't no more crazier than I is, use to come to town sometimes, he don't no more, but he use to; come in the summertime wearin that long black overcoat wid that bullwhip slung over his shoulder, and folks let him alone, sayin he was tetched in the head and had his seasons turned round, didn't know summertime from wintertime, and all them chirren, white and colored alike, they'd jump out and holler 'Bynymo, Bynymo, hit him in the belly wid a fawty-foe,' and take and run and he'd swing that bullwhip after em. Popped one or two of em pretty good, too. But the grown folks let him alone, didn't bother him, and thass all he wanted, he wanted to be let alone."

"How you know that, Ned?" the boy said.

"Never mind how I know, I know. He didn't want to be no nigger, thass all. He black, all right, black as the ace o spades, but he ain't no nigger."

"That don't make sense," the boy said.

"Thass right, sense it don't make, just like it's a lot o things in this world that don't make sense. Why there used to be this old nigger round here named Greensboro, lived out there in Shortleaf, and six days a week he worked as a carpenter for Mr. Caswell Michaels, buildin houses, and on Sunday he used to strap on this big ol bass drum and go walkin all over town, up and down streets, just beatin on that drum, little bitty feller he was; I speck some folks wondered, but nobody that I know of ever axed him how come he did it, folks would just sit on their front porch on a Sunday afternoon and terreckly one of em would sit up and say, 'Here comes Greensboro,' and terreckly here he come by, beatin on that drum, just struttin along like a little old banty rooster." Ned dropped the file to the ground and stood up, grunting with the strain of it. "I speck I better clip some o this smutgrass fore yore mule-headed grandma gits all riled up," he said.

"But why'd he do it?" the boy had said.

"Why'd who do what?" Ned said.

"Greensboro."

Ned scratched his head with his middle finger, and the boy could see little balls of sweat across his forehead. "I done told you, boy," he said. "He knew, I speck, that for six days a week he had to be a nigger, but on Sunday, on the Lord's day, he ain't had to be one."

THE BOY STOOD at the window and watched as his grandmother handed the dollar bill to Ned, and he watched Ned bow his head and shuffle his feet with a great show of humility; he was wondering if maybe preaching was Ned's way of, as he put it, not being a nigger on Sunday, but here he was, drunk and beggin money on a day when he was supposed to be preaching. The boy watched him, nodding thank yous, as he went out the door and down the steps, his hat still in his hands, a broad grin on his face.

"Lordamercy," his grandmother said, coming back into the kitchen, "What am I gonna do with that nigger?"

"Ma-Ma, did you ever see Joe Bynymo when he came into town?" the boy said.

"Sure," she said, "Wasn't much way to miss him, in that overcoat and that cocked eye." She started in to wash the dishes. "He was a sight to see, all right," she said.

"Was he black?"

"What you mean, 'black'?" she said, "he's a nigger man."

"I mean was he real black or yellow or what?"

"He's a high yellow," his mother said from the table; she had lighted a cigarette, and it hung from her lips at an angle, the smoke curling up over her head and making her squint one eye at him.

"Ned told me he was black as the ace o spades," the boy said, and his grandmother laughed.

"He's liable to tell you anything," she said.

"Now tell me again what his name was before he changed it to Joe Bynymo, all right?" the boy said, and his mother said, "Armistead King, for the fifteenth time."

"And his mother was named Bertha King, and yes I knew her, but not very well, all that for the umpteenth time and I can't understand why you're so interested in that crazy old hermit like you are," his grandmother added.

"It's just an old story," his mother said, "boys just like stories."

"Mr. Sam said the wind picked him up and flung him across the river and rapped his head against a white oak tree and that's why his eye is cocked and he's got his seasons turned around," the boy said.

"He got his eye cocked across the river, all right, but it wasn't any white oak that done it, more likely it was a sawed off pool cue in the back room of some nigger beer garden."

"Oh Eva," his mother said, "let him believe what he wants to about that old hermit."

"I wonder why he never comes to town anymore," the boy said more to himself that to them.

"Probly stayin one step ahead o the sheriff," his grandmother said, and his mother laughed and snubbed out her cigarette. His grandmother continued to wash the breakfast dishes, and his mother got up and padded toward the door.

"I'm goin to lie down for a while," she said in a tired voice; and when she went out the door, he said, "Ma-Ma, I'm goin outside"

"Well, don't stray far cause you got to shell some peas for dinner."

"Okey," he said, and went out onto the porch; the morning was bright, and the sun was high, and he walked around the corner of the house, still on the porch, and sat in the swing. The chain squeaked gently as he rocked back and forth, looking to where the road curved away from the house toward the river.

THE AFTERNOON WAS already bitter hot, and Hallie stood in the grassless, sandy back yard, in her shorts and shirt, her arms hanging loosely at her sides, her face fixed in a state of intense boredom; she could hear the rattle and clatter of the dinner dishes that her Aunt Julia was washing, and she could taste the greasy fried chicken they'd had (her Aunt Lil had infuriated her by placing a drumstick on her plate) and the sticky sweet iced tea and the cherry pie she detested. "I hate cherry pie," she'd said, and her Aunt Lil had said, "Why, you just don't know what's good, does she Julia?" "Aunt Julia ain't eatin any," she'd said, and her Aunt Lil had said, "Julia never takes sweets, chile, they tend to bloat her." Now she stood in the back yard, the smells of dinner still lingering in the air; her Aunt Lil was upstairs lying down, lying, she knew, with a damp washcloth across her powdered forehead, her eyes closed against the heat, and the Sunday silence, broken only by the occasional tinkle or clink of dishes in the sink, was stifling to her. She stood looking around at the yard, at the empty garage that leaned slightly, as though one day it might fall in a heap on its side, at the old, unpainted tool shed with the door falling off its hinges, and there was even an old privy, it too unpainted, in the corner of the yard. ("We keep it for the servants," she'd heard he Aunt Lil say, "we occasionally still have a girl in in the Spring.") The yard was littered with bits of paper and slivers of blue glass that picked up the sun, glass from a broken Vicks bottle that had been scattered here and there, and she could still see, in the dust, arcs made by the brush broom that her Aunt Julia had made and kept in the toolshed to sweep the yard. The girl wandered aimlessly over to the toolshed and pulled open the creaking, crooked door; light came into the close little room through the cracks between the boards, and she could see the contents of the interior, an old churn covered with dust and cobwebs, in one corner, and against the back wall stacks of newspapers and magazines that her Aunt Julia periodically sold to Mr. Taylor at the junk yard. The floor was hardpacked dirt, and the girl went in, her sandals scaping on the littered floor; the air was musty and stale, but the little shed seemed cool after being in the sun, and she sat down on one of the stacks of magazines and leaned back against the rough planking of the wall. She could see the back of the house through the open door, the dark windows with their misty, chintz curtains, and she listened but she could no longer hear the rattling of the dishes, and she knew that soon her Aunt Julia would be settling herself into a chair in the living room, or the parlor, as her Aunt Lil called it, next to the radio and switch it on and begin her long Sunday afternoon of listening to the programs, the westerns and the mysteries that she never seemed to tire of; she would play it very softly, so as not to wake her sister, sitting with her ear almost pressed against the speaker, a strange smile on her face as though she were very pleased that no one could hear the programs but her. "It's gonna be a long summer," Hallie said out loud, and her own voice almost startled her in the silence. She was remembering the morning, the long, tedious church service with the hymns, her Aunt Lil's voice shrill beside her, and the image of Reverend Wallgood standing behind the pulpit, his little glasses straining to cover his face, great half-moons of sweat in the armpits of his suit, the fat rolling in bulges over his wilted collar, standing, his face tilted toward the ceiling, the cardboard fans in each pew going slowly back and forth, and she wanted to laugh when he cried out, at the end of his long, mumbling prayer, "Lord! Make me thy servant!," because he was so serious and funny-looking with his hair parted down the middle. And when they had left, going out the door, he had taken her hand in his and leaned forward, smiling at her and welcoming her into the congregation, and she had thought that his arms looked as though they came from around behind him, he was so fat, and his body, in his dark suit, reeked of sweat. "Now he's the kind of preacher I like," Aunt Lil had said, walking home. "He preaches the Bible, none a this nonsense that some a these younger fellers are always getting up there and spoutin, nossir, he preaches the Bible." And the girl had walked along in silence, her Sunday dress feeling sticky and strange on her body.

Now she stretched her legs out in front of her, trying to relax on the magazines; she felt secretive and odd sitting in the little tool shed, the darkness contrasting with the brightness outside; she felt tucked away, hidden from the world, and the sensation was a pleasant one. She was thinking of her father, of the firmness with which he had shipped her off as soon as school was out. "It's good for a growin girl to have older women around, at least some of the time," he'd said, "and you'll enjoy it, they'll spoil you." "Huh," she'd said, "I doubt that." "Whatever else Lillian might be, she's a lady, and it can't do you any harm to spend the summer with her," he'd said. The bus had been crowded with servicemen, the air inside rank and hot, full of the smells of them, body sweat and whiskey and cigarette smoke, and they talked in loud, rough voices and there was much laughter from some, while others seemed to be asleep, oblivious to the noises of their comrades.

Once, the driver, whose name, according to a little metal plate over the windshield, was Frank Dodd, which, during the boredom of the ride she had looked at and looked at and decided that it sounded like a tongue-tied person trying to say, "Thank God," once he had to stop the bus and threaten to put one of the soldiers, who had gotten very loud, off the bus. Most of the others had hooted and yelled at him, and he had muttered curses under his breath.

It had been a long, hot, and tiring ride. Toward the end of it, when she knew they were nearing Hammond, she had started to see a few road signs. Soon the highway was lined with big crepe myrtle bushes, in full bloom, the thick red blossoms reminding her, as they always did, of watermelon.

"Hallie Fisque," her Aunt Lil had said when she got off the bus, "if you ain't the spirit and image of yore grandma, there ain't a nigger in Mississippi!" And she thought about the thin, stern, blank face that stared out of the heavy gilt frame on the wall of her aunts' parlor, and she hadn't thought that it was much of a compliment. "Was it hot on the bus? I bet I know what you need," her aunt said, as they walked home, Hallie lugging the straw suitcase which kept knocking against her leg, "a cool bath and a tall, cold glass of water. I bet Julia'll have some ready for us when we get there."

Now Hallie stood up in the tool shed and stretched her legs; the afternoon had worn on, and she listened, and way off in the distance was a gentle, long roll of thunder. She hated to leave the little shed, but she saw that the light outside had dimmed, and soon it would rain, and she knew that the roof leaked, and she didn't want to explain to her aunts how she had gotten wet. She came out in the light and crossed the sandy yard to the house; she walked with a slight, barely perceptible limp, which, for some reason she got a kick out of feigning.

Five

Now the days passed slowly, merging into one another, dying in the redness of the twilight, fresh and crisp in the mornings when the leaves on the trees moved gently back and forth in the breezes. They seemed long and empty, with an aimless, wandering quality about them: wandering along the white-hot sidewalks, under the huge old trees, as on the day when he'd told her about thinking of the hermit as a young boy, and she'd said, "Lord, that was a long time ago wadn't it?" Afternoons spent at the swimming pool, jumping from the tall, wooden tower and laughing, and the changing in the cool, mossy urine reek of the wooden bathhouse to walk home and stand in her aunts' kitchen and drink Cokes and eat soda crackers to stem the hunger of the swimming. Or long hours at the back of Dr. Frank Rutland's drug store, sitting in the wire chairs, where he didn't mind if you read the funny books as long as you ordered something, Hallie doling out nickels from the money her father sent her for a steady stream of cherry Cokes; once they had stolen a book off the wire rack of paper-covered pocket books, one entitled WHAT TO TELL YOUR DAUGHTER ABOUT SEX, but they had thrown it in the canal when they discovered it contained drawings like the ones they'd seen in their science books.

"Shoot, Doctor Weinstein don't know as much about it as I do," the girl had said, and the boy said nothing, standing on the wooden footbridge watching the book float away down the canal towards the river.

They liked the dim quiet of Mr. Sam's store; sometimes his brother Phineas was there, to play checkers or dominoes, and an old man named Rhett Hunnicutt who wore bright red and blue ties. They would sit for hours watching the games, surrounded by all the smells of the store, watching and listening to Mr. Rhett carry on, accusing Phineas always of cheating him or kidding them about something or other. "Why ain't you younguns in school?" he'd say. "It's summertime Mr. Rhett," one of them would say. "Is it now? Well, I'll be dog, I'll just be dog, here it's done got to be summertime again, and you keep yore frisky hands on top o the table, Finny, I got me a frog sticker in my pocket just right for frisky hands and youngun's ears." Sometimes, if the boy were by himself, Mr. Rhett would say something like, "Hey boy, how yore hammer hangin?" and when they were together, when Hallie was with him, more than once he had seen Mr. Rhett's pale eyes fastened on Hallie's legs, or on the front of her blouse, and though he didn't say anything about it, once Hallie had said: "That old coot sure has got a mean way of lookin at somebody." They had taken to calling him Rhett Funnybutt behind his back.

It was Phineas that they really liked the best; he was tall quiet man who talked to them as though they were no different from him. He ran the farm that he and his brother lived on, and during the summer months he hung around the store a lot, helping out and playing checkers and dominoes. "Sam tells me you like old stories and pictures and such," he said to the boy. "I like old things like that; I got some Confederate money I'll show you sometime."

"I'd like to see it," the boy said, though his grandmother had some that she'd shown him.

"There was this feller, a Dr. Simpson, come over here from the University one day and tried to buy that old money. I told him I reckon not, and the old feller went off madder'n a wet hen."

"What'd he want to buy it for?" the boy said.

"Folks do that," Phineas said, "they come in here sometimes, fiddle around till there ain't anybody else in here but them, then they kind of sidle up to you and say, real casual like, 'Got any old money layin around, old coins or stamps or anythin, I got a collection and I'll pay cash for old worthless money.' And I always tell em no, I ain't, and they act like you bein real sly with em and they don't believe you. Course I ain't bein any slyer than they are."

So the days passed for them; the long, late afternoons when, as they walked, after supper, their tall shadows fell across the faded, faint hop-scotch squares scrawled on the pavement with limerock. Sometimes they would pass Miss Vera Dukes, who would be out walking her dog; she was the only person in town who kept a dog on a leash, a little brown and white fice that would growl fiercely at them as they passed, and she would smile and say, "Good evenin, he won't bite." They would pass down the street, under the shadow of the tall Confederate monument, whose wide-brimmed hat some high school boys, last halloween, had painted bright red; it was now a pale, pink color. Walking the streets of town they would pass the pool room and steal a glance through the propped-open door; once they had seen Ted Mack Lowery sitting on a pool table, his legs dangling, drinking an orange drink. Or they would pass the picture show, not yet open, and they would stop to read the posters, the bright red and yellow coming attractions, and sometimes the old Negro janitor would be sweeping the outside lobby, grumbling under his breath, and he would say, "Show ain't open yet," several times, almost as though he were muttering to himself. They usually had enough money to go to the show once a week, and it would be on Saturday afternoons, to see the double feature, a western and a Bowery Boys or war picture and a serial.

Just who had the idea first for what eventually got them into trouble they later couldn't remember; it might have occurred to both of them at the same time, the idea springing full-grown from their minds simultaneously. Almost every day, at some time or other during their wanderings, they would pass the junk yard, a sprawling heap of old car parts and stacks of junk paper covered with ragged tarpaulins, fronted with a little wooden shack with a crudely lettered sign on the front that said OFFICE. The yard sat next to the railroad tracks, and there was a limerock cave just behind it that ran under the railroad embankment, and sometimes they went there to smoke during the day; and the yard was run by an old man named Taylor, a grizzled, dusty old man who sat in a cane-bottomed chair in the doorway to his office, puffing dreamily on his pipe, a red, flat tin of tobacco protruding from his shirt pocket. Several times they had taken a squeaky-wheeled, rusty red child's wagon that they had discovered in Hallie's aunt's garage (that they later found out her Aunt Julia used for much the same purpose) and gone along the river, down near the city dump, gathering pieces of iron, old bolts, and rusty auto parts to sell as scrap iron to old Man Taylor.

The first time they had come squeaking and creaking up the road, pulling the wagon with its small load, and stopped in front of the shack, the old man had just sat there looking at them, nodding his head as though he were telling them something.

"How much for this load o scrap iron?" the boy said

"Load, huh?" the old man said. He leaned forward and peered into the wagon, still nodding his head, and for a moment it seemed that he might fall forward out of the chair into the dust. "Fifteen cents for the load, a quarter for the wagon," he said.

They looked at each other, Hallie's face very serious, the bridge of her nose pink and about to peel again. "What you mean, a quarter for this wagon?" she said, and the old man chuckled. He said,

"Oh, I thought that uz part o the scrap."

"It ain't for sale," the girl said.

"I wouldn't have it noway," the old man said, "the thang give me a headache just listenin to you come up the road with it."

"This scrap iron is worth more than fifteen cents," the boy said, and the old man sat up straight in his chair.

"Now listen here, who the junk dealer here, me or you? I done give you a appraisal, you can take it or leave it, I ain't spendin my time hagglin with no snotnose chillen."

So they had decided to take it, and the old man had stood up and counted out a dime and five pennies into the boy's hand and taken the bolts and parts and just tossed them over the sagging front fence of the place; they clanged loudly on a pile of metal. "Hurry back," he called, wiping his hands on his breeches and sitting back down, and they went off down the road, the wagon creaking behind them; once the old man leaned out and hollered at them. "Whyn't you earl that bastid?" he hollered. And they went on down the road without looking back.

They would go back, from time to time, with another load, and the old man would always say something like, "Here come that load o mice again," or "Miz Walker up the road there asted me to tell you to quit goin by her house with that thang cause you done scared her hens so they won't lay." And he continued to dole out the change to them in small amounts, tossing the scrap iron over the fence onto the pile that didn't seem to grow any. Once, and maybe this is where it had come from, the idea, he said, "Wher you chillen stealin all this scrap from?"

"We pick it up along the river," the girl said; and the old man said, "Don't you know you been robbin the U.S. government?"

"It's just old junk," the boy said.

"That river belongs to the U.S. government, boy," he said, "an all that's along it and in it too, cept for the fish they allow folks to cetch. But I ain't particular, now, I pays good money for scrap iron and I don't ast where it come from."

And that evening, at just about first dark, they were sitting on his grandmother's back steps; they could smell the honeysuckle on the back fence, and the sunflowers were black shadows, like licorice allday suckers, against the ash-heap. "Hallie," the boy had said, looking out toward the sunflowers, "think about this a minute. Where, in the whole town, is there the most scrap iron just sittin there, waitin to be picked up?"

The girl was leaning back against the steps on her elbows, her legs stretched out before her. She was quiet for a moment. then she said, "I been thinkin about it."

THE CRICKETS WERE loud in the high grass along the railroad track as they walked; the night was dark, and the girl, from time to time, would stumble, the toe of her sandals catching on a crosstie. "Dammit," she mumbled, and the boy motioned for her to be quiet. "He might sleep in that shack," he whispered. They each carried a croaker sack, and the rough material was stinging on their bare arms. "He might shoot the hell out of us, too," the girl whispered back, and the boy put his finger against his lips. "Come on," he whispered.

They went down a steep embankment, slipping and sliding in the loose dirt, making much too much noise, and once the girl giggled and he put his hand on her arm; they stood at the bottom of the fill, looking across a small pasture to the little stream that ran through the limerock cave under the tracks, the ground rising sharply just past the stream up to the sagging, board back fence of the junk yard. There was a slight glow from the front of the yard that came from a street light a block away, and they could see the gaps in the fence, some wide enough for a grown man to walk through. The boy motioned his arm and they went slowly across the pasture to where they could cross the stream and then up the bank to the board fence. They stood, looking through one of the cracks.

The yard was still and quiet; the mounds of junk metal rose up like black volcanoes, and they could see several silo-like stacks of worn-out tires, all bathed in the soft, yellow glow of the street light down the way, which they could see in the distance, with hundreds of fluffy luna moths fluttering silently around it. They stood looking into the yard for a few minutes; the little office shack was dark. "Nobody's here," the boy said, whispering, "but be real quiet." They slipped through the crack and approached the nearest pile of scrap metal.

They filled the two sacks, then discovered that they couldn't carry but one between them, and only if it were half full, so they had to replace some of the scrap. Then they went out through the crack, half carrying, half dragging the sack. "This ought to be worth something," the girl said, "it's sure heavy enough." "Shhhhhh," the boy said. They had already picked a place to hide it, a cave-like washed out indention in a ditch near his grandmother's house, and when they reached the place they were both covered in sweat; they put the metal back in the wash and covered it with branches. "Listen, I got to rush home," the girl said; and the boy said, "See you in the morning."

Her Aunt Lil was sitting in the kitchen in her rose-colored dressing gown when the girl came in. "Do you know what time it is?" she started in. "Do you? It's almost ten o'clock, and here you are sneakin in. Where you been?"

"I wasn't sneakin in," the girl said.

"Where you been?" her aunt said, "up to no good, I know that, but where?"

"I been playin out," she said. Her aunt sat straight in the chair, looking at her, her face tilted slightly to the side; she had a book closed in her lap, her index finger stuck inside to mark her place.

"I swear, Hallie," she said, "why are you such a trial to me? Why can't you be like other young ladies your age, learnin to be a lady instead o playin out in the dark. What you been playin, hide an go seek, or what?" Her aunt was peering at her, a peculiar, narrow-eyed expression on her face. "Well?" she said.

"We been tellin ghost stories," Hallie said. "Over in Billy Malone's back yard. There was some other kids over there," she added, not quite sure why, except that her aunt's expression made her uneasy.

"What kinda ghost stories?" she said.

"Billy told about that old hermit that lives over there in the swamp across the river," she said, "he's the king of the hermits."

"Armistead King?" her aunt said, "that old nigra?"

"Yessum," she said.

Her aunt sat very still; the small, naked bulb that hung on a cord over the table made her skin look yellowish, and there was no sound in the room except for the occasional thump of a moth on the black windowpanes.

"I declare," she said, after a minute, "I do declare," and her voice was little more than a whisper. "Did I ever tell you about the time we had all that company for Christmas, and me and your Aunt Julia and your daddy all slept on the floor in the parlor, and Santa Claus stepped on your Aunt Julia's hand during the night?"

"Nome," the girl said. Her aunt was looking at the window, a wistful, lost expression now on her face.

"Why, we used to sit around the fire, listening to your granddaddy tell ghost stories, sittin there on the floor hearin his voice, he could really tell em, hearin the fire poppin in the grate and the grown folks' rockin chairs creakin and creakin, and fore long all the younguns would be droppin off to sleep, one by one. He could really tell em."

"Yessum," the girl said.

Her aunt looked back at her, her eyes misty, her head looking slightly lop-sided because the curls on one side were flattened where she had been lying down. "You go on to bed now, Hallie," she said, "an be real quiet so you don't wake Julia, hear? She works mighty hard, mighty hard."

"Yessum," she said, and she left the kitchen and started up the stairs, walking very carefully so as to keep the old boards from creaking.

THE MORNING WAS cool; it had rained during the night, and the loose-wheeled, rusty little wagon made little wriggly, worm-like trails in the damp dirt of the road. It was loaded with the scrap iron from the night before, and they fell silent as they approached the junk yard, both noticing how much different it looked in the sunlight of the morning. It was quiet, as quiet as it had been during the night, but now, as they approached, they saw a little puff of smoke come out of the doorway of the office shack.

"Well, well, well," the old man said as they came up to the shack, "if it ain't Mister and Miz John D. Rockiefeller." He sat in the chair, looking at them, his pipe drooping from his mouth at an angle.

"We got a good load for you this morning," the boy said.

"Have you, now?" the old man said.

"At least a dollar's worth," the girl said.

The old man leaned forward from his chair looking over the load. He stared at it for a few moments, his head nodding up and down, and they looked nervously at each other. "Hmmmmmmmmmmm," the old man said. He continued to nod his head, studying the contents of the wagon, the small pile of rusty metal. "Well, now," he said.

"How much?" the boy said.

"Let me study on it for a minute," the old man said. He sat up and drew on his pipe and blew a puff of smoke toward the ceiling; he watched it crawl up among the rafters. "Eighty cents," he said, "an thet's my final offer."

"Sold!" the girl said.

DURING THE NEXT week and a half, they sold the old man four more loads of his own scrap iron before he caught on, and when he did, they realized almost immediately that they had been both greedy and careless. They had split the money down the middle, and it had gone mostly for cigarettes and cherry Cokes, a couple of movie magazines, and four twelve-gauge shotgun shells that had just happened to strike the boy's fancy at Golson's store. And they had also bought a small can of Three-In-One oil which turned out to be, in the end, the cause of their downfall.

"Because you see," the boy had said, "if we can oil the wheels down real good so that it don't make any noise, we can take the wagon up there and get us a good, big load."

"I don't know," the girl had said.

But they had done it, and one night had taken the wagon to the junk yard and filled it and pulled it boldly out the front gate, which they had discovered the old man didn't even lock, and looking carefully up and down the street, had pulled it, the wheels still wobbling but barely squeaking now, to the wash in the ditch and hidden the iron, wagon and all, under the brush.

The old man seemed startled when they suddenly appeared before him the next morning; he had been sitting in the shack with his eyes closed, the sun warming his feet, when they had come up, and he had opened his eyes and jerked upright in the chair, blinking at them.

"Mornin," the girl said, and the old man looked from them to the wagon, then back to them.

"Earled it, huh?" he said. "You got rid o a right smart o noise." Then, still blinking his eyes, he looked at the load in the wagon; it was piled high with the rusty iron, so that the little wagon couldn't have held any more. It had made deep, slightly wobbly ruts in the dust. The old man stared at the loaded wagon, not saying a word.

"We got you bout a three dollar load this morning," the boy said, "or four."

The old man stood up, slowly, and stepped down onto the ground. He bent over the wagon and inspected the scrap iron carefully, picking up several pieces and peering at them, then dropping them back on the pile. "Uh huh," he said, "Uh huh."

"How much?" the boy said, and the old man said nothing. He put his hands on his hips and stared off down the road, his eyes following the trail of the wagon, his eyes squinting against the morning sun. His head nodded slightly, and he made a soft little chewing motion with his chin. Then he walked over to the front gate that was propped open with a stick of fire wood and looked down at the ground, and the boy and girl exchanged glances. He stood there, very still, looking at the ground.

"What you doin, Mister Taylor?" the girl said.

He stood there a moment longer, not saying anything, and then he said, "Just carryin on a conversation wit a fool, thass all," and the boy and girl exchanged glances again, and the old man looked at them and said, "Would five dollars be all right?"

"Sure would," the boy said, "that's bout what we figured."

"Well now," he said, going toward the door of the shack, "You'll heveta take a check, I don't keep that kinda money round the office, what wit outlaws about, you know?" He rummaged around on a cluttered desk and found the checks and sat heavily in the chair; he took a stub of pencil from his pocket and licked the lead. "All right, now, who do I make this out to? The Rockiefeller Junk Gatherin Company or who?"

"Make it out to Billy Malone," the boy said, and the old man wrote slowly on the check, pausing now and then to lick the lead.

"And?" he said. "Since you in bidnis together, I speck I better make it out to both of you, thass the proper procedure in a case like this."

"And Hallie Fisque," the boy said, and the old man wrote, his mouth forming the letters of her first name.

"Spell that last un for me," he said, and Hallie spelled it out and then pronounced it for him, and he finished writing with a flourish, filling in the amount and signing his name. "What kin are you to Miss Lillian and Miss Julia Fisque?" the old man said, tearing the check off the pad.

"They're my aunts," the girl said, and the old man said:

"Uh huh," and he looked at the boy. "I speck you Miz Eva Malone's grandson, ain't you? Woody Malone's boy."

"Yessir," the boy said, and the old man handed him the check.

"Take care o that check, now, cause it's Wednesday an the bank ain't open, hear?" And the old man sat back in his chair and began to stuff his pipe.

It was early that afternoon, when they were sitting in his grandmother's back yard, planning what to do with the five dollars, when his grandmother had stuck her head out the back door, and he had known from the expression on her face that something was wrong. "Hallie," his grandmother had called, "you better go home, you Aunt wants to talk to you," and they didn't even have to ask why, because it occurred to both of them at once what was wrong. "And Billy," his grandmother said, "you get yourself in this house this minute!"

HER AUNT LIL was sitting in the parlor when she got home, and she went directly there. She entered the room and her aunt looked up, and they stared at one another for almost a minute; her Aunt was fresh and crisp looking from her afternoon bath, and there was a faint scent of lilac perfume in the air. Her hand, holding the oriental fan, lay motionless in her lap.

"We have had common nigras here," her aunt said, slowly, "that we have had to let go for doin much less than you been up to."

The girl looked at her, a set, stoic expression on her face; her eyes were narrow, and she stood with her feet spread apart on the rug, waiting.

"Childish pranks are one thing, your granddaddy always said that children would be children, and though I ain't married and I ain't got any of my own, I'm smart enough to know at least that. But they's two things I need to say to you right here: one, that wasn't no childish prank, stealin from that ol man like that, and number two you ain't no child. You know what I mean?"

The girl stared at her. "I reckon I do," she said.

"Maybe this ain't a good time to bring this up, cept for the fact that we are talking, and this is one o those rare times you're here, but your Aunt Julia tells me you been spottin your stepins, which don't mean but one thing, and that's that you're fixin to become a lady sure enough, and it's high time you started to act like one."

"Yessum," she said; her expression hadn't changed, and she continued to stare at her aunt.

"I declare," her aunt said; she suddenly fanned herself with her Oriental fan. "You do know all about what's fixin to happen to you, don't you?" she said.

"I read about it, yessum," the girl said, "but it ain't gonna happen to me."

"Who do you think you are, the Queen of Siam or somebody? It happens to everybody, ever lady that grows up, it's the plague of bein a woman, it'll lay you out so bad sometime you'll think you got the polio; come in here talking bout it ain't gonna happen to you, well, I got some news for you, it's happenin to you."

"No it ain't, either," the girl said, "it ain't and it won't and you can hush up about it."

"Now you hold on there, young lady, don't you be gettin huffy with me, you ain't too old to get the daylights whupped out of you." She stopped and fanned, then put the fan on a table beside the chair; her elbow hit the table and made the green fringe on a lamp shade jiggle back and forth; that was the only movement in the quiet room for a minute. "But that ain't what I wanted to talk to you about, anyhow, though it is related," she said. "I had a nice, embarrassin phone call from Mr. Taylor informin me that my nice little niece who's visitin for the summer has been stealin scrap iron from him and then turning around and sellin it back to him. Now that sho is a nice, ladylike pastime for a young lady, wouldn't you say? I don't believe I've ever been so embarrassed as I was getting that phone call, and that old man laughing over the phone like he thought it was the funniest thing he ever did hear of, laughing mind you, at me, because it had to be my niece conductin herself like a common thief. And you just might want to know that he said he debated a long time bout whether to call me and Eva and let us handle it or call the sheriff and just turn the both of you over to him, and if he'da done that you woulda had the honor o bein the first Fisque to ever sit in the Hammond jailhouse, surrounded by drunk nigras and all sorts of other trashy riff-raff. I reckon you'da loved that, wouldn't you?"

"Nome," the girl said.

"I declare," her aunt said, "I declare, Hallie, you are a trial to me, I wish to the Lord your mother had lived, maybe she'd know how to deal with you, cause it sho musta been from her side that you got the kinda blood that would make you turn into a crook."

"I ain't a crook, and you stop talkin about my mother," the girl said, and her aunt looked quickly at her, her eyes darting.

"What do you call yourself, then?" she said.

"I don't know," the girl said, "but I ain't a crook."

"Well, you committed a crime, and folks that do that got to pay a penalty," her aunt said, and they looked at each other for a moment. "I don't know what I'm gonna do with you, I might get Julia to whup you, tan the daylights out of you, or I might make you stay in your room."

"For how long?"

"I don't know that yet either. Maybe a month," she said.

"A month?" the girl said.

"We had a nigra once that got caught stealin, and the judge gave him thirty days, and I figure you have let yourself in for the same kinda sentence."

"I know one thing," the girl said, "I ain't stayin in that ol room any thirty days, that's for sure."

"I declare," her aunt said, "I ain't ever heard of a judge yet that let the crook decide on the sentence."

"I ain't a crook and you ain't a judge, and you better stop callin me that." Her aunt's eyes, over the little quarter-size spots of rouge, were level on hers and she stood with her fists clenched at her sides, a strand of blond hair hanging across her face.

"If you ain't a hellion," her aunt said, "I ain't never seen one. You got bad blood in you girl, you know that? You standin there like you gone hit me."

"I'll knock the hell out of you if I take a notion to," the girl said.

"You would, too, wouldn't you?"

"I said I would, didn't I?"

"A hellion, that's what you are, a little thievin hellion. Thank God your granddaddy ain't alive to see this."

"That ol man's probly in hell where he belongs," the girl said; she still stood in the exact spot, her feet apart, her hands at her sides. Her aunt stood up, her eyes flashing.

"Take that back," she said, and the girl said:

"I ain't takin anything back."

"Take it back!" her aunt said.

"Make me," the girl said.

"Make her take it back, Julia," her Aunt said and the girl wheeled around and saw her Aunt Julia, standing in the door to the parlor; she wore the gray, shapeless dress and the bedroom slippers, and she was holding a broom like a staff. Her eyes were narrow in her putty-like face, and she stared at them, looking from one to the other and back again.

"Ain't either one of you got any respect for the dead," she said, "fightin like two ol cats."

"Did you hear what she said?" her Aunt Lil said; her voice was high and tense, and she seemed about to break into tears at any minute.

"I heard it," she said, "and the Lord hisself heard it, and will damn the soul that uttered it, even if He ain't had cause enough to damn it already." Her voice was quiet and steady in the tense air of the room.

"Amen," her Aunt Lil said, nodding her head up and down, and the girl backed away from them so that they formed a triangle in the room, and she, now, looked from one to the other.

"I know one thing," she said, her voice calm, "I ain't ever gonna be like you two ol things." And her Aunt laughed, a high, cackling laugh, and she said:

"You know what, Julia, you know what she said? She said that she ain't gonna havta put up with the curse!" She cackled again, but her Aunt Julia just looked at her. The light in the room was dimming as the afternoon wore on, and she could see the sheen of sweat on her Aunt Julia's face in a strange light.

"Didn't you tell her I've done found the spots?" her Aunt Julia said. She seemed almost proud, accusing, as though she had found something else yet that could damn the girl's soul, and the girl stood in the dim parlor, looking at them, and she felt very dirty and unclean. The two aunts looked at her, the one, dumpy, standing just inside the door where she had moved, still holding the broom like a staff, the other taller and thinner, with the rouge spots and tiny curls all over her head, smiling at her, her head reared back on her shoulders like a jaybird eyeing a squirrel.

"I ain't ever gonna be like you old bitches," the girl said. "Ain't nothin gonna happen to me, I'll see to that."

"A hellion and a thief and dumb to boot," her Aunt Lil said, "it ain't

Fisque blood, is it, Julia?"

"You better leave me alone," the girl said, and she suddenly felt helpless, almost defenseless, before them; the feeling lasted but a moment, then she carefully, with a sidelong glance, measured the distance to the door, the distance to escape from them. "You just better leave me alone," she said, with more conviction. She edged toward the door. "You ain't got any cause to call me dumb," she said, "you ain't got the sense the Lord promised a mule, cause you think niggers are gonna stay down." She looked at her Aunt Lil, and she seemed stunned; her Aunt Julia straightened up and raised the broom in front of her like a weapon. "You dumb ol ass-holes," the girl said, and she dashed for the door; she raced across the hall and up the steps, her sandals pounding on the creaking boards. She heard her Aunt Lil yell something after her in a shrilling, high voice.

"I always knew your mother's people were goddamned carpet-baggers!"

Later, after her aunts had come upstairs to their room, she lay across her bed in darkness. They had not called her to supper, and she had lain, in the still quiet, watching the darkness fall and darken the thick foliage of the oak tree; she had heard, from time to time, their vague voices murmuring downstairs, and then, long after dark, their footsteps on the creaking staircase, the footsteps going by her closed door, a still, chill silence in the hall outside, so that she could picture, in her mind's eye, her aunts pressing their fingers silently to their lips as they went by.

She lay thinking of the unpainted, creaky old house, with its sandy yard and its locked trunks, the mustiness with which the days passed within it, the lingering scent of lilac soap mixed with ammonia, the afternoon baths and long naps in the darkened rooms behind shutters closed against the heat. Her aunts seemed to be strangers to her, and she felt very alone on the high bed; she thought of what her Aunt Lil had said was happening to her, and she clenched her fists and shivered in the darkness. And she made a silent, hopeless vow.

Later, when the old house was deathly still and quiet, she took her small, straw suitcase from under the bed and put an extra shirt and a pair of shorts into it, then, being careful as she walked on the creaky floor, she got her toothbrush from the bathroom and put it in. Then, holding the suitcase high against her breast so as not to knock into anything, she went quietly down the steps; the moonlight filtered through the stained-glass transom over the front door and gave the little entrance hall an eerie, red and green cast, and she silently opened the door and slipped out. She crossed the porch and went down the steps and into the yard, and then paused and looked at the house; it sat, dumb and quiet, its windows black, its unpainted boards bathed in moonlight. A nightingale suddenly sang, from the Cherokee roses across the road, and she started; then she went across the yard, taking long strides, the suitcase knocking against her legs. She paused at the edge of the road, then she turned and walked toward her friend's house, hearing the sound of the crickets, steady and grinding, somehow comforting to her in the night.

Six

THE BOY WAS lying on the bed in the dark room; he was half-awake, aware of the steady hum and rattle of the pump in the pump house, knowing when it suddenly stopped and there was only the sound of crickets and the far-off call of a nightingale. He had been sent to bed directly after supper ("No more of this 'playin out' as you choose to call it," his grandmother had said) and he could still feel the welts across the back of his legs where one of his father's heavy black leather belts, wielded by his grandmother, had struck him. It had been very bad, with his mother leaning her elbows on the table, crying and complaining of a headache, while he lay across the kitchen chair, his breeches pulled down around his ankles, anticipating the flesh-biting blows as they fell, one by one, his grandmother red-faced and straining. ("You're not gonna whip him?" his mother had said, and his grandmother had said, "You're darn right I'm gonna whip him, I'm gonna flail the very tar out of him!" "My head is killin me," his mother had said, and his grandmother had said, "It's something else that's gonna be killin him, and if it'd been worn out more when he was littler, maybe I wouldn't be havin to do it now to a more than half-grown boy!") His grandmother had taken the check and torn it into tiny bits and made him flush it down the toilet. "And you're gonna work in this yard till you make back every bit you cheated that feller out of, you understand?" she'd said. "Lordamercy." Then she had laughed, and he'd not known why she was laughing. "Lordamercy," she'd said, "if you don't get more like your daddy every day, I swear, but it looks like you're forming all his bad habits and mighty few of his good."

Now he lay quietly, relaxed; he was wondering what his grandmother had meant, wondering about his father's habits that she had mentioned when he felt himself drifting off to sleep. He was wondering if his father had ever pulled the same thing on Old Man Taylor; the pump came back on and hummed, and slowly he was aware of another sound, a soft scratching on top of the pump-sound, a sound that he couldn't for a moment identify, and he listened to it; then he sat up in bed. He could hear a scratching on the screen of the open window, then a voice said, in a whisper. "Billy, it's me."

He slid off the bed and went to the window; the girl was standing outside, in the garden, and he could see her plainly in the moonlight, standing under the window against a row of thick, green turnip greens. He squatted there, looking down at her, and he noticed the straw suitcase sitting in the dirt beside her.

"Were you asleep?" she said. "How'd it go?"

"I got a lickin," he said. He looked at the suitcase. "You musta got one too," he said.

"Naw, they're scared to lay a hand on me," she said.

They were quiet for a minute, the only sounds the song of the crickets and the hum of the pump. Then, the boy said, "Where you goin?"

"I don't know," she said, "but I stopped by to see if you wanted to go with me."

"Out of town?"

"I don't know, somewhere, I thought about Birmingham."

The boy looked at her for a moment. "I sure don't want to go to Birmingham," he said.

"I don't either," she said, "I thought about goin home, but he wouldn't do nothing but send me back up here, and I ain't spending another night in that house with them biddies."

"I don't blame you for that," he said. He squatted, peering through the screen; he could see the moonlight glinting on the shiny green leaves of the high corn behind her. "I ain't got no suitcase," he said.

"You can put yours in with mine, I didn't bring much," she said.

"Wait a minute," he said and he left the window and crossed the room and eased open the bureau drawer; he took out a pair of folded jeans and a shirt, then on second thought, he went to the closet and pulled on a pair of high top tennis shoes. He dressed slowly in the darkness, putting on the clothes he'd worn that day.

She was waiting for him in the back yard when he eased himself out the door, holding her suitcase at arm's length; the yard was bathed in moonlight, and he could clearly see the blossoms on the honeysuckle that grew over the back fence and the tall sunflowers at the edge of the ash-heap. The sky was thick with stars, and the night was quiet and still; no sound or movement came from his grandmother's house. He crossed the yard toward her.

"This is the first time I ever did anything like this," he said, when he came up to her; she was standing under a twisted chinaberry tree.

"Me too," she said.

"Maybe we ought to set here and think about it for a minute," he said; he looked at her, and the night was bright enough so that he could see her green eyes, and they looked levelly at him.

"Listen," she said, " you can go on back in the house if you don't want to go with me."

"I didn't say I didn't wanta go with you," he said. "I meant think about where we goin."

Suddenly a bathroom light came on in his grandmother's house, and he said, "Shhhhhhh," and they moved around the chinaberry tree and into the shadows; they watched the lighted window for a couple of minutes, then it went out and the house was dark again.

"I hope she don't look in on me," the boy said, "she gits up all durin the night to pee."

"Well, less get goin," the girl said, impatiently.

"Ain't any sense goin till we know where we goin, is it?" the boy said. "I'm figurin on it." They sat on the grass in silence for a moment. "We can't get a bus, that's for sure, cause that one-arm man that works down there at night knows Ma-Ma."

"We can hitch-hike," the girl said.

"How far you think we'd get fore they caught us?" he said. "They gonna send the sheriff lookin for us just as soon as they find out we gone."

"The sheriff?" the girl said.

The boy sat thinking, his arms around his legs; he was quiet for a long time, the crickets chirping around them. The girl heard, in the distance, a dog barking at the moon, a faint, agonized howling that made her skin crawl. She looked at the boy, and he seemed to be lost in thought, staring off across the yard. "Listen," he said, "there's one place we can go where I don't think they'll find us."

"Where?" she said.

He looked at her, and both their faces were in shadows. "The swamp," he said. He tried to see her face, her reaction, but he couldn't, and after a moment she said,

"Where that ol nigger hermit is? No thank you."

"But listen," he said, keeping his voice low, "he won't hurt you, I know he won't, and besides, we probly won't even see him." She didn't answer for a moment. "He ain't crazy." He added.

"They got alligators over there," she said.

"No they ain't," he said, "I been over there lots of times, deer huntin, and I never saw one. It ain't even really a swamp, it's just woods, folks just call it that."

"I don't know," she said.

"Part of it, anyhow, but I know my way around. We wouldn't get lost or anything, an if you don't like it, well, we'll walk up to the highway at the river bridge and catch us a ride somewhere."

"Then what about the sheriff?"

"He'd be more likely to be lookin for us in the mornin than he would the next day, wouldn't he? We can just hide out over there for a couple of days, if you want to."

"Suppose we got lost?" she said. "And how we gone get over there, anyhow?"

"We'll swipe us a boat, I know where lots of em are tied up," he said. She was silent for a moment, and he tried to see her face in the shadow.

She appeared to be thinking, and her watched her still form, in silhouette. After a few minutes, she said,

"Lord, we getting to be real sure-enough crooks, ain't we?"

THE ROAD WAS almost as bright as day, and the limerock ditches on both sides glared white in the moonlight. Once a dog had run out at them, from under a porch, yapping loudly, so now they walked in the middle of the road, the boy carrying the straw suitcase; they walked rapidly, the boy talking short, quick steps, the girls longer strides not quite matching his. They were headed for Rowan's Landing, so called because once it had been a riverboat landing for John O. Rowan and Sons' Gin; now it was used as a skiff tie-up for the Negroes who fished for the catfish that came to feed on the town's waste that was dumped into the river just above. They had passed through the silent town, the streets deserted, the sparsely placed street lights hanging crookedly over their intersections and surrounded by yellowish-white moths that danced about them. There had been one car, parked in front of the pool hall in a rectangle of the light that fell from the open door, and once they had had to shrink back into the shadows to watch Lee Gossit, the night marshal, guide the police car slowly down the street. As they neared the river, on the other side of town, they had passed the jailhouse, a squat, gaunt brick building with bars on the windows; in the light of a naked bulb over the door they could read the sign, cut in stone: HAMMOND CITY JAIL, and there was a light burning inside.

"The got somebody in there tonight, I reckon," the boy said; and the girl said, walking very close to him, answered: "Probly some drunk nigger."

The road curved down sharply to the river, cutting between limerock bluffs on either side, and as they came over the final rise, to where the road widened and dropped down to the water, they stopped. The river seemed very still and wide, with a few ripples near the bank that picked up the moonlight like little silver flames; they could see the dense trees of the swamp on the other side, and, as they stood there, the thick, sour smell of river mud reached their nostrils and they began to hear the smooth flow of the current, barely discernible above the crickets. The night had darkened a bit, and the boy noticed for the first time, looking across the river, that the stars in the Western sky were obscured by a bank of clouds. He held her hand and they went stealthily down the limerock incline; there were several rusty, iron spikes driven into the limerock and tied to each one were five or six flat-bottomed wooden skiffs, each one pulled halfway onto the bank, their ropes forming a fan out from the spike. The boy looked around, studying the boats.

"Shhhhhh," he said suddenly, and the girl grasped his arm: he had noticed, for the first time, that there was a skiff out in the current. It was tied to one of the moored skiffs by a long rope, and it moved gently back and forth against the river's flow, and the boy peered at it; he could make out the form of a man, hunched over in the skiff, and when the figured moved he saw a kerosene lantern in the far end, its orange glow forming a round pool of light on the water.

"Who is it?" the girl whispered, close to his ear, and the boy motioned to her. "Get down," he whispered, and they squatted at the edge of the water, their forms hidden by the line of skiffs. They heard a dull thumping as the man moved his feet on the bottom of the skiff, and for a moment there was only the sound of the current, the gentle lapping among the skiffs.

"Who dat?" a voice said, breaking the stillness.

The girl tensed beside him, and the boy whispered, "It's a nigger, night fishin."

"Who dat up dere?" the voice said again.

They heard the thumping again, then a metallic, scraping sound as his foot hit his bailing can. They squatted in silence, hearing the steady lapping of the water, the occasional soft bump as one of the skiffs shifted and rubbed against another. "What's he doin?" the girl whispered. Just then there was a louder bump, and the man stepped into it, and they were suddenly covered with orange light from the lantern. They looked up and the Negro was standing over them, holding the lantern up high, looking down at them. He was tall and thin, dressed in overalls, and though he held the lantern away from his face, he appeared to be very old.

"Fo' God," he said, "what you chillen doin?"

They continued to squat at the edge of the water, looking up at him, and he raised the lantern higher and they could see that he was old, with a long, thin face and a caved-in mouth, and his head was completely bald; he had on no shirt under the overalls, and his skin was orangish-brown in the light of the lantern. He stared at them, his head nodding forward on his long, thin neck; then he looked at the suitcase, sitting on the bank between them.

"Goin on a trip, I speck," he said.

"That's right," the boy said.

The old man grinned at them, his lips curving inward into his toothless mouth. "Well, you waitin at the wrong place," he said, "riverboat ain't stopped here in thutty years." He sat down in the boat. "You chillen gone get the leg cramp sqattin dere like dat," he said. So they got up and the boy swung the suitcase into the skiff next to the one the old Negro was sitting in and they got in and sat down; the old Negro moved the lantern so that it was between them. "You ain't got no snuff in that ere box, is you?" he said.

Before they had left his grandmother's, the boy had sneaked back into the house and gotten a paper sack full of cold biscuits and a box of fig newtons and three packages of cigarettes that he had hidden in his closet, so he said: "No, but we got some cigarettes," and the old man said: "That ud do." The girl fumbled in the suitcase and came up with three cigarettes and passed one to the old Negro, and the boy lit theirs with a waterproof match. They watched the old Negro carefully peel the paper from his and deposit the tobacco against his gum under his lower lip; he rolled up the paper and tossed it into the river. He smacked his lips and spat once over the edge of the skiff.

"Who does this boat belong to?" the boy said.

"Dat dare boat, less see, dat dare boat belong to Buddy Ed," the Negro said, his chin making a rolling motion.

"Who?" the boy said.

"Buddy Ed, you know, he clean up down to the show."

"Oh, yeah."

"But he ain't gwine sell it, I don't speck, not lessen you wants to pay aplenty for it."

"I don't want to buy it," the boy said. They puffed on their cigarettes, and the old Negro sat there, rubbing his chin and looking at them; every now and then he would tiredly blink his eyes. "Reckon he'd mind if we borrowed it?" the boy said.

"Depends, I speck, on how long a trip you plannin on goin on," the old Negro said.

"Just across the river," the boy said, and the old Negro continued his chewing motion, staring at them. He looked first at the boy, then at the girl, then at the suitcase between them. The night had grown progressively darker, and the moon was now half hidden by the cloud bank, but they didn't notice it sitting in the circle of light from the lantern.

"Ain't nothin over dere," he said. "What you wanna go over dere for?'

"We just do," the boy said.

The old Negro seemed puzzled; he continued to study them, his chin making the steady rolling motion. His knees, in the worn overalls, stuck sharply, almost to his shoulders, and he let his arms droop between them. "It gwine storm," he said, and the boy looked to the West, above the trees on the other side; the clouds were higher, and as he watched there was a flicker of yellow light across the top of the cloudbank. He took a draw from the cigarette. The girl sat quietly beside him in the boat.

"Listen," the boy said, "there used to be an old hunter's cabin about a hundred yards back in the woods; is it still there?"

"It ain't much more'n a shed," the old Negro said.

"If you row us over there, I'll give you a dollar," the boy said.

"Thass a long haul against the current," he said.

"And five cigarettes," the boy said.

The old Negro seemed to be considering the deal. He hadn't moved from his original position, his shoulders hunched. "If'n yall gwine back in dem woods," he said, "yall gwine need a lantern." Because of the moonlight, the boy had forgotten to bring one, and now he looked across the river at the black woods; he could barely hear, way off, a roll of thunder. "Cose I got an old one here I can let you have for fifty cents, and I'll fill it up wit kerosene fo you." The boy looked at the girl, and she took a small, black snap coin purse from her shirt pocket and opened it and took two quarters out and handed them to the Negro. He put them into a pocket on the bib of his overalls and carefully buttoned it. "Cose most ferry trips is payment in advance," he said, and the boy handed over a wrinkled dollar bill, and the old Negro, just as carefully, placed it into the same pocket, his long, thin fingers caressing the rough, faded blue cloth of the flap.

He seated them on the rear seat of his skiff and placed his lantern on the front, securing it in place with a length of wire; they sat stiffly, the boy holding the suitcase in his lap because the bottom of the skiff was wet. The old Negro untied the rope and swung the wire stringer with his fish over the side; there were several small catfish, and they flapped against the bottom of the skiff, their skins green and shiny in the lantern light. Almost immediately the current caught the skiff and they began to drift, and the Negro seated himself with a grunt between the oars and began to pull.

"Put us out on that long sandbar over there, right past where that big willow grows out over the water," the boy said.

The Negro's face was in darkness, his back to the lantern; he was pulling steadily at the oars. "Some folks is crazy, some ain't" he said, "and it ain't for me to decide which one is which." His remark was punctuated by a long, steady roll of thunder.

They went slowly across the river, seeming not to make much progress; the oar-locks squeaked loudly and steadily in the night, and they could hear the Negro's heavy breathing, and every now and then he would grunt with the strain. Slowly the trees on the other side seemed to grow taller, and as they began to get close to the bank, a white crane rose from the sandbar with a great flapping of wings and soared away over the water and down the river. Some roosting birds, back in the woods, set up a sudden chatter and then were quiet, and gradually they could hear the gentle swish of the water on the sandbar; and with a final, heaving pull of the oars, the old Negro let the boat grind to a stop on the sandbar. They sat in the skiff a moment, the lantern in the prow casting a soft light over the still sandbar; there was a trotline tied to the big willow, and it moved gently up and down with the current, but the woods, the towering black trees and thick undergrowth, were still.

"Sho is dark in dere," the old Negro said, and he set about filling the extra lantern with kerosene, and while he worked the heavy-leaved trees rustled with the first breeze of the storm, and they could smell rain. The girl slapped once, then once again, at her leg, and the old Negro stopped his work and looked at her; he had moved the lantern so that he could see to fill the second, and he moved it again toward the back and spilled some of the kerosene into his hands and leaned toward them and began to rub it on the girl's leg. She shrank back.

"Muskeeters in dere big enough to carry you both off," he said. He rubbed the kerosene onto her other leg with both hands. "Muskeeters now, dey don't bother colored folks, some say dey don't like dark meat, but fair-skinned chillen like you they pick up and take home to serve to de preacher." He motioned to the boy, and the boy spilled kerosene over his hands and rubbed it onto his arms; the smell was thick and oily in the air. "Don't be sticken no match to yourself, dough," he said.

He lit their lantern for them, and they stepped out onto the soft, damp sand of the bar, the girl now holding the suitcase, the boy swinging the lantern, its light flickering off the thick green foliage. "We sure do thank you," the girl said; and the old Negro said, "Fo, God, the lil lady do got a tongue in her haid after all, ain't she?"

"That shed is right back in there, ain't it?" the boy said, and the Negro pointed.

"Rat to the right of that clump o bamboo is a path, you'll see it, just follow dat, it ain't fur, but you better git movin if you gone beat dis storm."

He pushed the skiff away from the sandbar, and the girl called out, "Wait a minute, you forgot your cigarettes," and the Negro said, "Yall keep em, I ain't gone need em like yall is." He was already a bodyless voice near a pool of orange light out on the water, and they heard the squeaking of the oarlocks, and they stood there as the sound grew dimmer and dimmer and the pool of light grew smaller, until it was only a tiny speck out in the middle of the river and they could no longer hear the oars. The trees over their heads rustled again, louder, as a gusty breeze hit them, and the sky flickered with light and the thunder came. They stood close together on the sandbar, in the light of the flickering lantern.

"I don't like this worth a damn," the girl said, and the boy said,

"Come on, we'll be fine in that cabin, we can spend the night there and go on in the mornin." They moved toward the clump of bamboo, a thick cluster of cane rising up and disappearing into the branches overhead, some of the stalks as big around as one of their legs.

"Go on where?" the girl said.

"Wherever it is we're goin," the boy said, and they entered the dark woods. The boy held the lantern high, its light penetrating the wilderness maybe ten feet, and they could see the narrow path stretching out before them. The mosquitoes buzzed around their heads, but the reek of the kerosene kept them off, and the boy, holding the girl's hand, led the way through the undergrowth, the bushes slapping at their arms and grabbing at their ankles. Deeper into the woods away from the riverbank, the undergrowth thinned, and in the weird, flickering light they could see the trunks of the huge trees rising up before them and the strange shapes made by fallen timber covered with vines. They could move a little faster now, and the girl held tightly to the boy's hand, the clumsy suitcase slapping and knocking into the now-sparser undergrowth. A streak of lightning that lit up the entire sky flashed over the trees, followed quickly by an ear-splitting clap of thunder, and the girl said,

"How much further is it?"

"Come on, it ain't far," the boy said.

The top branches of the trees swayed in the stronger wind, and the first drops of rain hit them as they came into the little clearing and looked across at the hunters' shack: it was a tiny one room structure sitting up on stilts, with a front-slanted tin roof, and as they crossed to it, the doorless front opening yawned darkly at them. The boy held the lantern up and they looked in at the rough plank floor, and at what appeared to be a pile of old, dusty croaker sacks in one corner. There was an empty beer can lying on its side in the middle of the otherwise empty floor.

"It ain't much, is it?" the girl said, and the boy said,

"At least it's got a tin roof on it."

They could hear the heavy first drops drumming on the tin roof; the cabin floor was about waist high to the boy, and he swung the suitcase in and helped the girl climb in, then he pulled himself over the threshold. The lantern lit the interior well; there was no windows, and the door-less opening faced East, so the cabin seemed to be fairly dry. The rain beat heavily on the roof; and just outside the door, as far as the light from the lantern penetrated, they could see the rain crossing the clearing in sheets.

"Boy , we just made it," the girl said. The rain had dampened her hair slightly and it clung to her head around her ears. "And the roof doen't even leak," she said, and suddenly she threw back her head and laughed.

"What's so funny?" the boy said looking at her in the flickering lamplight; he was sitting with his back against the rough boards of the wall, and she stood near the doorway.

"I was just thinking of the expression that's gonna be on Aunt Lil's face when she finds out I've left," she said, and she laughed again. "Aunt Julia, she'll just stand there in her old house dress, blinkin, and Aunt Lil'll have one o her faintin spells probly."

The boy sat quietly for a moment. "Ain't any telling what Ma-Ma'll do; but it won't take her long to have the sheriff out after us, I know that."

"You reckon he'll look for us over here?" the girl said.

"Naw," the boy said, "don't anybody know we're over here but that ol nigger, and he ain't gone say anything cause he rowed us over here."

The storm had reached its intensity, and the rain beat heavily on the roof of the little cabin. "It's pretty snug in here," the boy said, "we better try to get some sleep." He settled himself, his back against the wall, and the girl came and stretched out beside him.

"Damn, these planks are hard," she said.

"I would say less put those croaker sacks down, but sure as the world they're fulla ticks," he said. He leaned forward and blew out the lantern, and they were suddenly plunged into the darkness; they were blind for a moment, then their eyes could gradually make out the outline of the door and a few branches against the black sky. The wind moaned in the tree-tops, and the rain hit the cabin in wave-like sheets.

"Storm's passin," the boy said, "goodnight."

"Goodnight," the girl said, and they both sat, their backs against the wall, their eyes open in the darkness.

* * *

Ted Mack Lowery had been standing at the window of a darkened cell when they had passed the jailhouse, and he had thought to himself, "There goes Woody Malone's boy." The cell was dim and heavily shadowed from the one small light bulb that hung in the narrow hallway that ran along beside the row of four cells, and he had been standing in the shadows, looking out at the quiet street when he'd seen them go by. He realized, suddenly, that he'd said it out loud, when a voice from the next cell said, "Wha?"

"I ain't said nothing to you," Ted Mack said. The cell he was in was tiny; there was a wooden bunk with a naked, rough mattress on it, and against the brick wall, next to the window, was a yellowed, stained washbasin; next to that was a seatless toilet, its water full of frayed cigarette butts. The brick wall was covered with markings, scrawled with limerock, obscene drawings of huge male sexual organs and initials and dates. "I ain't said nothing to you," Ted Mack said again, "So you keep your black-ass mouth shut." He squinted his eyes and peered into the dark shadows of the next cell; he could barely make out the form of the Negro woman, her huge form sitting on the bunk.

"Wha you gwine do bout it, white man?" the voice said; it was heavy and masculine in the darkness. The entire little jailhouse smelled heavily of urine and musty, damp bricks, and Ted Mack stood, seething, in his cell. He could see the Negro woman only in form, and the deep voice seemed to come from all around him.

"You stink to high heaven, nigger," Ted Mack said.

The voice in the darkness made a chuckling sound. "I smell like pussy to you, white man," it said, and Ted Mack stomped his foot, his heavy brogan thumping loudly on the dirty brick floor.

"Goddam you nigger," he said, "you done done it now, you hear me?" The form sat quietly in the next cell. "You done done it now, you ain't knowed I's a member of the Klan, did you?"

"You ain't a member o nothin," the voice said, "cept maybe the pissin-on-the-street ciety."

"Keep on," Ted Mack said, "Just keep on, hear?"

"If I couldn't figure out nothing better to get throwed in jail about than pissin on the street, I believe I'd jest go off somewhere and hide."

Ted Mack paced about in the cell, his heavy shoes scraping on the floor; the bulk in the next cell was quiet, and he knew that she was watching him. He took a package of Camels from a pocket on the bib of his overalls. "You want a cigarette, nigger?" he said, and the next cell was quiet. "Well, you ain't gone git one."

Just then there was a flash of lightning outside and the interior of the little jailhouse was lighted momentarily, and Ted Mack could see the woman clearly, sitting on the bunk, her huge, fat legs spread, with ragged stockings rolled down around her ankles, her eyes bulging and her lips looking like two fat sausages across her wide face. She was sitting very still, her hands in her lap peeling what, in the instant flash of the lightning, looked like an orange. A long roll of thunder followed the lightning, and, as it died, Ted Mack heard a car stop outside, and, in a moment, the heavy iron door pushed open. Lee Gossit, the night marshal, stepped into the little hallway, a heavy flashlight in his hand.

"What you doin, telling this nigger woman I uz pissin in the street?" Ted Mack said.

"You tol her yourself, and everybody else that'd listen to you, when I brung you in," Gossit said. He was tall, and around his waist, where the blue shirt was tucked neatly into the darker blue pants, was a little, hose-like roll of fat. He wore a shiny, chrome-plated pistol low on his hip. "You done sobered up yet?" he said. Then he shined the flashlight into the Negro woman's cell. "What you eatin, Justina?" he said.

"Orange," the Negro woman said.

Another flash of lightning lit the inside of the jail, and Ted Mack could see the policeman's face, gray, pasty cheeks under little black eyes that looked like small lumps of coal, and his hair black and cut short and tinged with gray. The badge glittered on his chest in the glare of the flashlight. "Say," he said, shining the light at Ted Mack.

"Git that thang out'n my face," Ted Mack said, and the policeman lowered the light. "I'm sober as I ever was," he said.

"That sho ain't sayin nothing," the Negro woman said.

"You hear that, Lee?" Ted Mack said, "She ain't got a bit a respect for a white man."

"Hush up, now, both of you," Gossit said. "They's a storm comin up, so I'm gonna let you both go on home, the roof leaks in this place so bad it ain't fit for a sorry dog." The policeman shined the light into the Negro woman's cell; she sat heavily on the bunk, munching on the sections of orange, methodically raising one section to her mouth, chewing, then leaning forward to spit out the spent pulp before putting in another. "I talked to Mr. Tate on the phone about it awhile ago," the policeman said, "an he said, Justina, that you can go home if you'll promise to stay outta the Five and Dime from now on, as far as you're concerned, it ain't even there."

The Negro woman spit out a mashed section of yellowish pulp. "Mistah Elmore got so much stuff, look to me like he'd want to share it wit po folks," she said.

"Well he don't," the policeman said. "You promise?"

"I sure does," she said. "Tell Mistah Tate that my roof leaks, too."

"I'll do that, Justina, I'll pass the word along to him," the policeman said unlocking the cell. Then he turned to Ted Mack's cell. "An you got to cut out drinkin that shinny," he said, "next time we catch you takin a leak on a main down-town street we gone send you to Kilby."

"I don't drink nigger whiskey," Ted Mack said.

"Huh," the Negro woman said; with a great, panting effort she had stood up, and now she was gathering several wrinkled, brown paper sacks together. "My roof leaks, too," she said.

"Don't nobody care nothin bout your roof," Ted Mack said.

"Didn't I say hush up all that?" Gossit said. "Now come on, I'm gonna take you both home in the car."

"It ain't fur," the Negro woman said, "it's jest down de road here, I can walk."

"You sure? That storm'll be here in a minute."

The Negro woman had already started down the road, holding the brown parcels against her heavy breast; she moved more rapidly than it appeared she could. "Evenin," she said.

"I'd stay in jail fore I'd ride in any car with any nigger, anyhow," Ted Mack said, getting in the front seat.

"Would you, now?" Gossit said, cranking the car. "Well, next time

I'll let you do that," he said.

They had just driven into the front yard of Ted Mack's little maroon shanty when the first drops splattered against the windshield; they had driven in silence, the dash lights reflecting off Gossit's badge and the little metal buttons on the front of Ted Mack's overalls. The sky crackled with lightning and boomed with thunder, and the trees along the dark streets bent with the wind.

"Looks like it's comin a gulley-washer," Ted Mack said, and the policeman said:

"Yeah, I sure wouldn't wanna be caught out on a night like this," and he watched Ted Mack sprint across the littered yard to the dark porch of the shanty, the legs of his overalls flapping as he ran, his hands over his head against the rain that now began to fall in wind-tossed sheets.

Seven

THE BOY WAS the first to awake; he was gradually aware of the chatter of the birds around the cabin, and for a moment, forgetting where he was, he was confused. He opened his eyes and they were dry and scratchy, and he realized that, finally, he had dropped off to sleep. His body was stiff and sore from the rough planking of the cabin and the early morning chill that had followed the thunderstorm, and he moved slowly and carefully so as not to wake the girl beside him. She lay on her back, her hands folded across her stomach, sleeping peacefully, her head pillowed on his rolled-up shirt. He couldn't remember when they had finally dropped off to sleep; he only remembered their lying there, in the darkness, talking very little and his attempts to make her more comfortable. For a few seconds he sat still, listening to the almost hysterical-sounding chatter of the birds in the otherwise quiet woods, and he could smell the fresh crispness of the rain-clean air that drifted through the open doorway.

The boy stood up and crossed to the doorway and looked out at the woods; the sun was not yet up, and the woods were still and gray, and there was a fog-like mist around the roots of the trees. While he stood there, a soft breeze stirred, and a long stream of the mist, like the trail of a wedding gown, drifted slowly across the high grass and ground vines of the clearing. He heard a squirrel bark, high up in one of the trees, and he was remembering the squirrel hunts he'd been on, the stealthy entering of the dark, dripping woods to find a hidden seat on a fallen log, and the gradual, eerie way the tree trunks and bushes and forms in the woods would take shape, gray and colorless at first, the colors, greens and yellows and bright reds, slowly drawing their substance from the lightening air. And the deer hunts, at the edge of the big swamps, sitting long on the stand, peering alertly into the gray November woods, his body shaking, partly from the damp chill of the morning, partly from the lonely sounding, almost pleading song of the hounds striking deer far back in the thick woods. He thought again of the insignificance he'd felt, looking at the towering trees, and a chill passed up his spine as he felt anew the excitement that came with the hearing of the legend of the old black hermit; and he stood, feeling and knowing how far away from the town, sitting just across the river on its high bluff, he now was. He could imagine the first stirrings of the town: the milkman going slowly down the street, from house to house, nodding to the Negro maids who passed him, going to enter the darkened kitchens to start the breakfasts, carrying the now empty brown paper bags folded under their arms and the rolled-up parasols that would be used against the afternoon sun on their way home; Mr. Sam Golson, opening his store, his Negro boy sweeping out, Mr. Sam already doling out the soft drinks to the Negroes returning from the night shift at the lumber mill; the old Negro garbage man, harnessing his mule to the red wagon to begin making his way slowly up and down the alleyways of the town. He could hear, in his mind, Hess stirring in the kitchen, and, after a while, his grandmother padding through the house, the glasses in the dining room cabinets tinkling as she walked across the linoleum and he could smell the homey, comfortable smell of coffee in the air — all of it very distant to him now, standing in the doorway of the little cabin at the edge of the swamp, the only smell the clean smell of rain-washed woods.

The sun was coming up and the rays penetrated the thick trees in little shafts that danced on the mist. He was reminded of a picture he'd once seen, of a tall stained-glass window in a huge cathedral, the sun behind the window sending hundreds of shafts that fanned out on the floor of the church, and he thought that the little clearing in the woods, under the new sun, had the same stillness, the same feeling of quiet sanctuary, that the cathedral had. And now it was not a picture; he was here.

He half-sensed and half-heard a stirring behind him, and he turned to look at the girl; she was sitting up, looking at him, her hair tangled about her head, her eyes only half opened against sleep. "Good morning," he said, and she sat up straighter, "sleep good?"

"I'm stiff," she said, "is it still rainin?"

"No, it's a beautiful day," he said. "The sun's up already."

"I'm hungry," she said. She sat rubbing her bare legs; there were several small cuts from the briars the last night. "I wish to hell I'd known we were goin to the swamps fore I dressed to leave home," she said.

"It won't be hard on you in the daytime," he said.

"Less hope not."

The boy had noticed a rusty tin bucket sitting on the ground outside the cabin, and now it was three quarters full of rain water, almost as though they had placed it there for that purpose; he jumped down to the ground and tested it for leaks, then hoisted it up to the floor of the cabin. The water began to seep into the plank floor. "Fresh water and everything." The boy said. "It leaks, but not very fast."

"It looks cloudy," the girl said.

"That's just where it dripped off the roof," the boy said. "We ain't got to drink much of it, we'll find us a spring this morning." He dipped his fingers into the water and wiped his eyes with it. "Cool," he said.

The girl wet her hands and washed her face, then she leaned over and dried it on the front of her shirt. She opened the straw suitcase and took out two of the cold biscuits and gave him one. "I sure am glad we brought these along," she said.

They sat and chewed the cold, half-cooked biscuits in silence, every now and then cupping their hands to reach into the bucket for water, making slurping sounds as they drank if from their palms. When they had finished, they edged away from the bucket to avoid the dampness seeping into the planks, and they sat, looking out the door at their clearing, brighter now in the higher sun. The foliage was very green, and the branches of the trees twisted and intertwined to form a canopy that extended out almost to the cabin.

"We can move on anytime you're ready," the boy said, and the girl continued to stare out the door. Then she looked at him; she was sitting with her knees drawn up, her arms around her legs, her chin on her knees, and her eyes where narrow green slits in her face. She had brushed her hair back neatly from her face. "What's the matter?" the boy said.

The girl hesitated for a moment. "I got to be excused."

She had not changed her sitting position, but she shifted her eyes back to the door, and the boy said, "Round behind the cabin," and the girl was very still; then she looked back at him, moving only her eyes, and the boy could see the color in her cheeks, and he suddenly remembered the first time he'd seen her, standing on his grandmother's front steps twisting the handkerchief between her fingers. "Use leaves," he said, and the girl, without looking at him again, got up and walked to the door and jumped clumsily down to the ground. "Just make sure you don't get no poison oak or anything," he said, and the girl stopped and stood where she was, looking off at the trees, and he could see her thin back in the shirt and her streaked hair pulled back behind her ears. She just stood there, very still, her back to him. "Wait a minute," the boy said and he went to the door and jumped down; she didn't look at him. There was a large bush with broad green leaves growing at the corner of the cabin, and he tore off a branch and handed it to her. "Here," he said.

"Thank you." The girl walked around the corner of the cabin without looking back at him.

Miss Lillian Fisque came down the stairs at exactly seven o' clock, as she was accustomed to doing; she rose every morning except Sunday at six, had a quick bath, dressed and made up her face before coming down for coffee. Her sister served breakfast at exactly seven fifteen every morning, and Miss Lillian respected her for that; it made for a neat and punctual household to start the day, each day, in such a manner. She entered the kitchen on this morning, and Julia stood at the stove as she always did, and a cup of hot coffee sat on the table if front of her place; she sat in her chair, straightening her pink linen skirt about her legs, and took a first tentative sip.

"Delicious, as always, Julia," she said, "an how are you this morning?"

The kitchen was bright, cheerfully full of sunlight, and Julia, with a long, wood-handled fork, slowly turned pink strips of bacon in a heavy, black iron skillet, the bacon's sizzling increasing as each strip was turned.

"Quite a storm we had last night," Miss Lillian said, "I didn't sleep well at all, what with the thunder and lightning, you know how nervous it makes me. I declare, I suppose I'll be irregular again." She sighed. "The Lord has placed another burden on our shoulders, and I decided, lying awake and suffering last night, that the thing to do is carry it to the Lord Hisself. I'm goin over to see Reverend Wallgood this morning. It wasn't meant for two ladies like us to have to tame a wildcat." Miss Lillian sipped at her coffee and sighed again, and the bacon continued to sizzle in the skillet, its aroma filling the room. "How is Miss Prissbritches this morning?" she said. "You wake her up or decide to let her sleep out her conniption?"

"Her bed ain't been slept in," Julia said.

"What you say?" Miss Lillian continued, "you'll have to speak up, Julia, that bacon, and that storm's ragin in my head."

"I say her bed ain't been slept in, and that straw satchel she brought with her is gone, and she's taken that pink toothbrush, too," Julia said.

"She's gone?" Miss Lillian said; Julia was turning the bacon again, holding it high and letting the grease drip into the pan before stretching the bacon back into it.

"Looks that way," Julia said, "She ain't here, anyhow, and ain't been here since last night looks like."

"I declare," Miss Lillian said. She sat, staring straight ahead, her coffee untouched before her, little wisps of steam rising from it. After a minute, she said, "Where's she gone off to, you reckon?"

"Maybe she's done returned to hell, where she come from," Julia said. She forked the strips of bacon out onto a platter and she cracked two eggs on the side of the skillet and dropped them into the bacon grease. While the eggs were frying, she opened a can of peaches for her own breakfast. "Anyhow, she ain't here, and good riddance, I say."

"She's a hellion, all right," Miss Lillian said.

"I kinda liked her some at first, reminded me of her daddy, but she cussed the memory of her own granddaddy, my daddy, an that come from a black soul, a soul already doomed to hellfire and damnation, I say." She put the plate of eggs and bacon before Miss Lillian and sat down before her bowl of peaches in syrup.

"I declare, that hellcat's got you stirred up, Julia, I ain't heard you talk so much in twenty years," Miss Lillian said, and Julia sullenly began to spoon her peaches into her mouth, staring at the table top. Miss Lillian began to eat, then she put her fork down.

"We can't just let her go off without knowin where she is," she said, "she is our own flesh and blood."

"She ain't none o my flesh and blood," Julia said.

"You reckon she's headed home? Maybe we ought to call long distance," Miss Lillian said.

"Waste o money," Julia said, sipping at the canning syrup, "good riddance, I say."

"I bet that's where she's gone, caught her a bus and gone home to her daddy. I bet Ralph calls tonight to tell us she's got there," Miss Lillian said. "And he'll be a mad un too," she added.

"Waste his money," Julia said.

"His courting and all, and that little rapscallion poppin on him outta the blue, no wonder he wanted us to keep her while he courted, there ain't too many women want a ready-made family anyhow, and that Hallie, sweet Jesus above," she said.

"I hope this un don't drink," Julia said, staring morosely at the near empty bowl in front of her, and Miss Lillian cocked her head, her fork halfway to her mouth. She pursed her lips and peered, bird-like, at her sister. "Julia," she said, "you know good and well Sara didn't drink."

"She must have," Julia mumbled, her mouth partly full of peaches, "how else did she get that bastard in her if she didn't?"

Miss Lillian shook her head slowly back and forth and lowered the fork to the plate. "I declare, Julia," she said, staring at her sister. "No, sir," she said, "no sir, a fool he mighta been for marryin her, her and her high-falutin ways, but a play father to some woodshed chile he ain't, and you know that good as I do."

Julia sullenly finished the last of her peaches and stood up and took the bowl to the sink.

"I don't think I'll have any more breftus, Julia," Miss Lillian said, "I'm gonna sit in the parlor and wait, but I know nothin's gonna happen. I declare, that chile has made me irregular both comin and goin. You might have to fix me some hot broth for dinner, Julia." And she walked delicately out of the kitchen as Julia started in washing the dishes.

"He was gone when I got up this morning," Eva Malone said. "Probly sulkin down along the river over that whipping." She sat across from the boy's mother, the remains of breakfast between them.

"Ain't like that boy to miss his breakfast," Hess said; she was clearing the table, scraping the dishes and stacking them in the sink; the boy's mother wore the pink chenille bathrobe, and she was smoking a cigarette, a fresh cup of coffee in front of her.

"He didn't miss it," Eva said, "he took practically a whole plate of cold biscuits with him. I swear, I never saw a boy act as strange as that one this summer."

"He need a daddy, what wrong with him," Hess said, and Martha said,

"Well it ain't my fault, Sometimes you act like it was my fault that Woody got killed."

"I ain't said that, Miss Martha," Hess said, "but it's a long time for a girl your age to go without a man."

"Oh, Hess, not again," Eva Malone said.

"Dat boy growin up, he feelin his manhood comin on him, an he don't know what to make o it."

"He's just a boy," Martha said.

"It's dat girl, Miss Lillian's niece, what got him all stirred up, you can bet on dat."

"She's a strange one, all right," Eva said, "goin out walkin all the time, not playin, walkin, walkin all over town. And Billy rummaging around in my closets, goin over all those old letters and pictures for hours, a pretty day outside and everything. And bein fascinated by those old stories about Joe Bynymo. It's almost like he don't know what to do with himself."

"He feelin a stirring in his britches," Hess said.

"Oh, for heaven's sake, Hess," Eva said, "he ain't but twelve years old."

"Goin on thirteen," Hess said.

Later that day, around noon, Eva made two phone calls, one to Miss Lillian Fisque, and the other to Bubba Tate, the sheriff. She had come into the kitchen just as Hess was putting a steaming plate of field peas on the table. "Seen anything of him?" she'd said, and Hess had said, "Not hide nor hair." So she had given the operator Miss Lillian's number.

"Is Hallie there?" she said, when she got Miss Lillian on the line.

"Lord, no," Miss Lillian said, "she's gone off somewhere."

"Gone off somewhere?" Eva said, "what you mean, gone off somewhere?"

"She packed her suitcase and lit out," Miss Lillian said.

"When?"

"Last night, near as we can figure, Eva, she's just ungrateful, that's about all I can say for her, ungrateful and spoiled rotten."

"Where'd she go?" Eva said.

"We don't know where she went," Miss Lillian said, "probly gone home to her daddy, we figured he'd be callin tonight to let us know she arrived, mad as a wet hen probly, knowin him, but ain't no telling where she's gone, Julia just keep sayin 'good riddance.'"

"You mean she ran away, by herself, and yall ain't called anybody or anything?"

"Ain't anybody to call. I was goin over to see Reverend Wallgood this morning after breftus, to talk it all out with him, but I don't see any sense in goin over there now, bein she ain't here any more, I tell you, Eva, that chile has been a trial on me, cussin and smoking and carryin on, and yesterday, right in front of Julia, and you know how Julia loves the memory o her daddy, right in front of her cussin the memory, comin right out and sayin he was in hell. I declare, Eva, she ain't fit for decent company."

"Hold on, Lillian," Eva said, "How'd she go?"

"On the Mobile bus, I reckon."

"Lillian," Eva said, "there ain't any Mobile bus runnin at night."

"I don't know how she went, then, hitch-hiked I reckon."

"There ain't any telling who picked that poor girl up," Eva said, "besides, I think Billy's gone with her; he ain't here."

"Sweet Jesus above," Miss Lillian said.

"Some pervert, probly," Eva said. "Listen here, Lillian, hang up the phone; I'm gonna call Bubba Tate and get him out looking for em."

"The sheriff?"

"The same one you shoulda called at six o'clock this morning, or whenever it was you discovered she was gone; sometimes I think you ain't got the common sense of a mosquito, Lillian."

"I declare," Miss Lillian said, and she hung up the phone.

"Damnation," Eva said; Hess was standing across the room, watching her, a dish towel clutched in her hands before her. "Give me Sheriff Tate's office," she said to the girl when she came back on the line.

By the time the sun was high they had gone deeper into the woods; they found an old logging road, little more than parallel paths in the underbrush, overhung with thick branches from the trees overhead, and they had followed that for part of the morning, stepping over the fallen logs and clumps of ground vines that grew across it. The boy carried the straw suitcase and the girl the cold lantern, and they plodded on, passing intermittently through the deep shadows and into the dappled sunlight that filtered through the foliage high overhead. The sun had warmed the morning, and the mist was gone, and they had both begun to perspire; the boy led the way, and they had made good time until the logging road faded and then petered out into a canebrake beside a narrow creek. The landscape, by then, was becoming increasingly lower, and they had rested on the bank of the creek, sitting on a naked limerock bank watching the sunlight play over the ripples of the water; the birds still chattered in the still trees around them.

"Smell that dampness," the boy said. "That's the smell of the swamp, we on the edge of it."

"You sure you know where we are?" the girl said. She was looking across at the thicker undergrowth on the other side, tall ferns growing out over the water and thick bushes that grew in tangles, the trees more heavily covered with twisted vines.

"This is Maconaco Creek," the boy said, "it gets wider down towards the river; folks fish it."

"Look mighty snaky to me," the girl said.

"We'll go upstream, to some higher ground, where we can cross," the boy said. "But we ain't in any hurry, we got all day."

The girl sat with her bare legs out in front of her, her shirt hanging out, the lantern sitting beside her. She was digging absent-mindedly at the crusts of limerock on the bank; she could smell the murky, damp smell in the air around her.

"Maybe we shoulda tried to make Birmingham," she said, and the boy said,

"You know where we'd be right now if we had? Right back there in Hammond, getting fussed at all over again."

"I know what you got in mind," she said, after a minute. "You want to find that ol hermit, don't you? Well, I don't."

"You want to go back to your aunts' house?"

"No," she said, "but we gotta come outta here sometime, don't we?"

"Why? He didn't, he lives in there, just cause he wants to, that's all, and he ain't crazy and he won't hurt you."

"How you know he ain't crazy, runnin off and livin the swamp like that?"

"Well, we ain't, are we?"

"I don't know for sure," the girl said, "I sure don't."

They sat in silence for a moment, the only sounds the birds and the whispering of the water in the creek. "Come on, less have us a cigarette and then get started," the boy, opening the suitcase.

Later, as they made their way upstream at the edge of the creek, the ground began to rise sharply, and they came to a fork in the stream. In the crotch of the fork was a high, pointed and rocky bluff, and they stopped for a moment, the boy surveying the stream and the bluff, looking carefully at the rock-strewn bottom, and then he said, "We'll cross here and follow that ridge, it'll be easy goin." They went across the narrow, shallow creek, stepping carefully on the slippery stones, the water cool on their feet. And the boy helped the girl scale the rocky hill on the other side, grabbing at the trunks of the bushes that grew between the stones, dragging the suitcase and the lantern awkwardly behind them. Once at the top they could see the ridge stretching away into the swamp, topped by its high, thick trees, and off to their left, across the branch of the creek, the low lying, steaming swamp itself. The ridge was relatively free of undergrowth, covered with a thick carpet of pine needles, and they started out, walking briskly now; they could see more of the sky, and it was a deep, clear blue, with only a few high, cottony clods very high against it. The ground was level and soft, and the boy felt very good as he walked along, the suitcase swinging back and forth. "Oh, I been workin on the railroad, all the livelong day," he sang out, and the girl laughed and skipped along to the music.

"You feelin better?" the boy said.

"Sure," she said, "It's a beautiful day."

"I feel free as a bird," he said. "Come on, let's run."

And the two of them went running along the ridge, their laughter echoing in among the thick tree trunks, the birds fleeing their perches with squawks, the squirrels barking back at them from high among the branches overhead. The boy's sneakers pounded the needle-covered ground, and the girl almost slipped in her sandals once or twice, but she kept up with him. Once they stopped, breathing heavily, giggling, and the girl looked out over the treetops of the swamp. "Shiiiiiit!" she yelled, and they listened, and a faint echo came back to them, and they laughed, throwing their heads back. "Shiiiiiit!" she yelled again, the sound of her voice dying over the swamp; they laughed and broke into a run again, the suitcase and the lantern swinging at their sides. The ridge began to taper and descend, and they pounded along, the sound of their breathing heavy in the early afternoon stillness, and then the girl began to slow.

"Wait a minute," she panted from behind him, and he stopped and went back to her; her face was white, and little beads of sweat stood across her forehead and across her upper lip. "I got to rest a second," she said, and she sat down heavily on the needles; she breathed deeply, her eyes narrowed, looking out across the swamp.

"What's the matter?" the boy said.

"Nothin," the girl said; she sat very still, and the boy sat down beside her.

"Are you sick?" he said. "Are you gone throw up?"

"No," she said. The boy watched her, and after a minute she looked at him. "I ain't gone throw up, so quit lookin at me like that," she said.

"Well, somethin's wrong with you, you ain't actin right," he said.

The girl narrowed her eyes again and looked out over the swamp. "I hurt, that's all," she said.

"Where, your stomach?" the boy said.

"No, dammit, my chest," the girl said, and the boy said,

"Oh." He stole a glance at the front of her blouse, and she pulled her knees up to her breasts and sat, looking out over the swamp; she seemed, for a moment, to have forgotten that he was there. Then, after a minute, she said:

"Billy, do you think there's a God?"

"I guess so," he said.

"Well, I don't," she said, "I think that's all just a lot o hog wash." Then she stood up and picked up the lantern. "Let's go," she said, "it's hot in this sun."

They were going downhill now as the ridge tapered off, and the undergrowth was getting thicker again; soon they left the ridge and were in the swamp again, the ground growing damp beneath their feet, and they pushed their way into the bushes looking for the branch, along which, the boy knew, they would find a spring. The thick, leafy branches overhead cut off the sun, and the gloomy swamp was almost night dark; once there was a sudden crashing ahead of them, and the boy saw, in a little dappled clearing beyond a jagged pile of brush, the flicker of white tail disappearing into the dim woods.

"Deer," he said, "we flushed him off his bed."

"Lord, that scared me," the girl said.

She retrieved the lantern, but she held his arm as they went across the little clearing, and the boy stopped and put his finger against his lips and they listened; they could hear the gentle trickle of water, and the boy said, "Spring," and they pushed their way toward it. The ground was almost muddy now, and the girl's sandals slipped, and she held to his arm as he pushed the branches out of the way, moving through the thick, stinging undergrowth, and suddenly the boy pushed the last branch aside and they came out into a little clearing and stopped, looking around them.

They were standing on a bright, clean sand bar that curved, to their right, in a semicircle around a clear, cool looking pool; across from them was a bank of rocks, partly covered with vines and ferns, and water ran, from several springs back in the rocks, in shiny, slick streams into the little pool. The high trees formed a wall all around them, their branches extending out over the pool, reflecting there, and the sunlight streamed through the opening, like a skylight, directly over the center of the smooth water. The little clearing was quiet, and they stood, hearing only the trickling, lapping water as it seeped down the rocks and then out of the pool to form a small brook at the other end that wound its way down to the branch below them and to their left.

"It's like an enchanted forest," the girl said, her voice shattering the stillness of the scene, and they walked out onto the firm, damp sand of the bar. The spring-fed pool was smooth and still; the water was perfectly clear, and they could see the shadowed, sandy bottom.

"I reckon we found us a good place to eat our dinner, all right," the boy said.

"It's beautiful," the girl said; she sat down on the sand and took offer her sandals and wiggled her toes. "I'm glad we came, now," she said, and the boy sat down beside her and opened the suitcase and took out the box of fig newtons, and they began to chew, the silence of the little clearing all around them. A slight breeze picked up, and the leaves moved softly back and forth; the willow trees across the pond from them, their long, whip-like limbs trailing in the water, swayed gently. They finished half the fig newtons, then went to the edge of the pool, near the place where a spring entered, and cupped their hands and drank the cold, almost icy water; the air in the little clearing was fresh and sweet after the moldy, sour smells of the swamp, and they stretched out, lying back on their elbows, looking up at the patch of sky that showed through the trees. The sun came almost directly down on them, warming the sand, and they stretched their legs out full length in front of them.

"Boy, I could stay here for the rest of my life," the girl said, sighing.

Her hair was pushed back behind her ears, and she had her head back and her eyes closed against the glare of the sun.

"Maybe we will," the boy said, "just set up camp right here in this clearing, build us a little lean-to hut right over there against that rock and just stay here. Sometimes at night we'll sneak out an rob that store over on the highway near the river bridge, to get us some food and fishin stuff and cigarettes, and we'll get us some beer, too."

She look over at the boy, at the wet sneakers and the muddy, wrinkled blue jeans and dirty tee shirt with one sleeve flapping where a briar had torn it. "You don't look like robbin any store," she said, "What you say we take us a bath in our own private swimming pool?"

The boy sat up and looked at her; then he looked out at the still pool, without answering her.

After a minute, she said, "It don't matter, I ain't got anything you ain't got."

"Yeah," he said, "but I got something you ain't got," and he looked at her; she was staring at him strangely, the same slit-eyed expression that she'd had in the cabin that morning showing on her face. Her cheeks reddened for a moment, then she said, "We can wear our underwear, what you gettin so heated up about? It ain't any less than we wear in the pool, anyhow, almost, anyway."

"I ain't heated up," he said; she stood up and wiggled her toes in the now dry sand.

"I sure am dying to get in that water," she said.

"Well, go ahead," he said, "ain't anybody stoppin you."

"What we gone do, be hermits the rest of our lives and not ever go swimming?" she said. She was looking down at him, and he began to unlace the sneakers, and he pulled them off and stood up and pulled the tee shirt over his head.

"Billy," she said, standing there in front of him.

"What you waitin on?" he said.

"Listen, Billy," she said, and he looked at her, and he could see the glow rising behind her tanned cheeks, "don't embarrass me, hear? I'm modest, so don't look at me, you know? Up here?"

"What I want to look at you for?' he said, unbuttoning his blue jeans, "you ain't got nothing I ain't got."

"You can be about the contrariest person I ever saw," she said, and she turned her back to him and began to unbutton the shirt. She dropped it to the sand, and he looked at her naked back, very thin, her shoulder blades almost like sharp wings, and he could see the white skin that had been left beneath her bathing suit. She unbuttoned the shorts and let them drop and stepped out of them, and he turned his eyes away from her thin butt in white panties. He stepped out of his jeans, and, in his undershorts, he walked down to the water. He looked back at her, and she followed him, stepping gingerly in the sand, one arm folded across her breasts.

"I bet it's cold," she said, and she stuck her big toe in and shuddered.

"Spring water always is," he said. "Geronimo!" he turned his back to the pool and fell backwards into the clear, icy water, laughing; the sudden cold took his breath away, and he sat up, splashing. "Whew!" he said, "it's great!"

She was still standing at the edge of the water, her arm across her breasts, her white panties pale against her tan legs. "Come on in!" he yelled, and , laughing, he splashed water on her, and she jumped. "Stop," she said, "I'm comin," and she waded into the water; she squatted slightly and, with her free hand, splashed herself with the water. "It's cold as hell," she said. "All at once," he said, "thass the only way to do it, come on." "I can't," she said; and he said, "Come on, Hallie."

"All right," she said, "here I come." She closed her eyes tightly and stretched her arms out in front of her, and as she began to fall forward he could see the gentle swells of her breasts, pink-tipped, not much bigger than marbles, and he stared at them as she splashed into the pool beside him.

"Eeww, shit," she said, sputtering as she came up, her hair plastered to her head. She splashed about in the water, ducking her head and coming up to spit water at him laughing; "This is better'n any swimmin pool," she said.

They splashed each other for awhile, then they lolled about in the shallow water, sitting on the sandy bottom with only their heads sticking out. They stayed in the water a long time before they walked back up on the sandbar, the girl again being careful to keep her left arm folded across her breasts, and they stretched out on the sand to dry; the sun had moved across the sky, and the afternoon was hot, but the little glade was still and quiet, and the girl said:

"I believe I'll catch me a little nap," and they lay in silence while the afternoon wore on, breathing gently, both of them on their backs, the boy's damp undershorts sticking to him, the girl with her left arm folded carefully across her naked, tiny breasts.

She was the first to awake, and she sat up and put on her shirt; the sun had gotten low in the sky, and the glade was full of shadows, and while she buttoned the shirt a bullfrog in the bushes across the pool began to croak. Then it plopped loudly into the water, and the girl jumped and woke the boy.

"What's the matter?" he said, sitting up, and she said "Somethin splashed over there."

"Ol bullfrog, probly," he said.

"What made him jump in the water?" she said; and the boy said, "He probly saw you movin around over here."

THE BOY RUBBED at his eyes, and the girl looked around the clearing; there was still plenty of light, but already the crickets back in the undergrowth had started and the surface of the pool was a pale, mirror-like gray. "I guess we'll just spend the night on this sandbar and go on in the morning," the boy said. "I'll get us some wood for a fire fore it gets dark." The boy stood and put on his pants and put on his shirt; "I'll be right back," he said, and he went toward the woods.

The girl sat in the still clearing; she could hear the steady gurgle of the water and the buzzing of crickets, and every now and then she jumped as she heard the boy rummaging in the woods. She heard then, way off, the mournful, lonely crying of an owl, and she remembered the one they'd heard that night along the river, and she wondered, for a moment, if it might be the same one; then she thought of the hermit, and she looked around. She felt goose pimples appear on her arms and legs, and she stared at the thick, dark woods around her, sensing a stillness, a heavy silence behind the green-black façade of growth. The boy appeared, carrying an armload of dead logs.

"These ought to do us," he said; and she said: "Billy I'm scared."

"Don't be scared, ain't nothing gonna bother us on this sandbar."

"There's somethin out there watchin us," she said.

"There ain't nothing out there but a cane-cutter rabbit or two," he said. "And hush up talking like that."

The sun was getting very low, and the small patches of western sky that they could see through the trees were bright red; it was getting dark in the clearing, and the boy set about making a fire. He was stacking the wood when the girl said, "What was that?"

"What?"

"Shhhhh," she whispered, and they sat in silence, listening to the hum of the crickets, the gurgle of the water. Then they heard a movement, a shuffle in the darkness along the brook that ran from the little pond. "You hear it?" she whispered. She moved over next to him, and she grabbed his arm when they heard the shuffling movement again, and the boy said: "Who's that?" and there was only silence above the crickets and the water. "Who's that out there?" the boy said again. They sat on the sand, still as death, and slowly began to make out a form. It moved out of the bushes and slowly made its way toward them, moving with an awkward, plodding gate, and the girl's hand gripped the boy's arm tightly.

The form moved closer to them, and they could make out, in the half light, that it was a man; he came slowly closer, until he was standing almost over them, looking down at them, and he was moving his hands in front of him, and suddenly there was a scratch and a match spurted into flame, and they shrank back; they were looking up at a huge Negro man who stood staring down at them, a grotesque right eye cocked to the side and bloodshot, an old, black felt hat crammed low over his ears. He stood silently, while the match burned down, glaring down at them; and they could see, in the dying flicker of the match, that he had on a thick, black overcoat that hung all the way to the ground.

His hands moved in front of him again, and another match spurted; they could smell the thick, sulfur smell of the flame. The flickering light glinted on the cocked eye, and they could see tufts of steely-gray hair sticking from under the hat; the man spoke, and his voice was deep and gravelly.

"You can say it," he said, and they crouched, looking up at him, locked rigid in their positions. "G'wan, you can say it if you want to."

"Say what?" the boy said, and his voice was little more than a whisper.

The old Negro spoke slowly, "Bynymo, Bynymo, hit im in the belly with a fawty-foe." Then as the flame of the second match died, in the returning shadow, the boy and girl were shocked as they realized, could see, that the old Negro was grinning at them.

Eight

Late that afternoon, when the Western sky was just beginning to take on its red glow, Bubba Tate, the sheriff, parked the patrol car in front of Mrs. Eva Malone's gate and got out and went slowly up the front walk. He was tall and wide-shouldered, and his gait was self-confident, and he wore a wide-brimmed, Western-style hat tilted at an angle over his right eye. He knocked and then took his hat off and held it over his chest, and, after a minute, Mrs. Malone opened the front door.

"Well?" she said, and he stood looking down at her, his brown eyes narrowed in the leathery skin of this face.

"No luck," he said, "yet."

She pushed open the screen door. "Come in, Mr. Tate," she said, and the big man moved through the door and entered the room, standing first on one foot, then the other, turning the wide-brimmed hat around and around in his hands.

"If they headed for Prichard, they ain't arrived there yet," he said. "They didn't take any bus anywhere, Dub Ford'd have remembered em, he says he sold four tickets to Bessemer last night, all to niggers. Course they coulda got a couple o niggers to go in and buy em for em, knowin that Dub would remember em, but Dub believes the niggers was all together. We checked out the bus station in Bessemer, course nobody remembers seein em, the bus company's tryin to locate the driver now."

"Sit down, Mr. Tate, and I'll get you a glass of iced tea," Mrs. Malone said.

"Nome, thank you, I can't stay long, but I will sit for a minute," he said, and he sat on the sofa and crossed his long legs; he wore high-heeled cowboy boots with the legs of this khaki breeches stuffed into them. The boy's mother came into the room, in the chenille bathrobe, a wadded handkerchief in her hand, and sat in a chair across from him. Her eyes were red-rimmed and cloudy, as though she had been crying. "Martha," he said, nodding to her.

"Any news, Bubba?" she said.

"No, not yet. But ain't anything happened to em, if it had we'd of heard."

"Unless some pervert picked em up and left em in a ditch somewhere," Mrs. Malone said.

"Oh, Eva, shut up," the boy's mother said.

"They'll turn up, ain't any reason to worry too much," the sheriff said. "Have you thought of anywhere else they mighta gone, anywhere around here?"

"I don't know," Mrs. Malone said, "they could be hidin out anywhere around here, couldn't they? They played some in those ol caves down by the river."

"I'll have Lee check em out when he comes on," the sheriff said. "Seem to me like somebody woulda seen em last night, it couldn't o been all that late, two chirren goin down the street totin a suitcase; they musta left before that storm. Anyhow, wouldn't nobody strike out on foot in a storm like that."

"I wonder where they were durin it, that's what I'm worried about," the boy's mother said.

"Did you talk to Lillian and Julia Fisque?" Mrs. Malone said.

"Yessum," the sheriff said. "They couldn't tell me nothing. They just figured she'd head home to her daddy, but they'da been there by now, surely. I tell you, Mams, I believe they right around here somewhere, hidin out scared. Them caves might be just what we lookin for." He stood up, clutching his hat in front of him. "Lee'll be comin on in a few minutes, " he said, "and we'll git back to work on it. Yall don't worry no more'n you have to, we'll find em." He was taking long strides toward the door, and Mrs. Malone followed him.

"Let us know, now, first thing you find out," she said; and the sheriff said, "Yessum, we will, now yall don't worry no more'n you have to."

The front door closed softly behind him, followed by the rattling slam of the screen door, and the boy's grandmother turned back into the room. The boy's mother had her head thrown back on the back of the chair, breathing deeply, her hands clasped around the wadded handkerchief in her lap. "That girl," she murmured, "that girl."

"Now don't go blamin that little girl for all this," the boy's grandmother said. "You can blame me and the belt all you want to, but don't go blamin that little girl. A boy don't run off from home, at least not one his age, for the likes of any girl."

"He never did anything like this before," the boy's mother said.

"There's a first time for everything, Martha," the boy's grandmother said, "a boy grows up, he changes; you can say it ain't our fault that we had to raise him in a world where the only two men in his life were a half-drunk, preachin nigger yard man and a fairy-tale hermit livin back in the swamp, but sayin it ain't our fault don't bring him back safe right now, and trying to find somebody else to lay the blame on, like that poor little girl, don't do it either."

"I wasn't blamin her," the boy's mother said. "I just don't understand him, that's all."

"I don't reckon you do," the boy's grandmother said. "I reckon Hess was right, he's a boy changing into a man, and that something me nor you neither one can never really understand." She looked at the boy's mother, at the red-rimmed, bloody eyes. "But that poor little girl, now, that's another matter entirely, ain't it?" she said. And the two women looked at each other in the darkening room.

Bubba Tate parked the patrol car in front of the court house and went up the front steps through the narrow front door of the old building; the sun was almost set, the sky in the West a bright, orange-red color that reflected off the whitewashed brick walls of the courthouse, a square, narrow building with a belfry on the roof that resembled a church, that had in fact at one time been one. He passed a bright red white and blue sign, a picture of Uncle Sam, pointing, the caption reading "UNCLE SAM NEEDS YOU," and next to that a poster with a large red cross, under which someone had scrawled in crayon, "County Health Nurse Office, Tues., 2-4." He pushed open the door to his office, and Lee Gossit was sitting behind a single desk, his blue shirt open at the collar, smoking a cigarette.

"Bus company called from Birmingham," he said, "said the driver o that bus said they definitely wasn't any white boy and girl on his run last night."

"Figures," the sheriff said. "Know'd they wasn't anyhow." He came on into the room and sat down across from his night marshall.

"Where you reckon they are?" Gossit said.

"Study on it this way," the sheriff said, "where would you go if you was twelve years old and run away from home?"

Gossit drew on the cigarette, then studied the glowing tip. "I didn't never run away from home when I was a young un," he said.

"You ain't much help," the sheriff said. "You sure you didn't see em last night?"

"Wadn't nobody stirrin but Ted Mack Lowery, and Justina Beasley, I let em both outta jail right fore the storm hit."

"Maybe they saw em goin home," the sheriff said.

"Naw, Justina lives up the road from the jailhouse and I drove Ted Mack home in the car, if he'da seen em I would."

"After while I want you to take the car and go down there and check out them caves down along the river. Don't forget that one behind Old Man Taylor's junk heap," the sheriff said.

"Right," Gossit said, "I'll go right now, fore it gets too dark."

"Set there a minute," the sheriff said, "ain't any hurry, whyn't you wait on the moon, be just like day."

Gossit shrugged and took out another cigarette. "What'd they run away for, any reason?" he said, and the sheriff said: "Shit, just kids, I guess."

IT WAS LATER, after the moon was high, and the sheriff was sitting in the little office when he heard the patrol car pull up outside and two doors slam, and he thought, Goddam, he's done found em. He heard talking in the hall outside and he stood up behind the desk, and just then the door opened and Lee Gossit walked in, followed by Ted Mack Lowery, his hands jammed into the pockets of his overalls and a scowl on his tanned face.

"Nothin in them caves but spiders," Gossit said, and the sheriff said, "Who's your buddy here?"

"Found him prowlin round down in niggertown, I done told him and told him to stay way from there," Gossit said.

"One o these mornins we gonna find him in a ditch, his goddam throat cut, an it might be a good thing for this town if we did," the sheriff said. "You check that one behind Taylor's?"

"Ever one, not a sign of em," Gossit said.

"Iss a free goddam country, ain't it?" Ted Mack said.

"Lowery, you bout the sorriest hunk o goddam white trash I ever run across; if you ain't pissin on a white man's street corner you sniffin round a nigger man's woman. Now sit down over there and shut that goddam rotten mouth o yours!" the sheriff said.

"You ain't got no cause to talk to me like that," Ted Mack said, "I minds my own bidnis." He sat heavily in the chair, his hands still jammed into his pockets, his feet, in the dusty brogans, crossed at the ankles. "Besides, I seen them chirrin Lee uz lookin for, seen em lass night."

The sheriff looked at Gossit and the night marshall shrugged. "Claims he seen em go by the jail last night, fore I come to let him out, but they ain't no sign of em in them caves. He thought they uz goin toward the river, towards Rowan's landing," he said.

"You sure it wadn't a parade o pink and blue circus elephants you seen?" the sheriff said.

"They uz carryin this yellow lookin suitcase, Woody Malone's boy and some girl a little taller'n him, and I seen em clear in the moonlight, and I remarked on it, you can ast that nigger woman, she heard me remark on it when they went by."

"Rowan's landin?" the sheriff said, "you don't reckon they

headed for Mobile on the river, do you?"

"They sure didn't get far in that storm if they did," Lee Gossit said, and the two men looked at each other.

"I'll be damn," the sheriff said, and just as he said it the telephone on the desk rang and he picked it up. "Sheriff Tate speakin," he said.

"Mr. Tate, this is Eva Malone," the voice on the other end said. "Mr. Tate, my yard man Ned Clay is at the back door, and he just told me that that old nigger they call Navajo told him this evening that he rowed Billy and Hallie across the river last night for a dollar, just shortly before the thunderstorm hit."

"Across the river?" the sheriff said.

"Let em out on that sandbar right across from Rowan's landin, they told him they were headed into the swamp, an I shoulda thought o that before now, Mr. Tate."

"What'd they want to do that for?" the sheriff said.

"I . . . I don't know, really Mr. Tate," she said, "but that's where they are, probly lost by now, or no telling what's happened to em by now, but I reckon we got to find em."

"All right, Miz Malone, we'll find em, I'll get together some fellows that knows that swamp like the back o their hand, we'll find em. Lemme make some plans, and I'll call you back, hear?" he said, and he hung up the phone and looked at the two men, who had been watching him curiously while he spoke on the phone.

"I reckon you did see em, Lowery," he said, "an they picked about the best place I know of to lose themselves in; they over in the swamps."

"The swamps?" Gossit said.

"Goddam it," the sheriff said, "just plain ol out an out goddam goddamit!"

THEY HAD BEEN unable to move, and the old Negro had picked up the lantern beside the girl and lighted it, then he sat down on the sand across from them, across the little pile of logs the boy had prepared for a fire and placed the lantern between them. They were now sitting in a circle of yellow light that made the woods around them seem much darker, and the flame of the lantern reflected off the silver surface of the little pool. He continued to gaze at them, a half-smile on his face, his legs crossed Indian-fashion in front of him; he had been carrying a croaker sack, with a rope tied onto it for a shoulder strap, and it was bulging and full and had clattered as he dropped it onto the firm sand near the beginnings of the fire. He reached into the folds of the overcoat and took out a pipe and a red tin of tobacco and slowly began to pack it, watching them, his face varying, now and then, from a half-smile to a broad grin; then he stuck the pipe into his mouth and lit it with one of his heavy kitchen matches, sucking at the stem until great clouds of gray smoke rose about his head and drifted off. He took the pipe from his mouth and smacked his lips.

"Indians give us tobacco," he said, "you know that? They's a lot of things the Indians give us. Corn and what not. Squash, too. I bet you ain't knowed any of that. White folks come over cross the water and took all their land from em." He looked around the woods, scanning them, as though he were searching for something. "Ain't no Indians round here at all any more. Where you spect they gone?"

The boy and girl just looked at him, not answering, and he said, "What you chirren doin over here? Where you come from?" He kept tilting his head slightly to the side; as though better to get them into focus with his good eye.

"Hammond," the boy said.

"What you doin over here?" he said, and they sat in silence for a moment.

"We just came over here to look around," the boy said, and the old Negro nodded his head.

"Yall on vacation," he said, then he tilted his head back and peered at them in the lamplight. "Yall married?" he said.

"We ain't married," the girl said, and the old Negro grinned at her; his teeth were brown and tobacco stained. He puffed on his pipe for a moment, regarding them through the smoke, over the bowl.

"Yall know who I is?" he said, after a minute.

"Yes," the boy said, "you're Armstead King."

"No, I ain't," the Negro said.

"I mean, you're Joe Bynymo," the boy said.

"Thass right, thass me, Joe Bynymo," he said. "Yall scared o me?"

The two of them looked at each other, then back at the old Negro, who still sat facing them, Indian-fashion, his pipe hanging from his teeth. "Kinda," the girl said.

"Well, you sho oughtta be, I got me a black snake whip in that sack yonder quarter o a mile long, and sometimes I take it inta my head to haint folks," he said, "an you gotta buil a fire fore you can heat beans and boil you some coffee, now ain'tcha?" He sat looking at them, and they didn't move. "Boy," he said, "you got a look in yo eyes ud stop a bear in his tracks. What you got to eat in that satchel?"

"Fig newtons and cold biscuits," the boy said.

"Well, less get us a fire started, I brung the beans, you brung the dessert and the bread, what you waitin on?" the old Negro said.

He pulled the croaker sack to him and began to rummage around inside, and the boy finished his preparations for the fire. "Make it flat as you can, we'll buil it up after we gits through cookin on it," the Negro said; he seemed to have everything they needed in the sack; first he brought out a heavy, black cast iron skillet that stood up on legs, then a battered and stained coffee pot. "Supper ain't supper lessen you got coffee to drink wit it, is it?" he said. He pulled out a can of pork and beans and a can opener, and followed that with a cloth sack of coffee. "Whyn't you git us some water from the spring, lil lady, whilst I puts these beans on?" he said, and the girl took the coffee pot and filled it, and when she returned to the circle of lantern light the boy had the fire going. The old Negro had opened the beans and he dumped them into the skillet and sat back, grinning at them. "Soon as it die down some, we have us a good supper sho nough," he said. "Yessir, it sho is nice to have some company." He drew on the pipe, and tilted his head back to blow the smoke at the sky; the moon was up now, and the sky was bright and thick with stars, and crickets chirped steadily in the undergrowth all around them.

"It is?" the boy said, and the old Negro said,

"Sho is, I gits tired talking to my animals all the time, squirrels and rabbits and deers, they smart, smart'n most folks, but they don't talk back too plain sometimes."

"I thought you was a hermit," the boy said, and the old Negro took his pipe out of his mouth and stared at them.

"I is," he said, blinking the good eye at them. "Whyn't you tend to your fire, boy, me and the lil lady there gittin hungry."

The old Negro had but one tin plate, and he gave that to them and then took it back and gave the boy a fork and the girl a spoon. "I ain't got but one o everything," he said, "so I eat wit my fingers, but I ain't burnin em on that hot spider."

They ate in silence, the boy and girl eating out of the skillet sitting between them, their utensils scraping on the iron, watching the old Negro cram the beans in his mouth with his fingers; when he was finished he sopped the tomato sauce up with one of the biscuits and stuck it into his mouth and chewed, looking at them with his head tilted to the side; then he took the box of fig newtons and shook them out into his palm and inspected them, then crammed them both into his mouth and began to chew. When he swallowed, he said, "Figs make a good cake, don't they?"

"Yeah," the boy said, "they do."

"I useta have me a fig tree," the hermit said. "Had me a little house. Had me a wife, too, prettiest little thing." He looked at the girl. "You puts me in mind of her, cept of course she wasn't no white girl. But that was a long time ago." The old man closed his eyes. "That fig tree sho nuff had the figs on it, I tell you, great big old juicy figs that'ud break open they so ripe, and the squirrels and the birds come from everywhere, just a barkin and squawkin and fussin to get at them figs. We didn't care, cause we'd already got all we could eat and all my wife could make preserves out of. We'd eat them preserves on big old cat-head biscuits all winter." He smacked his lips. "Yes sir, sparrows, blue jays, mockin birds, all of em come, to get at that sweetness. Yall ever ate fig preserves?"

"Yeah," the boy said.

Later, after he had carefully washed the skillet at the edge of the water, spilling sand into it and scrubbing with his knuckles, he washed the bean can and brought it back to the fire for their coffee, he poured his into a tin cup and sat back, legs crossed, and stuffed his pipe and lit it, blowing smoke at the glowing coals of the fire. "We'll buil that up fore we bed down, keep the wild animals away," he said, and the girl said,

"What kinda animals you mean?"

"Bobcats and bears and wild hogs." The old Negro said, "this here swamp is runnin with wild hogs."

"It ain't either," the boy said, and the old Negro stared at him, sitting across the fire from them, his black hat pushed back on his head, his gray hair matted like steel wool on his head. He puffed his pipe several times, then he said, "You a smart one ain'tcha?"

"Don't scare her like that," the boy said.

"I didn't go to scare her," the old Negro said. He grinned at them, and they sat across the fire from him, watching him puff on the pipe, the stem making little sucking noises that blended with the crickets and the swishing flow of water and the occasional nightbird that cried out back in the swamp. The fire was low, and the lantern flickered dimly. They sat for a while, and then the girl said:

"Why do you wear that old heavy coat, hot as it is?"

"Ain't you heard? I got my seasons turned around," he said.

"Don't you get hot?" she said.

"I gits hot in the winter, cold in the summer, right the opposite from what most folks gits," he said. The boy and girl were staring at him over the glowing coals of the fire. "I reckon I'm what they call crazy, ain't I? Course you can call hot cold, and you can call cold hot, don't make no difference what you calls it, folks just made up them words anyhow. Like callin me crazy; maybe you crazy and I ain't, maybe you cold in the summer but you so crazy that you think it's hot, so you run around in them short pants freezing to death, all the time thinking you hot. Folks just told you you was hot, and all this time you mighta been cold." He was looking over the pipe bowl, his good eye fixed on them. "Most folks don't do nothin lessen other folks tell em to, noway," he said, "nor feel nothin, either." He leaned forward and put two logs across the coals, and tiny flames began to lick at them. "You take that war over there cross the water, what all them folks over there killin one another for, if it ain't cause other folks done told em they had to do it?"

"My daddy got killed over there," the boy said; the old Negro was poking at the fire with a stick, and he paused and looked up at the boy, the new flames bright on the fierce, cocked eye.

"Thass a shame," he said. "Folks is crazy, I ain't, they done done it twice since I been livin over here, they sho crazy."

"I ain't crazy," the girl said, and the old Negro said,

"I ain't said you was, I said folks is crazy, you ain't folks, you chirren," he said, and he dropped the stick on the sand beside him and leaned back, tilting his head to look at them. "Leastways, I think you chirren," he said.

"What you mean by that?" the girl said.

"Well, you both look like you got the juices flowin in you," he said.

They looked at each other. They didn't understand what he was saying, and yet they did, too. Billy thought of Hallie at the pool, jumping into the water, holding her chest. What was going on inside his own body was still a mystery to him, but he knew enough to know he had the juices flowing. Whatever exactly the old hermit meant by that. Hallie thought of her spotted panties, the look on Aunt Julia's face when she had discovered them.

"You mean we're growing up," Hallie said.

"Somethin like that, yeah," the hermit said.

"How old were you when you ran away?" Hallie asked.

"Older'n you, bigger'n you, and blacker'n you," he said. "I ain't got no age. My life ain't measured in years, like most folks's. Ain't no time over here. You see a clock or a calendar around someplace?" He grinned at them. "You ain't told me what yall doin over here."

"Just lookin around, I said," the boy said.

"Yessir, you did say that, didn't you," the old Negro said, and he looked shrewdly at them, the pipe sticking from the corner of his mouth at an angle. "Course we don't git many tourists over here, mostly what we gits is folks runnin away from home an all like that," he said. "Course what yall doin over here, I reckon, is your own bidnis, cept for the fact that yall trespassin."

"This land's posted?" the boy said.

"I don't reckon you could rightly call it posted," the old Negro said, "but I done laid claim to it, I done took it and give it back to the Lord, an I'm just the caretaker, lookin after it for Him, and He don't want no folks comin in here and messin it up. He want it to stay just like it is."

"How do you know that?" the girl said.

"He made it like this, didn't he? Soon as you let a man come in here, first thing he gwine do is cut a tree down, folks can't stand to go in nowhere without cutting down a tree; they see a creek, first thing they gwine do is seine it; find a new patch o woods, first thing they do is run a pack o dogs through it to make sure ain't nothing in there they gone miss shootin at. Listen here to me," he said, peering at the girl, "you know how long it take the Lord to grow a tree?"

"No," she said, "a long time, I reckon."

"An it take two men wit a cross-cut saw bout three minutes to cut it down, now that don't seem right, do it? They see a tree up, like it spose to be, like the Lord put it, and they figure it oughtta be down. Now is hot cold or is cold hot?"

"All right," the boy said, "but spose He meant for it to be cut down, you ain't got any way o knowin He didn't."

"No, I don't reckon I do, cept for the fact that it's there," the old Negro said, "an the way I figure it, if He'da meant for trees to turn into boards He'da made em grow that way, now tell me how come He didn't."

"Sounds like a lot o hog-wash to me," the girl said, and the old Negro took his pipe out of his mouth and pointed it at her.

"Hog-wash it ain't," he said, "besides, hogs don't wash, folks do that, washin and washin to get the stink o the earth off of em, while the ol sow just lay around in the mud, blinkin her eyes and sleepin and gettin fat, boss man come in twicet a day with a bucket brimful o good old slop for her, all she got to do is lay there in the mud an take it easy."

"And end up in somebody's fryin pan," the boy said.

"Everybody end up in one kinda fryin pan or another." The hermit stuck the pipe back between his teeth and puffed the coal alive again, and the boy and girl sat very still across the fire from him; he seemed to be lost in thought for a moment, staring into the crackling fire.

"Who are you?" the boy said suddenly, abruptly. "I mean . . . what

". . . what are you?"

"I a crazy ol nigger hermit," he said. "A black man is a nigger, don't make no difference who his daddy was, nor who his mammy was either; a nigger ain't but a nigger, call him what you want to. White folks, now, they got their own ideas bout what a nigger is, and niggers got a different one, and don't either one of em really know what they talkin about."

"Ned Clay told me that you wadn't a nigger," the boy said, and the old Negro said,

"See there, I don't even know no Ned Clay, and here he done tol you somethin bout me like he know what he talkin bout; I ain't got no more use for folks than a boar hog has tits, and they ain't no good at all, an thass somethin yall gone find out soon enough." The fire was crackling between them, and they could hear the steady hum of the crickets back in the brush. "That is, if you ain't already found it out, runnin off like you done; I know how it is, I run off one time, too, only I stayed and laid claim to this swamp and give it back to the Lord, and He give me a full time job just caretakin it for Him, and thass a heap more than most ol niggers can claim, ain't it?" He grinned proudly at them. "Now put us another log on that fire," he said, "I can see it's gone be a long night."

Ted Mack reappeared at the courthouse with several of the other men, carrying a long, double-barrelled rabbit-ears shotgun with a length of bailing wire wrapped around the hand-grip of the stock.

"That goddam thing is gone blow up in your face," the sheriff said

Ted Mack answered, "They don't make shotguns like this here no more."

"You're damn right about that, all right; what you plannin on shootin with it?"

"I seen that ol nigger one time, I'se seinin up on Maconaco Creek one time an he come bustin out yellin some kinda African talk at me, run me off."

"Just remember, it ain't open season on niggers; you can come along, but keep your lip buttoned and your trigger finger up your ass-hole."

Now they were all standing in a little group, half-way up the incline at Rowan's Landing; Miss Julia Fisque stood slightly apart, wearing the same gray, shapeless house dress, but she had replaced the bed-room slippers with a pair of high-top, lace-up shoes; her sister was a part of the group, a knitted shawl around her shoulders, hugging herself against the dampness of the river and the night. Mrs. Eva Malone was talking, saying something about the crazy old hermit who lived over there, and the young sheriff, who was holding a flashlight and chewing a match stick, just nodded. Several men stood or sat around the group, most holding flashlights, some holding rifles and shotguns. She jumped as she heard the shotgun blast from the river; every now and then, about every five minutes, someone in a boat on the river would fire into the air; the roar boomed across the water and echoed against the high, chalky white bluffs and died, in reverberations, over the thick, black, forbidding trees on the other side.

"We can't keep this up all night," the sheriff was saying, "not scarce as them shells are; not even the law can get em in any quantity."

"But maybe they'll hear it," the boy's mother said.

"If they ain't already heard it, they ain't goin to," the sheriff said. "A couple of us went in as far as this old shack an there was signs of em, some biscuit crumbs and cigarette butts and like that. I figure they spent lass night in there; if they did, they was high and dry. Ain't any use goin in any farther tonight, we'll just hafta wait till daylight."

"They's quicksand in there," a voice from the shadows said, and they all turned; they could make out the form of Ted Mack Lowery, sitting on a limerock bank, a long shotgun across his knees.

"What'd I tell you when I let you come along?" the sheriff said, and Ted Mack sat sullenly on the limerock at the edge of a ditch, the moonlight glinting on the long barrel of his gun. "All right, then, keep it shut."

Turning to Miss Lilian, the sheriff said, "Ted Mack's just talkin. There ain't much that could happen to em; the worst is they got lost and get scared; but it's only a matter o time fore we find em."

"But that crazy ol nigger Bynymo," Miss Lillian said, "What'll he do with em?"

"I always heard there was snakes bigger'n your leg," Miss Julia said, "an snakes is the instrument of the devil."

"Oh Julia, hush up," Miss Lillian said.

"What would he want with em?" the sheriff asked.

"Some say he's a cannibal," Ted Mack said, from the shadows; and Eva Malone said, "Don't pay no attention to him; he's drunk probly."

They all jumped when the shotgun went off again, the sound echoing hollowly around them. "Sweet Jesus above," Miss Lillian said, "they sho ought to hear that, lessen they clean outta the county by now."

"Sound don't carry good back in them trees," the sheriff said, "not like it does on this water.

They stood silently again, looking across at the black stillness of the swamp, the river flowing smoothly by in front of them; the silver moon glinted on the wrinkled surface of the water. Several other people had gathered, standing apart from them, talking quietly, and they could see some people standing along the top of the bluff, up river from them, holding flashlights, and there was an occasional spurt of a lighted match. Once there was a long peal of laughter, as though somebody had told a joke; and then silence, the gentle swishing of the water, and then once more the sudden, shattering roar of the shotgun. Occasionally, someone in a boat down on the river would shine a spotlight along the line of thick undergrowth, but there was no movement, no life among the leaves and vines.

"Yall might as well go on home," the sheriff said, "an come back at first light. Ain't any sense in tirin yourself out like this."

"We'll stay awhile," Eva Malone said, "they might come walkin out any minute."

"They might at that," the sheriff said, and he shifted the frayed match to the other side of his mouth, chewing on it, and looked off across the river, his hands propped casually on his hips.

There were several Negroes down near the river; Ned Clay squatted on his haunches, drawing little designs in the limerock dust with a stick; he peered at the old bald-headed Negro in the overalls who was sitting in a skiff, watching the point of the stick as it moved about. "Yo neck gone be worth bout two cents if them chirren dead," Ned Clay said, "an they just might be."

"Ain't nothin happened to em," the bald-headed Negro said.

"Wher dey at den?" another Negro said.

"They'll find em, don't you worry none bout it, they'll find em," he said.

"That libel to be the hardest dollar you ever earned," Ned Clay said, "I sho wouldn't wanna be in yo shoes when they do finds em over there snakebit and dead."

"They ain't dead, so git on wit you," the bald-headed Negro said. Sides, I'm goin over there wit em in the mornin, I'll find em."

"Maybe they'll let you pick out your own tree to hang from," the other Negro said; he was standing with a twisted, rolled cigarette drooping from his lips. Ned Clay laughed, and the bald-headed Negro sat slumped in the boat, not answering, staring straight ahead.

"It just ain't any use," the boy's mother said; "I just got a feelin . . ." and Eva Malone said, "Hush up now, Hess is comin with some coffee."

"I need a couple o aspirin," the boy's mother said; and the sheriff said, "They's some in the car, I'll git em for you. Don't you wanna set down over here?"

The four women moved toward the car; when they were seated, they stared through the windshield at the broad river, at the spotlight playing futilely across the thick growth on the other side, the blackness and mystery that had engulfed the two helpless children; and the boy's mother started to cry, quietly, her shoulders slumped, her curved palm caressing her forehead. The moon had started its downward slant, and more people had gathered along the river, the lateness of the evening causing them to lapse into silence, their eyes staring at the dismal swamp that lay always just across the river. There were soft whispers and rumors that ran back and forth: "They said that old hermit kidnapped em." "Naw they just ran away from home." "There ain't no hermit over there noway, that ain't nothin but a story made up to scare chillen." "What the hell you talkin bout? I seen him with my own eyes." They moved about quietly, watching the spotlight move back and forth, hearing the spaced shots from the shotgun.

"Lord I hope daylight hurries up and gets here," the boy's grandmother said. There was no answer from the back seat, and she turned to look at the two sisters; Julia was staring out the window, a sour, almost sinister frown on her flat, round face; and Lillian, sitting primly with the shawl about her shoulders, was fast asleep.

"Why'd you run away, Joe?" Hallie asked.

"Bout the same reason yall did, I spect. Only yall lucky: you got each other for company."

"I thought a hermit didn't want any company," the boy said. "I thought you wanted to be all alone."

"You a smart one, ain'tcha? I done told yall I'm glad you come a-visitin." He poked at the fire with a stick. "What you want and what you got ain't always the same thing. I reckon yall have done found that out by now, surely."

"Yeah," the girl said. Her voice was dreamy, sleepy. The fire snapped and whispered. Bullfrogs had set up back in the swamp, on the other side of the pool, their croaking providing harmony to the crickets and katydids and the trill of the waterfall. The music was a rhythm, a natural melody that lulled them all toward sleep, that drew them deeper into the very essence of the swamp. The boy and girl could feel its dampness, could smell its rich, pungent muck mingling with the sharp woodsy smoke of their fire.

"Yeah," the hermit said after a while. "I had me somebody to keep me company one time, had me a little house down there in Frogbottom. And that fig tree I'se tellin yall about. Had me a peach tree, too, lawd those peaches was sweet, sweeter'n these wild persimmons I eat out here, that's for sure. A persimmon'll turn your mouth inside out and downside up, but they good enough, now. It ain't like I'm complainin bout what the Lord put out here for me to eat. We had us a chinaberry tree, too, right there in the front yard. She liked that for decoration. And a chicken yard, for eggs and fryers. Wasn't much we wanted for."

"What happened?" the boy asked.

"Well," the old hermit said, "didn't much happen."

"You said 'she,' " the girl said.

"Yall bout as curious as a month-old kitten," Bynymo said. He shook his head. He chuckled. Then he looked sad, haunted. "Like I said, she was a pretty thing." He paused again. "Ain't nothing perfect in this world," he said, "yall gonna know that soon enough, too, I reckon. Folks is mean, and selfish, all wrapped up in theirselves. When I go into town little chirren jump out and shout at me, and I get my bullwhip goin on em, too. I can't walk three blocks without somebody hollerin at me. But I walk them streets cause they just as much mine as they are theirs. Or they used to be. Before I give em back. And took up over here."

"What happened to her?" Hallie asked. Her voice was hushed, breathy, as though she didn't really want to hear an answer.

The hermit busied himself with snapping several small dry limbs into pieces which he arranged on the fire, moving as slowly and carefully as if he were a sculptor fixing some permanent design on top of the glowing ashes. Tiny flames began to lick around the sticks. "I lost her," he said. He fixed his good eye on them. "She taught me everthing I know about love, and I lost her. Nemmine how or why. One day she was as much a part of me as my right arm, and then she was gone. I was a young man then, crazy in a different way from what I am now. We was both crazy happy, and I thought it'ud always be like that, that once you had somethin nobody could take it away from you, but I found out that'uz wrong." He sighed. He was silent for a long time, the only sounds the music of the swamp. "You can be young like yall are," he said finally, "and fine. An yall bout sweet and pure as yall ever gonna be. But it ain't gonna last. Nothin good gonna last, and you just haveta keep on livin and hopin that what you makin outta livin is good, and have faith that it is, whatever you doin with yourself, but that ain't easy atall. Because folks is just mean."

The shadows were deeper, the night inky dark now. The sticks sputtered and flamed up as a knot caught and flared. They watched the brief dancing of the flames, all three of their faces in black darkness, indistinguishable one from another.

"Yall more than welcome to come over here and be hermits with me," the old man said.

"We might just do that," the girl said.

Then the fire died down once again. The moon was lower in the sky. They sat for a long time without speaking, until there was a sudden sound, a far off pop, something odd and alien to the serenity of the woods. Another. The pops were barely discernable above the frogs and crickets.

"What was that?" the girl asked.

"Sounded like a shotgun," the boy said.

The old Negro said nothing, still sitting across the fire from them, his heavy black coat draped over his knees.

"Why would anybody be huntin this time o night?" the boy said; and the old Negro said, "Depends on what they huntin, I speck."

The boy and girl looked at each other, then at the old Negro, who sat holding his cold pipe in his hands before him. They waited, their ears cocked, hearing the soft sound of the water; in a few minutes, the sound came again, just barely discernible on the air.

"It comin from the river, to guide yall back," the hermit said, "But ain't no sense in tryin, not lessen yall got some more kerosene in that satchel."

"We ain't goin back," the boy said, "they can't find us in the dark."

"They ain't gonna try, they'll wait till mornin, then they'll find you, they'll be here, there ain't anything they can't find once they set there minds to it."

"But how'd they know we were here?" the girl asked.

"They know," the hermit said, "an come mornin, they'll be all over this swamp. I can hide from em, cause they ain't lookin for me, but yall can't, ain't no way you can hide from em, they'll find you quicker'n you can say scat." The hermit seemed wistful and sad as he picked up a stick and poked at the fire. "I don't like em comin in here, I tell you that, but it don't matter much, I a old man, I ain't gonna be round to take care o it too much longer, noway. I done had to be a nigger part o my life and a crazy man the other part, an I ain't learned much more than cold is hot, and hot is cold, an folks don't want to believe nothin that ain't wrote down or that they can't chop down or shoot."

"Listen," the boy said, "I'm sorry about em comin in here."

"It ain't your fault, you didn't go to bring em in here, they'd come anyhow, sooner or later," the hermit said; and the boy and girl looked at each other again. A hush seemed to fall over the little clearing; even the crickets seemed silenced. "Folks just hates one another most o the time, an when they do do what they call love, they does it for the wrong reasons," he said, the good eye fixed on them. "Just remember that if you can."

The hermit started to pack his pipe; "One more pipeload," he said, and the boy sat watching him, thinking of the image he had so often imagined, the young Negro standing against a sapling high on the town-side bluff, looking out over the brown, sun-lit river at the silent swamps; then he thought of the Saturday crowded streets, the laughter and the smells and the high noon sunlight glinting in the street; and remembering the afternoon that he and Hallie had sat on the steps of her Aunt's house and watched the homeward-bound wagons going by; he thought of the time, once again, when he and his grandmother had visited Hess when she was sick, the spoon being raised to the thin, quivering lips, the slurping sounds within the dark, thick Negro smell of the tiny cabin, and he felt the same sadness, the same sense of feeling of loss that he couldn't place but that left him hollow and yearning inside.

"Is that really true, Joe?" the boy said and the Negro puffed at his pipe, then he looked at them and grinned his wide grin, and his face seemed to relax under the grotesque, cocked eye. "Thank God for chirren and hermits," he said, grinning at them, then he set about putting more wood on the fire. "We better buil this up and git us some shut eye, don't you speck? It gittin late, and I speck I'll just walk you part way out in the mornin, keep em from comin in this far, anyhow."

"Sure," the girl said, and her voice sounded strange to the boy. A deep-seated fear, a wavering, a premonition swept through him and disturbed him. He looked at her; she had leaned back on her elbows, and her face was in shadow, so that he couldn't really see her, but he knew, was sure, that she had felt it too.

Nine

A MOVEMENT WOKE them at the same time; an early morning breeze brushed the leaves around the little clearing, and on it they could smell coffee. They sat up and looked at the hermit, who sat just as they had last seen him sitting the night before, grinning at them, and they could hear the soft bubbling of the water in the pot; he looked less sinister than he'd looked in the firelight, even though now they could see the faded scars on his cheek, two lines that ran from under the bloodshot, twisted eye, one down to the corner of his mouth and the other curving under his chin, and the black overcoat was dusty and caked with mud around the bottom. "Mornin," he said.

The boy was rubbing his eyes. "What time is it?" he said; and the hermit said,

"I done told you we ain't got no time here, got mornin, noon, afternoon, evenin, and night, and what anybody need anything else for?"

"That coffee sure smells good," the girl said.

"It ready, hand me that can, ain't nothin like coffee, is it?"

The sun was already high, and the clearing was bright with sunlight; the sky was a pale, clear blue, with no clouds in sight, and the steady breeze moved the leaves back and forth and wrinkled and rippled the surface of the pool. The flames of the fire danced in it, and the boy could see that the hermit had gathered more wood while they slept, and the boy said, "It's late."

"Don't matter. They gone be movin real slow," the hermit said. The boy sipped at the coffee and handed it back to the girl; her hair was tangled, and her shorts and shirt were dirty and wrinkled, and the hermit sat watching them, looking from one to the other, and the boy noticed the overalls under the coat and the thick-soled rubber boots. "I ain't got no bacon an eggs," the hermit said, "but I speck yall gone be eatin eggs and grits fore long, anyhow."

"I wouldn't mind stayin out here with you," the girl said.

"An I wouldn't mine havin yall, cept they ain't gone let you alone. Yall ain't lucky like I was, wadn't nobody to come lookin for me," the hermit said, and the boy and girl looked at each other; and the hermit said, "What you stealin them looks at each other for? I mean what I say."

"I reckon you do," the boy said.

"It gone rain fore the day's out," the hermit said, "I can smell it on that breeze, smelled it when I first woke up this mornin."

"I reckon we better get started, then," the boy said; and the hermit said, "Ain't no hurry, they ain't gone do like yall did, they gone cross the creek and head right out through the swamp, they ain't got sense enough to find em a ridge."

"How'd you know we come down a ridge," the boy said; and the hermit said,

"Cause that girl wouldn't have no skin left on them bare legs if you hadn't. Sides, you wouln'ta got this far comin through the swamp. Drink yo coffee."

They sipped at the hot, steaming coffee, and the boy could feel the stiffness going out of his legs; his clothes felt clammy on his body, and he stretched and yawned. The hermit slurped his out of the tin cup; he sat holding it with the tips of both fingers, his head down, and they watched him as he slurped at the hot liquid several times; then he looked up. "I bet yall's folks won't letcha swizzle like that, will they?"

"My Aunt Julia does," the girl said. "She won't eat nothin that don't come out of a can, and ever mornin she eats a can o peaches for breakfus and then drinks the syrup outta the bowl. She ain't got any sense," she added.

"Don't sound like it," the hermit said.

"Listen," the boy said, "how'd you get your eye done like that?"

And the hermit said, "You know how it happened, you know everything else."

"No, really," the boy said.

"Rilly," the hermit said, mocking the way he said it, "Rilly, I got my head whopped up side a white oak tree, knocked me cockeyed and I been that way ever since."

"Ma-Ma said somebody hit you with a pool cue," the boy said; and the hermit said, "Yo Ma-Ma don't sound like she right bright either." He sipped at his coffee, his good eye watching them over the cup. Just then there was the pop of a shotgun, way off, and the hermit said, "There they go, shootin them guns for yall again."

"Sounded like they were closer," the boy said.

"Naw, they ain't come in very far. They probly really don't wanna come in here no more'n we want em to; they scared o the swamp, cause they don't understand it." He turned and swung his arm tossed the dregs of his coffee into the brush. "That's why fore too much longer it ain't gone be here any more."

He leaned over and took the top off the coffee pot, then poured the remains of the coffee on the fire. "Whyn't you take this thing, lill lady, down there and wash it, and be careful, it's hot." He stood up and hefted the croaker sack and put it back on the sand. "Ain't any sense in totin this thing, I'll jest come back after it when I get yall out," he said, looking at the boy; "One thing for shore, ain't nobody gone steal it, is they?"

The girl came back with the coffee pot and the hermit put it away in the croaker sack; he rummaged around and came out with a long black bullwhip with a wooden handle that was worn smooth from his grip, and he dusted the sand off the back of his overcoat and slung the whip over his shoulder. "Yall waitin on me, you backin up," he said pushing sand over the fire with the toe of his rubber boot, and they dusted the sand off their clothes; the girl picked up the straw suitcase, and the boy said, "You want this lantern?"

"Well, it ain't often I got kerosene," the hermit said, "but I thank you, I speck I can use it."

The hermit led the way, his big, floppy rubber boots shuffling in the vines and undergrowth; soon the little clearing was behind them, and they could no longer hear the gurgling of the springs or the whisper of the brook. The ground began to rise, and soon they were on the edge of the ridge, going along under the tall pines and hickory-nut trees; once they stopped and the hermit swung his arm in a big arc, out over the view of the swamp. "That's a mighty heap o trees, ain't it?" he said.

They stood there, the three of them looking out over the green swamp, the clear expanse of pure blue sky above it.

"It don't look to me like it's gonna rain," the boy said.

"I forgot, you the smart one, ain't cha," the hermit said.

"Well, there ain't a cloud in the sky," the boy said.

"I done told you, it'll rain fore evenin, ain't I smelt it?"

"Sometimes I think you just say things," the boy said.

"Sometimes I do," the hermit said, "an sometimes I don't."

He stood, his feet apart, his head cocked slightly to the side, surveying the swamp that stretched out before them; his black felt hat was pulled forward to shield his eyes from the high sun and the bullwhip was thrown casually over his shoulder, the worn handle dangling against his chest and the tip dragging in the pine needles behind him. "Look yonder," the hermit said, pointing, and they shaded their eyes and followed his point, and over the trees, in the distance, was a long, thin column of black smoke. "Thass the lumber mill," he said, and the boy felt a strangeness creeping up his spine, a tingling with the sudden realization that the mill was operating, the whistle had blown on time, people were still walking the streets of the town; he felt, suddenly, that they had been away a long time.

"It don't seem like it's been just two nights and a day, does it?" the girl said, and the boy looked at her; her green eyes were squinted against the sun and her hair, still tangled, was brushed back clumsily behind her ears. Her shirt was hanging loose, and he could see the small swells of her breasts beneath it, and he thought of the sight of her, her eyes closed, arms outstretched, the tiny breasts on the little-girl-like body exposed, falling forward into the clear, clean water of their pool.

"No, it don't," he said; and she looked at him, and smiled.

The hermit was going on along the ridge, and they followed him; they had begun to perspire in the sun, but it didn't seem to bother the old Negro; his legs worked steadily, his heavy rubber boots lifting and falling rhythmically on the pine needles and loose rocks. They were nearing the bluff where the creek forked, where they could cross and follow the stream to the old logging road and turn back toward the river, toward the men who were looking for them.

There were more people at the landing and along the bluff now, and the group stood where they had the previous evening. They were still surrounded by the almost holiday-like atmosphere, but the crowd had become more subdued as the morning had worn on and the heat had risen. There was still an occasional spurt of laughter, and now and then a shout of "Look!" and pointing and a sudden surge to the bluff to see someone, one of the men, come out of the brush on the other side to stand on the bank, leaning on his gun, and a sudden sigh of disappointment would sweep among them. The crowd nearest the group stole sympathetic glances at them, and whispered among themselves, and the boy's grandmother said once, "Why don't they just go on home?" And Miss Lillian said,

"Why Eva, they're our friends, they're very concerned."

"Humph," the boy's grandmother said.

Earlier, they had stood in the misty dawn and watched the men prepare for the search; the sheriff, his hat cocked on his head at an angle, his boots freshly shined, had come up to them, a fresh kitchen match protruding from his lips. "We'll have em out by noon," he'd said, "so yall don't worry no more'n you have to." They had watched in silence as the men loaded into the skiffs and then went slowly over the river, the long barrels of the shotguns and rifles sticking up over their hunched forms; they made strange, bulky silhouettes against the thin mist that hung over the river.

"They ain't gone find nothing over there," Julia had said, "cause there ain't nothing over there to find."

"How do you know so much?" the boy's grandmother had said.

"I know," Julia had said, and she stood, apart from them, watching the skiffs nearing the other side, her black eyes almost defiant in her round, flat face.

"Don't yall just love Bubba Tate? He sho did turn into a nice young man," Miss Lillian now said.

Nobody answered her. She straightened her shawl more securely around her shoulders. Her face was freshly yet hastily made up, and the severity of the quarter-size spots of rouge on her cheeks was even more pronounced than usual. She fidgeted and twisted at a wisp of a handkerchief that she held in her hands.

The sun climbed in the sky, and occasionally they could hear the pop of a shotgun, muffled by the thick trees across the river; the river flowed tranquilly on, and the crowd along its banks shifted restlessly in the bright summer sunlight. Julia still stood apart from them, her shapeless grey dress hanging crookedly from her paunchy body, and they were all startled when she suddenly began to sing. "Shall . . . we . . . gather . . . at . . . the . . . riiiiiver," she sang, her voice deep and rough, "The beautiful . . . the beautiful . . . riiiiiver." The people nearest them were all looking at her, standing flatfooted, staring.

"Sweet Jesus above," Miss Lillian said, "Julia can't carry a tune in a bucket."

"Shall . . . we . . . gather . . . at . . . the . . . riiiiver," Julia sang on, "That flows by the throne of Gooooooooood!"

"Hush up, Julia," Miss Lillian said, "folks are lookin at you."

"I invite em all to join with me," Julia said, and a voice, a boy's voice, from back in the crowd, said,

"You doin all right by yourself," and there was young men's laughter. "Sing 'The Old Rugged Cross'!" the voice called out, and there was more laughter.

"Why don't you boys git on away from here!" the boy's grandmother called out, "we didn't ast you to come down here."

The line of people nearest them were still staring; they seemed embarrassed, and they shifted from one foot to the other, looking from Julia to the boy's grandmother to the river. "Don't mind them boys, Eva," an old man said; he was hunched over, leaning on a cane, and his adam's apple bobbed up and down when he spoke. Standing next to him was a short, dumpy woman with washed-out blonde hair; she was holding the hand of a little girl, almost an exact replica of herself, and she was glaring at Julia as though she hated her. "Come on, Helen Grace," she said, jerking the little girl's hand, and they marched off up the limerock roadway, the woman's back stiff, the little girl struggling to keep up.

"We're all God's children," the old man said, his adam's apple bobbing up and down, "so don't mind them boys."

"We just ain't in any mood for jokes," the boy's grandmother said, "Martha's sick and all this is wearin her out."

"I can see that," the old man said, "the Lord will provide."

"Well, I wish he'd hurry up," Miss Lillian said, "it's gittin hot out here."

"Patience is the goldenest virtue of em all, Miss Lillian," the old man said; he seemed to be bowing forward over the cane, his head nodding up and down. "Some of us must endure many years fore the gates of Heaven are opened up to us."

Miss Lillian cocked her head to the side and glared briefly at the old man, then motioned to her sister. "Come on over here with us, Julia," she said, "an less don't sing any more, all right?"

"Look to me like you'd wanna be singin hymns," a woman at the edge of the crowd said; she wore a red dress and a red straw hat decorated with wooden cherries. She had the look of one who had dressed to come to town and had come to see what the excitement was about. "Look to me like you'd be prayin," she said.

"Reverend Wallgood was with us last night," Miss Lillian said; then the woman said,

"Wher's he at now?" And she shifted a worn shopping bag with string handles from one hand to the other and exchanged glances with another dressed-up woman beside her.

The crowd seemed to fall silent at just that moment, and suddenly there was a loud blast from a shotgun, not too deep in the swamp, and it was followed quickly by another, and the eyes of the group and of the crowd swung toward the still woods on the other side. There was a hush, then a long, shrill yell, almost a cheer.

"Yeeeeeeeeeeooooooooooowwwwww," The long cry came.

"They musta found em," someone in the crowd said; and the old man said, "Sounds like they jumped a deer and shot it."

Ten

They went along the creek toward the old logging road, the boy now in front, carrying the straw suitcase; the hermit was bringing up the rear, and the boy could hear the clomping of his heavy boots as they walked.

"I believe I'll just walk along wit you for a little piece," the hermit had said when they had crossed the creek. "But we gittin mighty close to the river, it ain't any way once we git to that ol road."

The boy had said, "An they'll be all over the place." "What do it matter?" the hermit had said, "they ain't after me, they after yall." Maybe they don't understand you either, the boy had thought, but he hadn't said anything, and he had taken the lead.

Now they drew nearer to the road, and the boy could make out the tall stand of cane that marked it, showing through the trees and undergrowth, and he stopped.

"Yonder's the road," he said.

"Look out!" the hermit said suddenly, and the boy, half turned toward them, felt the body of the girl slam into him, and he grabbed her, trying to hold her up, seeing only a vague flash of blackness as the hermit moved away from them, and suddenly the boy's ears were filled with the shattering roar of the shotgun and he let himself and the girl fall to the ground. The gun roared again, its boom echoing among the trees, and the boy and girl huddled together on the ground, already smelling the tart burnt smell of the powder of the first shell even as its twin followed it, and he heard the girl say, "Joe!" The boy looked up, and as he did, a wild almost primitive yell, or scream, filled the air, a long, shrill and piercing, savage cry; it ended abruptly, and the sound of it died away into the trees, and the boy heard someone yell,

"I got the sumbitch, I got im!"

The boy sat up, holding the girl's arm; they couldn't see the hermit anywhere, and they heard a crashing in the undergrowth, and suddenly Ted Mack Lowery, holding a long, double-barreled shotgun, the barrels of which were still smoking, was standing along the creek bank, looking at them, hefting the shotgun and grinning his toothless grin at them.

"I reckon two loads o double ought buckshot oughtta fix anybody," he said, "even a nigger hermit."

The boy and girl sat stunned, looking at the toothless, grinning man in overalls before them, sharp-nosed and his face burned deep brown by the sun; he hooked the thumb of his free hand through the strap of his overalls.

"That's all right," he said, "yall safe now."

"You're a drunk bastard!" the girl screamed, and the grin faded from Ted Mack's face.

"I ain't either drunk," he said, "I ain't had a drop."

"You goddam drunk bastard," the girl said, and just then the sheriff stepped out of the bushes, stumbling as he did and cursing under his breath: there were other men behind him, and the boy recognized Phineas Golson, and Phineas was looking at them with a calm, almost sad expression on his face. The sheriff stood, his hands on his hips, a matchstick rolling around in his mouth, looking from the boy to the girl to Ted Mack to the bank of the creek. He took out a handkerchief and took his hat off and wiped his forehead, then put it back and carefully adjusted the tilt.

"Lowery," he said, "you're under arrest," and Ted Mack said, "What for?" his voice high and whining.

"For killin that nigger," the sheriff said.

"He killed him," the boy said, and the sheriff looked at him, his hand still on his hips. The boy could hear a bird start in singing back in the brush.

"I oughtta arrest you too, both of you. You done caused more trouble to more people than any law I know about allows," he said. "Now less get outta here."

"But what about Joe?" the girl said. The sheriff looked at her, tilting his head to the side, a puzzling look on his face. He pulled the frayed match stem from his mouth and flung it away from him into the bushes. "We'll take care of im, he's dead," the sheriff said. "And I got a few questions I'm gonna ask yall once we git outta this swamp."

"Dead?" the girl said. The boy held her arm while they stood up; when they were standing they could see the dark form, like a pile of old dusty cloth, crumpled at the edge of the stream. The girl turned her head away.

"He didn't do nothing to yall," the boy said.

"Everybody said he kidnapped em," Ted Mack said, "you heard em, Bubba."

"Just shut up, hear?" the sheriff said; he slapped at a mosquito on his neck. "We'll tend to all this later; now less go."

Eleven

They started down the old logging road, Ted Mack Lowery and another man leading the way followed by the boy and girl and then the sheriff. The other men were strung out behind them. They walked along in silence, the limbs of the trees twisting together to form an arching canopy over their heads, the bright noon sunlight filtering through in dappled spots along the narrow road. They passed through the clearing with the hunter's shack, and the boy looked at it and then at the girl, and she was staring straight ahead, the set, stoic expression that he had come to know and recognize on her face. They pushed their way through the thicker undergrowth along the river, along the path, and the boy spotted the cane that grew at the edge of the sandbar, and through the trees he could now see the almost blinding whiteness of the bluffs across the river, as they lay shimmering in the brilliant sunlight. Then they pushed past the canebrake and walked out onto the sandbar, and the sheriff stepped forward and waved.

The boy was unprepared; the bluffs across the way were lined with people, and with the sheriff's wave a sudden cheer went up, the voices sounding very close over the water. The boy's eyes scanned the bluff, the blues and reds of the dresses and parasols, the cars parked in a clump above the landing, the little group of people that he knew to be his mother and grandmother and the girl's aunts, and his eyes followed the bluff to where it curved away down the river, the lumber mill sitting right at the edge and the black smoke from the tall stack curling almost straight up in the stillness of the summer noon. Then he saw, behind the smokestack, way to the south, a great low bank of black clouds, and he touched the girl's shoulder and pointed and she nodded her head up and down and then looked at the ground, at her sandaled feet on the sand.

One of the men was bringing a boat around for them, and the cheers were still coming from the other side; the boy looked across at the landing, and there was a man, a figure, standing near the water's edge, and while the boy was looking, he raised his arm over his head and waved to them, a long slow wave that the boy could see was a wave of welcome. And he looked once again at the cloud bank, and then at the girl; she looked at him, and he could see the misty film in her eyes.

"Don't cry, Hallie," he said, and he put his hand on her arm and squeezed it gently. And they both knew what a futile and useless gesture it was.

New Stories

The Best of It
Birmingham: Mothers' Day, 1961
Brother Bobby's Eye
Passin' Side/Suicide
Walking Strawberry

The Best of It

WHEN MY FATHER calls me at my apartment in New York to tell me my mother has died, I prepare to make the trip again. It's not a surprise to either of us. I had just been down there. She'd been hospitalized: pneumonia. She was bleeding internally as well; in the hospital they discovered she had severe diverticulitis. But she got better. Her lungs cleared and the bleeding stopped, so we moved her to a convalescent home with neatly clipped lawns and tightly trimmed hedges. I flew back to the city on a Tuesday. She died the following Friday morning.

"Gideon," my father's voice on the phone says, "I'm afraid I've got bad news," and of course I know what it is.

"When?" I ask. I can hear him breathing, over all those miles. I can hear the high faint whistle of his hearing aid.

"This morning. She was eighty-eight years old. She lived a good life."

For a long time, I say nothing at all.

On the flight to Birmingham and the drive down to Hammond in my rental, I keep recalling a similar trip ten years before, when I had come down for my sister Celeste's funeral. I hadn't been back to visit but once since then, only one Christmas. I used as an excuse my extended stay in Cassis, in Provence, where I was working on a new play, but I was back in

New York from time to time and it was difficult to keep that a secret.

"Tom Whitfield's mother called and said you were back in the country last week," my mother whined by transatlantic wire. Tom and I grew up together in Hammond, and he lived two buildings down on West End in Manhattan. "You didn't even call. Why don't you ever come home?"

"Because I don't want to see him," I said.

"Oh, Gideon," she sighed. "Whatever am I going to do with you two?"

My mother still pretended my father and I were having a silly argument, just something between "the boys." She knew better, of course. In her deepest heart, she knew, just as I did, that my father had murdered my sister, just as certainly as if he himself had wielded the razor Celeste used to slash her wrists. He would not let her live.

My younger sister was mentally deficient, "mildly retarded" it was called back in the late forties when she was diagnosed. I was four years older, eight or nine when we found out, and though my parents whispered a lot between themselves, and though neither of them ever sat me down and explained it to me, I knew. I knew it from the way they acted, knew that our family had somehow been disgraced, that there was now something in our midst of which we should all be ashamed.

My father was a war hero. He was wounded in the South Pacific, at Peleliu. He lost his left hand, blown off at the wrist by a land mine. When he came home he wore on the end of his arm a strange chrome contraption like a hook with pincers. He strutted around town, holding the device above his head, proud of the sacrifice he had made, and he talked all the time about how his great grandfather had lost a leg at the Battle of Franklin up in Tennessee. He made speeches at the patriotic rallies at the Elks' Club. But at night I heard him cursing and crying. I heard their voices in their bedroom, murmuring heatedly, sometimes raging, and I was frightened of him. I heard my mother crying, and I heard what sounded like my father hitting her. Sometimes she had marks on her face that she covered with makeup.

By the time the war was over, my father had developed political aspirations. He never talked to me about them, but I overheard him tell my mother on more than one occasion that he would someday be governor of Alabama. He started with the office of mayor of Hammond, which he won. Easily. The Westlake family had been in Hammond for four generations, counting me and Celeste, and we lived in one of the biggest, whitest houses in town. My father also owned a great many acres of land, practically a whole county, which he and his younger brother — killed in action in Europe during the Battle of the Bulge — had inherited from their father, my grandfather. Though my father claimed that the family had come out of the depression "land poor," by the end of World War II — during which he had sold timber off thousands of acres — he had made quite a bit of money again, though how much I have no idea.

Celeste was a beautiful little girl, with a chubby body and soft brown eyes. She was bald until she was almost two, then her hair came out curly and dark, like our mother's. Her face was like a miniature of Mother's: high cheekbones, a narrow, pointed nose, and full, lush lips. But she never ran around like other children, and she played slowly with her dolls, very deliberately, her movements hesitating and calculated. She did not like to be read to, grew bored very quickly. A few years passed and Celeste did not begin to talk.

My mother had three years of college at a state normal school, where she had been studying to be an elementary school teacher when she dropped out to marry my father. She insisted they have Celeste tested.

"She won't be able to learn," she said, "we can't put her in school."

"No, I don't want to hear it," my father said, "there ain't a damn thing wrong with her. She's slow, that's all."

"That's right. Call it what you will. But she —"

"No! Not another word about it."

Finally she convinced him, but my mother had to take Celeste all the way to Atlanta to get her tested. My father would not hear of Tuscaloosa, nor even Birmingham, for fear that someone would find out. "In my position, I can't be havin folks knowin I've got a daughter that some fool doctor calls a retardate. All right?"

"For God's sakes, Franklin," my mother pled, "she's your daughter!"

"How the hell do I know that for sure? The only thing we know for sure is that she's your daughter!"

"Oh, go to hell," my mother said. The air crackled between them. Never in my young life had I seen such hatred as I saw in my father's eyes, but it wouldn't be the last time I'd see it. I could see how unhappy they were, and it terrified me. I heard his false hand clicking, like scissors snapping. It was a nervous habit, something he did when he was tense or anxious. It became a warning sign to me. Clinka, clinka, clinka.

"Do whatever the hell you want to do," he said to my mother. "Just keep it under wraps and don't bother me with it." He glanced over at me. "What the hell are you lookin at?" he asked sharply.

"Nothin." I ran out of the room before he could take a step toward me.

My father was something of a learned man, too, having attended that same state normal school before he dropped out to find a job in that bleak fading depression year of 1937. "I had to have some cash money," he often said in later years, "you can't eat dirt, no matter how black and rich it is or how much you have of it!" He went to work for his Uncle Ronald, as night manager of a small tourist court on the edge of Hammond. He was a voracious reader, especially of anything about the Civil War. He could sit in the little office and read all night. He read biographies of all the major figures in the war. He read the classics, and histories. He read contemporary novels and volumes of poetry, whatever he could get his hands on. There was quite a large collection of dusty books scattered around in our rambling old family home, an eclectic assembly of almost everything, from the Hardy Boys to Greek drama, from Forever Amber to David Copperfield, from Don Quixote to Gone With the Wind. My father claimed to have read Gone With the Wind sixteen times. I never doubted it. He carried a copy of it throughout his war experiences. He kept that particular book, with its warped cover and wrinkled pages, in a locked drawer of his desk.

One of the biggest quarrels we had when I was in high school was when I came home one day and told him that I thought Gone With the Wind was a piece of commercial trash. I was only repeating what my English teacher had said, but my father became so angry he turned crimson. He was a big man, heavy-set, strong and powerful, and he struck me across the face and knocked me half-way across the room.

Junior high school was a traumatic experience for me, a sudden plunge into a culture I had not known even existed. My father had sent me for the first six grades to a school called Northside Progressive Academy. It was run by a shriveled little woman named Miss Julia Whitfield (a great aunt of my friend Tom, who has also escaped to Manhattan), and it was part grammar school and part military academy. The boys wore uniforms: gray wool ones modeled on those of the Old Confederacy. And we had military drill every day. The girls wore regular school dresses, except on Fridays, when they wore crinoline dresses with long hoop skirts and wide brimmed straw hats. After the boys had marched in formation the three blocks to the statue of the rebel soldier in the downtown park and had laid a wreath and sung "Dixie," we returned to the house and had a dance, with old fashioned reels and waltzes, Miss Julia banging away on an old upright piano.

And on those Fridays, as part of the ritual, after opening the day by singing "The Bonnie Blue Flag" on the sun-porch, we paid a visit to Miss Julia's mother, an ancient old woman propped up in a huge four poster bed with yellowing linen. We held hands down the long dark hallways of what Miss Julia called her "cottage," gathered around the bed, and the old woman peered silently down at us. We all had learned that she was the widow of a Confederate officer; we knew the story by heart. Captain James Taylor Whitfield, who commanded the 9th Alabama Rifles at Gettysburg, had been severely wounded in that battle, so that when he returned to Hammond after the war he had walked with a pronounced limp, dragging his useless left foot behind him. He was an attorney, a bachelor, remaining one for many years until he married young Serena Simmons from Spring Hill when she was only sixteen. He was in his eighties when Miss Julia was born. It was hard for us to believe the old woman we saw every Friday morning had ever been sixteen.

As I sat with my mother in the hospital during her last illness, I thought of all the years that had passed and were gone. I thought of Miss Julia's mother, the way she had looked fifty five years ago. In the pictures in our well-worn old photograph albums, my mother as a young woman was a flapper, happy and mischievous. Her hair was thick and dark, her eyes dusky in the old sepia prints with their checkered borders. She looked as though she loved posing, sometimes mugging at the camera, barely able to suppress a laugh. There is a picture of her as a baby, maybe a year old, when she had won a Most Beautiful Baby Contest at the Choctaw County Fair.

In the hospital she was wasted, worn down. She had always been a private person, even prissy, and she was now robbed of all her dignity. She didn't seem to care anymore how she looked. I knew that even up to the beginning of this sickness she had had my father take her every week, him struggling to get the wheelchair out of the trunk of their Oldsmobile, to the hairdresser she'd been frequenting for years. Decades, I suppose. When I came home that one Christmas, as she sat in the den in her wheelchair reading or watching television, her hair was always perfectly coiffed, even though it was thinning so much on top her pink scalp glowed through.

"Do you want me to get Martha to come out here and fix your hair?" I asked her, and she shook her head no without opening her eyes. (The next time Martha would fix her hair would be in the funeral home, and though I didn't really know that then, I think my mother did.)

She had her lucid moments, but they were growing fewer and farther apart. Once she fixed me with her gaze and said, "You need to forgive him. You need to pity him."

"Can you do both?" I quipped and she frowned at me. She looked off out the window, at her view of the roof of another part of the hospital, a huge heating unit. I was later relieved it wasn't the last thing she saw in life.

"I am serious," she said. Her voice was weak, and it was an effort for her to speak.

"I'm sorry, Mother," I said.

"His life has been disappointment." Though my father had persisted, his political career was stymied. He never went beyond mayor of Hammond. He ran several times for the state legislature and twice for lieutenant governor, losing every time.

During my mother's final illness, my father didn't come to the hospital while I was there. He sat at home, in a darkened den.

"It's too much of a reminder," he said to me when I got back to the house.

I thought about that for a moment, and then I asked,

"Of what?" I thought he might possibly be referring to my sister's death, her funeral.

He looked at me, his eyes piercing. He sat with both arms resting on the arms of the recliner, a book turned face down and draped over his knee. His metal claw glowed dully in the light that spilled in from the kitchen. He would not get one of the new, more natural prostheses, just as he would not consider surgery for his fading hearing. He would not spend the money. He wore black horn-rim glasses that he had worn for thirty years, having new lenses put in when his vision changed.

"A reminder of my own mortality," he said. He said it as though I were completely stupid to ask.

He was two years younger than my mother. Eighty-six. He was still in pretty good shape, though he walked with a limp because he had broken his leg just above the ankle almost eight years before and it had never healed properly. He had slipped off a ladder when he was trying to trim some saplings in the yard.

"He thinks he can do anything with that hook," my mother said, "always has."

He offered me a drink, just as he had always done. It was a test. Always, all during my sixteen years of sobriety, he would still ask me if I wanted a drink. Part of him had never accepted the fact that I was an alcoholic, in much the same way he never accepted that Celeste was retarded. It was as though he were confident that God would never do anything like that to him, that it must be some mistake, that there was no conceivable way his two offspring could be that flawed, that maimed. I offered to fix him one — a bourbon and water, nothing else, ever — but he grunted and pushed himself up and shuffled into the kitchen. I heard him rummaging around in the cabinet. He returned to the room and sat back down with a sigh, holding the drink — dark, three ice cubes — in his right hand.

Sixteen years ago I had wound up in the psycho ward at Bellevue, with bars on the windows. That was where they put drunks in those days. A friend had found me in my apartment, in a near coma, badly in need of detoxing. When they transferred me to the treatment center out in

White Plains, where I was to spend the next thirty-four days, my father was skeptical. "You're no more an alcoholic than I am," he said on the phone, "they're just after your money." When I asked him and Mother to come up for family week, as my significant others, and to even bring Celeste, he laughed. "That's a lot of bullshit, Gideon. Just be a man. Have some will power. Know when to put the stopper in the bottle. That's all you gotta do." He had refused to come, and he wouldn't allow Mother to come, either. I don't think they ever told Celeste, who by then never came out of her room on the third floor of the big house. He had had the top floor remodeled for her, and I used to make him angry by referring to it as the attic.

"Typical southern family," I said one day, "keep our freak in the attic!"

"You shut your goddam mouth," he shouted, "don't you ever let me hear you refer to your sister as a freak again!" When I laughed, he threw his drink in my face.

He reached up and switched on the reading lamp. He picked up the book he'd been reading and opened it. He turned the pages with his hook. His forehead wrinkled, the tip of his tongue protruded from the corner of his mouth.

"What are you reading?" I asked, and he turned the book's cover toward me.

I could have guessed. It was The Collected Poems of Donald Davidson. His favorite poet. I knew what was coming next. He squinted at the page, pulled it closer to his face. He read aloud: ". . . the God of your fathers is a just and merciful God." He was reading his favorite poem, "Lee in the Mountains." He looked up at me then for a moment. His eyes went back to the page and he read along in silence for a few moments. Then, aloud again, "Never forsaking, never denying His children and His children's children forever, Unto all generations of the faithful heart." His voice quaked. He lay his head back when he was finished. He sighed and closed his eyes.

He looked then like a very old man, antiquated and gray, the years like ashen tarnishes on his wrinkling face.

While I was subjected to Northside Progressive Academy, from which

I never recovered, Celeste received no schooling at all. My father refused to let Celeste leave the house for most of her life. There was a short period, when she was twelve or thirteen, when she would ride her bicycle downtown to the picture show on Saturdays. I had already embarked on my young manhood of drunken, spinning nights, prolonged bouts of heavy drinking. I should have known then that I was alcoholic. I did know then, but it took another twenty years of hopelessness and desperation and a final splattering against a rock-hard bottom to rip the shrouds of denial from my eyes. I loved my sister very much. I had always been protective of her, taking care of her when we played out after supper during long summer dusks, carrying her home when the playing-doctor games started in someone's playhouse.

One Saturday afternoon, Celeste stood on the street in front of the theater, crying. She had been taunted by some high school boys, and when she'd come out after the double feature the front tire on her bike was flat. I happened by about then. I had been drinking beer with some friends all day. When I spotted my sister I knew immediately what had happened, and when I asked her who she told me. I went in after them, followed by my two friends who were just as drunk as I was. We got into a tremendous fight right there in the theater, and we wound up in jail. I lost several teeth and have worn a misshapen nose all these years since.

My father, of course, was mayor of the town at the time. He was horrified and scandalized. He took away my car, an old Plymouth that I'd bought with money from my job sacking groceries at the A & P. He not only confiscated it, he sold it, and pocketed the money himself. I was not allowed to go out on weekends for months, and Celeste was never allowed to go to the movies again.

"I won't have my children actin like white trash!" he said.

I have no way of knowing for sure, but I suspect that Celeste never left that third floor after that. All her meals were carried up to her on a tray. I would come home from time to time from the university, or from Houston, then Denver, then finally New York, and she would let me come up and visit her. She was pale and freckled, her eyes faded. She was terribly thin and her hands shook.

"I have to tell somebody about this," I said to her. "The police. Maybe that preacher at the church he goes to. He's keeping you prisoner!"

"No!" she would say and begin to cry. "Please don't! No! I'm scared of him!"

"What does he do to you?"

"Nothin! Nothin! I never see him. I haven't seen him for a million years."

"Does Mother come up here?"

"Yes. Mama comes up here."

Then she would stare at the floor, refusing to answer any more of my questions. She would not look me in the eye.

"She's happy enough," my mother protested.

"Happy?!" I blurted. "How can you say she's happy?"

"She doesn't know any better."

"Are you sure he doesn't keep her chained to the bed?"

"Gideon, stop it." My mother looked off out the window. "We live with what God gave us, Gideon. We make the best of it." I knew there was no point in saying anything else.

I could have saved Celeste. But I didn't. And I live with that fact every day. I think of it first thing when I awake, and it is the last thing on my mind when I finally fall asleep. I could have tried harder to break through my mother's denial. I could have spirited Celeste away in the night and carried her north with me, put her in a special school, given her a life. But I didn't have the courage to face my father. In the early years I was too drunk to do it, and after my treatment I was too busy tending to my own sobriety to have time for her. I knew that if I drank I would die and if I went home and became too involved with my family I would drink. In a way, I'm just as guilty as my father for what happened. And my mother. She sat by and watched it happen. She sat by and watched all our lives happen, the way mothers do.

I was rehearsing a new play at a tiny theater on Bank Street in Greenwich Village when the call came about Celeste's suicide. My mother traced me down at the theater by calling Tom Whitfield, after she kept getting my machine.

"She's dead, Gideon," my mother said, sobbing into the phone, "she killed herself."

"W . . . who?" I stammered. But I knew.

"Your sister! Oh, she's dead!"

"She . . . killed herself?" I felt as though the floor of the dusty lobby had disappeared and left me hanging there, dangling from the phone. It was like a surprise blow to the kidneys from behind, a heavy stick swung against the backs of my knees. I had never thought of Celeste dying, never even contemplated it. I couldn't quite grasp it. It seemed unreal, maybe a part of my play. As though something intangible and unsaid on the stage had spilled out and surrounded me.

So I flew to Birmingham and rented a car and drove to Hammond. It was a long trip that day, a perfectly clear and warm April day. The hills and ridges south of Tuscaloosa were splashed with dogwood and redbud. Everything was springing to life.

Except for Celeste. I drove straight to the funeral home. Bobby Simms, the mortician, an old friend from high school, showed me the stitches on the insides of her wrists. She looked beautiful and serene, still. I was too stunned and shocked to cry. "She bled to death," Bobby said. Yes, I thought, she bled. All of her life she bled. There were three huge sprays of flowers beside her coffin, white and yellow roses and mums and lilies. I knew my father had put them there. Celeste wore a green dress with long sleeves, lace at the cuffs, hiding the stitches.

I get the two funerals confused in my mind now. My mother was alive at one, nowhere evident at the second, except hidden away inside the dark-stained cherry-wood coffin, identical to the first, with its blanket of the same red roses. There is the same preacher, rotund and too young. The church is the same Presbyterian one I was dragged to as a child, except that now it is a part of the ultra-conservative branch, which I'm sure pleases my father. He probably led the secession. Only my father and I and my first cousin Miriam — daughter of my long dead uncle, my father's brother — sit on the folding chairs before the raw, open grave.

I'm sure there were people in Hammond who had no idea Franklin Westlake had a daughter until she died and had to be buried in the family plot in Riverside Cemetery. It would be whispered about and explained to them that she "was peculiar," she "was not right." Her stone, in the corner of the plot, still looks brand new when my mother is buried. It reads:

Celeste Land Westlake, March 4, 1942 - April 17, 1990. There is a stone angel-child on the marker, sitting, her flat blank eyes focused somewhere off toward the river, toward some world not this one at all.

Before I fly back to New York, he wants me to drive him over to Lauderdale County, Mississippi, to visit the old Westlake Family Cemetery. I agree to it because I know that when I leave this time I am never coming back.

The Oldsmobile seems huge after the rental car. We take back roads. He slouches on the seat beside me, his prosthesis propped on the dash as though to stop himself if I should hit something. He has had many of the devices over the years, but always of the same type; they were different shapes and sizes as they became more refined and improved. As a child, I thought he was Captain Hook. He was the insane murderer in the stories that teenagers told, the one who left his hook on the door handle of the lovers parked near the river.

"Turn right up here, boy," he says.

"When are you gonna stop callin me 'boy?'" I ask.

"When I'm dead."

We cross into Mississippi. It is not far now. Near the old Westlake Cemetery is a Civil War Cemetery, with hundreds of graves in perfect rows, marked by simple white wooden crosses. You come upon it suddenly, with no warning, right out in the middle of nowhere. The graves are almost evenly divided between Union and Rebel soldiers, most of whom were wounded at the battle of Shiloh in Tennessee and brought to a field hospital in nearby Daleville.

"Stop here," my father says.

He walks out among the graves. The grass is thick, neatly clipped. The white crosses stretch away toward a tree-line in the distance. The cemetery is manicured, well kept, and I note from a sign that it is cared for by the United Daughters of the Confederacy, Meridian, MS Chapter. I think of Miss Julia, her mother.

My father stands with his head bowed, and I know he is praying. I can only imagine what is in his mind, what he must be saying to his own concept of God. I have never seen him mourn, never seen him cry. I know nothing of what he thinks about anything. When he is back in the car we drive the half mile to the red clay hill where our ancestors are buried. Scrawny cedars and patches of Johnson grass and crab-grass dot the hillside. There is a sagging old iron fence, rusted, the gate long gone.

My father heads straight to the crest of the hill, his limp like a stagger, his hook glittering in the sunshine. I scramble up the rutted dirt road after him. Yellow butterflies dart about on the sparse areas of grass, fat bumblebees float lazily in the hot, moist air. He stops at a row of gravestones, gray and lichen-splotched, the oldest ones. He leans against the tallest of the stones and looks out over the valley to the west.

I come up to him and stand beside him. We can see the Civil War Cemetery, the row upon row of crosses that look tiny from here. Rolling Mississippi pastureland stretches away to the horizon; a creek with water oaks and willows and plum bushes lining its banks curves and bends through the pastures. From here we can see the old Westlake home place, marked by two lone magnolias, where the big house stood before it burned back in the thirties. There is a new house near it, long and low, ranch-style. Miriam's house. Mt. Zion Church, like a child's doll-church, gleaming white in the sunshine against the intense green of deep woods behind it, sits at the end of its gravel road.

I look at the stone my father leans against. Nathaniel Westlake, it reads. Born North Carolina, August, 1789, Died Mississippi, December, 1841.

"Your great, great grandfather," I say, "my great, great great grandfather." I have heard him point that out to me a thousand times. But this time his eyes seem locked on the horizon, the far distance, as though he does not hear me. I hear a crow back in the woods, the aimless chattering of a squirrel.

I look at another gravestone: Iva Ward Westlake, Beloved Wife, 1800-1851. These two, from whom both my father and I had sprung. And Celeste, too, I think, and Celeste, too.

I start walking then, along the ridge of the hill. After a while I stop and stand looking around me, at the thick woods, the hickory and oak and cottonwood trees, the kudzu that crowds the drooping fence. The green is fierce, the day now hot, the high sun like an unmuted spotlight. I can see my father still standing there against the stone, gazing serenely off across the Mississippi countryside. I think then of his hand, what was left of it decaying and returning to the earth of a distant island in the Pacific. I think of his great grandfather's leg, amputated in that field hospital in Middle Tennessee, likely without anesthetic, and buried there, left there, in a mass grave with the limbs of others, of strangers and brothers.

 The lush green earth stretches away in all directions, as far as I can see. The gravestones all around me lean at odd angles, many of the graves sunken, the names and dates obscured, washed away by the generations and the seasons. I stand still, unmoving, for a long time. I watch a gray-brown hawk circling over a field. Its glide, on outstretched wings, is smooth and delicate. It is graceful and beautiful. Then, like a sudden shaft of new sunlight it slashes toward the ground, toward its prey, and disappears from my view.

Birmingham: Mothers' Day, 1961

MARTIN, DOC AND MOLLY'S ONLY SON, lived in a home for retarded adults in an Atlanta suburb. He was forty two years old with the mental capacity of a four year old. As Doc was driving Martin back to the bus station in downtown Birmingham for his return to Atlanta after a visit, he was surprised to see the streets unusually crowded for a Sunday afternoon. Doc wondered if it had anything to do with this being Mothers' Day, maybe a parade or something. The holiday had been the reason for the timing of Martin's visit this time. He was to stay a month, but after only two weeks Molly decided she had had enough. "I just can't stand it, Bennie," she said, calling Doc by the name she had met and married him under, "everywhere I go in the house there he is. Sneakin up on me. I can't hear him when he walks. He sneaks. I look up from whatever I'm doin and there he is, not two feet from me, looking at me, and my heart jumps up in my throat. He makes me nervous! And he looks at me like everything is my fault!" She dissolved into tears, randomly spaced sobs wracking her body like little electric shocks. Doc knew exactly what she had experienced.

Doc heard Martin mumbling to himself in the passenger seat. Though Doc was ashamed to admit it even to himself, he, too, was relieved that Martin was going back early. Doc's son's attention span was so short he couldn't watch television or go to a movie or anything like that. He couldn't read, of course. He would simply stand there, at your elbow, gazing at you curiously, waiting for whatever was next. This went on during every waking moment. They had once bought him toys suitable to his mental age, and Martin had gone into a temper tantrum and broken them all. Every time Doc took him fishing Martin wound up with a hook in his arm or hand; once he had fallen out of the boat and almost drowned. Molly had given up years ago, but Doc still struggled to find something to entertain Martin.

When Doc glanced over at him Martin grinned broadly, showing two missing teeth, one on the top and one on the bottom. It gave him an off-center, jagged look. There were times when Martin seemed almost normal, when Doc would actually try to talk to him like to another adult, and on those occasions, after all this time, Doc's heart would soar briefly with expectation only to plunge quickly again into hopelessness and despair when he took a closer look at his son.

"What did you say?" he asked. Curtly. Abruptly. Sometimes you had to treat Martin like a disobedient child.

Martin looked away, out the open window. He mumbled again, his voice all but lost in the street sounds beyond the open window, but Doc clearly heard Martin say: "I need me a hot woman." Doc decided to ignore it. He had no idea where Martin might go with that idea. Martin had had a couple of girlfriends that Doc knew of in the more than twenty years he had been at Chattoochee Village. All the Villagers were sterilized, one of the conditions for admittance, so that there would be no tragic consequences of "dalliances" between them, and there would be "dalliances," Doc and Molly had been informed in their initial interview with Dr. White; after all, the doctor had reminded them, the Villagers were physically all adults. No consequences? Doc glanced at his son again. When Martin and his last girlfriend broke up, the boy (Doc could not help thinking of him as a boy) had beaten his rival so severely with a mop handle that the man was hospitalized for two weeks.

Martin was slight of build, only five feet four, and his stoop made him seem even more physically stunted. He had always walked like an old man, hunched forward, his overlarge head preceding him wherever he was going. Though Doc's own hair had turned white in his thirties, Martin had not a single gray hair on his head. But in the last few years Martin had developed a middle-aged paunch that rode just beneath his high belt line. The rest of his body was thin, his narrow neck pushing his face toward whatever he was looking at as though, Doc would think, he were nimbly curious or about to make a piquant observation. Until Doc looked into his flat, passive eyes, a kind of brownish gray, and saw that there was nothing in there.

The closer to the bus station they got the more crowded with cars and pedestrians the street became. Doc stopped the car at a red light. He and Martin both looked at the crowd of people, mostly men, milling in front of the station. He had a vague memory of some big event happening today, that he had overheard two men discussing in hushed tones in the waiting room of his optometry office, but he could not recall for the life of him what it was.

Doc wondered if he'd ever find a parking space. He thought of all the times he'd carried Martin's suitcase any distance. Martin, when he came home to visit, packed practically everything he owned in it. Doc had vowed to himself that he wouldn't lug the suitcase at all this trip. It was like carrying a suitcase filled with bricks. Martin would not carry it himself. He would simply refuse to pick it up and would walk off and leave it. He had lost suitcases in the downtown Atlanta bus station numerous times over the years, and each time they had to outfit him with an entire new wardrobe and set of toilet articles, which he rarely used anyway. Doc and Molly saw it as a useless and extravagant expense, but they had to do it, even though Martin would wear the same clothes every day until his house parent at the Village made him bathe and change. This time, Doc planned to make Martin carry his own suitcase.

Martin grinned at all the people out in the street. Crowds excited him and he clapped his hands, two quick raps. "Goin to church," he said, "gonna say the Apostles' Creed."

"No," Doc said, "they ain't goin to any church." The men looked rough and mean, the kind Doc always tried to avoid. They wore blue jeans and work clothes. They looked like steel-workers from out at Fairfield. Some laughed loudly with their heads thrown back; others scowled and frowned at each other. They were all moving toward the bus station. Police cars were parked all along the street, and Doc could pick out cops' uniforms in the crowd. "I don't speck these fellows are regular church goers, son. Looks to me like they're lookin for a beer garden that's open on Sunday."

Doc had an uneasy feeling about the crowd. He knew it had to do with what the men had been talking about in his waiting room. He had paid little attention at the time, and now he wished he had listened more closely. As he eased through, passing in front of the bus station, he knew the parking lot in back would be full. He would have to park on the street. This was not the best part of town. It was over close to the section of downtown where all the troubles had been going on, where the unrest was. The Negroes. Reverend Shuttlesworth and all. There were no colored people at all living out where he and Molly lived, in Center Point, so Doc didn't pay a whole lot of attention to the stories when they came on the television news. He didn't have the time to watch television much.

And he rarely read a newspaper. He had dropped that habit when he had taken his second job: he worked at night for a place called Deluxe Cleaners, on Roebuck Parkway, collecting bags of dirty laundry in the dorms of a junior college near their house and delivering in return bulky bundles of fresh clothes wrapped in brown paper. It sometimes took him most of the night. He had been doing that for over fifteen years now, though he never stopped to count. He would have been surprised to realize it had been that short a time, since he felt as though he had been doing it his entire adult life.

Doc had to go three full blocks beyond the bus station to find a parking space, and then he had to parallel park. Their old 1952 Chevrolet two-door coupe did not have power steering and it was a struggle. He left the front end protruding slightly into the street. He knew he didn't have to feed the meter on Sundays; maybe sloppy parking was forgiven, too. Anyway, he thought to himself, every policeman in Birmingham was back there at the bus station.

When they were on the sidewalk, Martin said, "I want a Krystal Cheese."

"You just ate," his father said, "right before we left the house."

"I want six Krystal Cheeses," Martin said, "with some French fries."

"No," Doc said. He unlocked the trunk and opened it. "Get your suitcase, son," he said. He knew what the reaction would be even before he said it. Martin just stood there, looking around, gazing up at the buildings around them. "I said, get your suitcase, Martin. I mean it!"

Martin gave no indication he had even heard him. If the boy was going to pack so much into his suitcase, then he should have to carry it. If he had to carry it he would learn his lesson, Doc thought. But Martin could not "learn" any lesson. How many times over the years had Doc presumed that he could, only to realize anew that the boy made no connection at all between cause and effect. Doc had mostly stopped trying, but his patience was thin today.

Doc could feel the beads of sweat popping out on his forehead. "You pack it so heavy, you carry it," Doc said angrily. "I'm not touching it." Martin just stood there. Martin shaded his eyes from the afternoon sunlight and peered up the street toward the bus station. "I mean it, Martin," Doc said, almost shouting. "Get the goddam suitcase out of the goddam car!"

Martin took a step or two toward the bus station, as though Doc had not said a word.

"Martin, I swear . . ." Doc began. He tried to quell his anger, to keep himself calm. "Look here, son," he said, his voice trembling, his breath short, "if you don't tote your own suitcase I swear I'm gonna get back in the car and leave you here, right here. And you'll never see me again." The boy looked at him with an odd and curious expression in his dull eyes. He looked hostile. Frightened, but defiant as well. He made no move toward the car and his suitcase.

"Get it out!" Doc said. "Now!"

"No," Martin said. He turned and started up the sidewalk.

"Goddamit!" Doc shouted. Martin kept walking. "Goddam you, boy!" Doc yelled to his son, bellowed to his departing back, as Martin was now loping steadily toward the bus station, his gait both awkward and determined. The boy walked purposefully, not looking back. His belt, which he had bought himself on one of the villagers' periodic trips to a department store in Dunwoody, had a ridiculously large silver buckle shaped like a horseshoe. The belt was several sizes too big for him and the silver tipped end hung and flapped beside him as he strode. Martin seemed not to be aware of the excess length.

Then Martin stopped and looked back at him. Doc slammed the trunk and went around to the driver's side and got in. He tilted the rear view mirror. He could see Martin standing there, watching him, waiting for him to catch up with him with the suitcase. "Goddamit," Doc muttered. His chest felt oddly hollow, and he was light headed. He started the car and ground it into gear and pulled out into the street. He adjusted the mirror again and watched Martin grow smaller and smaller, standing alone on the sidewalk. "I'll just show him," Doc said aloud.

Doc couldn't believe what he was doing. He was proud of himself, but his hands were shaking and his knuckles were white where he gripped the steering wheel. He made a right turn and went several blocks and turned back left. He began to tremble all over. He thought he was going to pass out in the traffic, mostly big trucks that rumbled all around him now that he was on First Avenue North. Up ahead he saw the Sloss Furnace belching smoke across the viaduct. He saw in his mind's eye the forlorn, hunched figure of Martin on the downtown sidewalk. Doc's mouth was dry and he could not swallow. "Jesus," he muttered. "Jesus H. Christ!"

Then he was in the billowing, acrid gray smoke that drifted into the open windows and around him like shredded clouds, and he could smell the hot sulfurous burning. He caught glimpses of the bright red molten iron as it was being poured, the hot crimson that would light up the night sky so brightly it could be seen all the way from where they lived. He could feel the loud metallic clanging of the foundry vibrating in his bones, felt it burning in his blood. He was crying, the tears running unobstructed down his cheeks. His vision was blurred. His heart was constricted in his chest, a tiny hard knot no bigger than a plum. As he passed through the smoke he felt that he was disappearing, that the other end of the viaduct would take him straight down into the bowels of the earth. He came suddenly out into the clear spring air.

He could not see clearly and when he was off the viaduct he had to pull to the side of the street and wipe his eyes. He sat there for a long time, the engine rattling. *It serves him right*, he thought. He remembered the bus ticket sticking out of Martin's shirt pocket. He remembered all the policemen. And it was then that he remembered what the men had been talking about: bus loads of colored people, coming into Birmingham. "Freedom Riders," they scoffed.

Doc eased back into the Sunday afternoon traffic, his hands quivering on the steering wheel. He turned off First Avenue, going south. He would double back, finding his way through the unfamiliar streets. He had to get back to the bus station, because something very bad was going to happen. He knew that. The sun was high, the air coming through the windows muggy and damp. Doc was so tired it was an effort to keep the car steady.

He could not remember a time in his life when he had not been tired. Even when Martin was over at Chattoochee he dominated their lives. He called collect several times a week to complain about the place, about the food or his new counselor. There seemed to be a tremendous and continuous turnover on the staff, which Doc could understand. Sometimes Martin would call and then refuse to say anything. He would call collect to pout silently, the phone company clicking off cash money by the minute.

It took everything he and Molly could scrimp from the basics to keep Martin at Chattoochee Village. Doc's income from his optometry practice would have been sufficient were it not for Martin's expenses. His office was in a strip of shops in Roebuck Plaza. It was a narrow space to begin with, and he shared it with a dentist who drank all day and — for all Doc knew — inhaled his gas too since by the end of the day he was always totally drunk. Doc would never have let the unpleasant man work on his teeth. But the dentist paid half the rent on the place.

He and the dentist had a sign out front with both a big white molar and a big blue eye on it. Doc spent his days giving eye exams to the blue collar people who lived in the area and selling them less expensive frames than the fancier chain optical companies that kept moving in. It was because of them cutting into his business that Doc had had to take the second job at night. Over the years Molly had had a series of jobs: as a minimum-wage aide in a nursing home, waitressing at several restaurants in the area until her legs and feet could no longer stand the punishment, selling tickets in the booth at the Roebuck Plaza movie theater. She now worked downtown in the women's clothing department at Pizitz and at night she did alterations, both for Pizitz's men's and women's departments and for Deluxe Cleaners.

Doc's anger had subsided now. It was replaced by a familiar sense of helpless disappointment that only heightened his fear and worry for his son. The disappointment was always with him because he knew that his life had been wasted, that it had never really been his own. He could be considering retirement now, like other men his age. He could be looking forward to resting after what could have been a long and fruitful career. But there was no way, because of Martin. It had not worked out that way at all.

Doc always felt a terrible and persistent guilt when he thought about how simple life would be without Martin. He found himself wishing, not for the first time, that the earth would just open up and swallow Martin, or that he would get on the wrong bus and wind up in California or Alaska or somewhere, that the boy could somehow simply disappear from their lives, painlessly and quickly. He considered briefly turning back around and leaving Martin to his own devises. Maybe something terrible would happen to him. Maybe he would get in the middle of whatever was going to happen at the bus station, with the colored people on the busses. Doc knew now the men collecting at the bus station were Klansmen, and they played rough. They were there to meet the busses.

The two of them had gone to church together that morning, because Martin always insisted on it. They went to the Presbyterian church Martin had grown up in, over in Woodlawn. They went without Molly. Molly would not go any more at all, and, truth to tell, the church had gradually lost everything meaningful for Doc as well. He had tried to maintain his beliefs, but he could not. He could neither understand nor believe in a God who would create Martin, who would make of his and Molly's lives such an empty and unrelenting journey. Better that Martin had died as an infant, during that brief interval of order and peace for them all.

Doc wiped the sweat from his brow with his finger and flicked it out the window. There is no spring anymore, he was thinking. We go right from the deep freeze of winter to the blistering of summer. He thought of the hallways of the girls' dormitories he was allowed to enter because of his second job, stepping off the elevator and shouting "Man on the hall!" The hallway would be deserted, but as he worked his way along, picking up the white bags of dirty laundry, girls would appear. Crossing the hallway in slips and transparent nightgowns, some even in only panties and bra. Or coming from the shower with just a narrow towel wrapped around them, sometimes a plump breast and a nipple peeping out at him, all of them cutting their eyes at him and giggling. Every year, with new girls, it was the same.

He didn't tell Molly about this experience. She would have a conniption if she heard about the college girls. She did not believe in sex for older folks. "My God, Bennie, it ain't fitten," she had said to him one night longer ago than he could remember, "that's for the young uns. I ain't got the energy left over for that!" On those few occasions when he had tried again —awkwardly, fumblingly, after one of his visits to the girls' dormitory — she had become angry and had spat at him that he was nothing more than an animal. The only time they slept in the same bed now was when Martin was home for his infrequent visits. Martin slept in the other bedroom, Doc's room, then. Doc snored, and Molly had complained that it kept her awake. Molly snored, too, but Doc didn't tell her that either.

He tried not to think about Molly too much any more. It broke Doc's heart that he had had to watch Molly grow old and faded so quickly, the luster of her hair and eyes replaced by a bitter tongue. He could not bear to recall the mere days, the briefest of moments, when they, innocent twenty years olds, had brought their new baby home from the hospital. Molly was still pretty then, not wearied and worn down. She still smiled and laughed; she was as fresh as a morning breeze in the springtime. They were happy, almost delirious: a family, exciting and comfortable and nourishing for each other. At the time Doc had been certain that it was all a tiny glimpse of heaven. And then they found out the facts, the truth about their son.

Doc saw the street in front of the bus station was blocked off, police cars parked diagonally across it. He sat there, trying to figure out what to do, the car idling. Where in the hell was Martin? In the bus station, Doc thought, of course. Then he saw a man with a big camera, a newspaper photographer from the looks of him, being chased by two men, who caught him on the sidewalk next to where Doc was parked. They began to beat him with bicycle chains. They picked up his camera and hurled it to the sidewalk, smashing it.

This was serious business, all right. Doc got out of his car, leaving it right there, very near where he had parked earlier. He watched the two men sprint back toward the bus station. Doc opened the trunk and got a tire iron. He could hear shouting in the distance, a roar, almost like a ball game. He saw Martin's suitcase there in the trunk, and his stomach gripped on him. He thought he might be sick.

He loped down the sidewalk toward the bus station, carrying his tire iron. A policeman stood on the sidewalk just outside the door. He pushed it open for Martin. "Go git em, buddy rubba," he said, grinning. Inside the bus station was chaos, pandemonium. He saw another policeman.

"My son," he yelled to him, "I'm lookin for my son. I got to find him!"

"Little feller? With a red necktie?"

"Yes! Yes!"

The policeman pointed toward the boiling crowd. The screams and shouts were deafening, echoing from the tile floor and the high, rounded ceiling. There were people on the floor. Bicycle chains whistled through the air. There were cries of pain, cries of anger. Doc waded in. "Let me through!" he exclaimed, "I got to find my son!"

"Them folks ain't no kin to you," one of the men said to him, laughing.

"Let me by!" Doc yelled, pushing the man out of the way.

And then Doc was face to face with an elderly Negro man. The man's eyes were wide, his mouth open. He was praying, the words faint, incomprehensible. He looked at Doc but Doc could tell he didn't see him. Doc didn't see Martin anywhere. Panic seized him and a white hot rage filled him to bursting. The intense anger came on so suddenly that it caught Doc by surprise. He forgot momentarily where he was. Then he swung the tire iron and hit the old man on top of his head. He heard the dull thud. He saw the blood begin to spurt as the old man dropped to his knees and then fell sideways to the dirty floor.

He came back to himself with a rush. "My God!" Doc blurted aloud. "My God!" He looked at the old man, motionless on the floor. Someone bumped Doc from behind, then he was jostled from the side. Hot tears sprang to his eyes. He thought surely this was some nightmare and he would awake. But he could smell the bus station, smell the rank of the bathrooms, the stink of sweat and blood.

He tossed the tire iron to the floor. His tears blinded him. He floundered, turning, groping back toward the door to the street. He could not comprehend what he had done, could not even call the old man's face back up in his memory. And yet he could still see his eyes.

He pushed out the door into the hot sunshine. The air revived him. He looked around frantically. There were sirens now, more policemen arriving. Doc turned back toward the bus station, but he was blocked. "Nobody goes in," said a policeman.

"But my . . . my . . ."

"Nobody. Sorry."

Doc staggered off down the sidewalk toward his car. He knew he looked drunk, but the policemen on the street paid no attention to him. His head was splitting with an ache so profound that for a moment he could think of nothing else, not even Martin, not even the old Negro he had hit. He prayed that the old man was not dead. He prayed that Martin was somehow all right.

And then, through the fog that shrouded his head, he saw him. The boy was sitting on the steps of the church near where Doc had left the car. Doc squinted in the afternoon sunlight. Martin sat calmly, peacefully, eating something. When Doc got closer, he recognized it as a Moon Pie. The boy sipped on a Coke; he did not see Doc. He did not even look up when Doc passed. Doc plodded on to the car, feeling the sweat run in cool rivulets down his sides under his shirt.

Martin would be with him forever. Martin would continue to be like a shadow at his elbow, like a shade of himself. His son: waiting expectantly for the simple clue of Doc's next move, for the direction of his most casual and innocent word.

Brother Bobby's Eye

THE EYE, as blue as a clear spring sky, was knocked completely out of his head at a construction site down near Causeyville and then buried in a canning jar in the cemetery behind the Shortleaf Church of God. Brother Bobby Loomis — whose eye it was — was the pastor at the church on Wednesday nights and all day Sundays, and during the week he drove nails for Davis Wayne Construction Company, which was building the Causeyville house. He was a master carpenter who could have worked for any home builder in the area, so good he was. And he was handsome, with long blonde hair that curled around his ears and flirted with the collar of the blue serge suit he wore to preach in, hair just busy and unruly and long enough to give him not just a youthful appearance but a sly hint of decadence.

The people in the congregation did not doubt that he had the Holy Ghost in him. Since he had accepted the call to preach there four years ago, their numbers had more than tripled. Brother Bobby had a high pitched, pinched voice that was more of a shriek, and he and his wife Bonnie often sang duets during the service. He had hired a young crippled fellow from over at the Junior College to paint a mural across the back wall of the church, around the window to the Baptismal pool, that showed in bright primary colors Jesus and John the Baptist standing knee deep in the Jordan River, surrounded by a heavenly choir and rolling green hills into the distance. Jesus, in the mural, looked a lot like Brother Bobby.

But it was his sermons that drew them. He screamed at them about what sinners they were, cajoled them about their behavior and damned them for it. The more he ranted, the more they came. He Baptized new people every Sunday. The church got so big they had to put up a new one, an aluminum butler building right next to the old white frame one, with an exact replica of the original mural. Brother Bobby himself framed in and built the steeple on the metal roof that distinguished the church from the warehouses that lined the road less than half a mile away. Things were going very well.

Until the accident with his eye and all that seemed — with some kind of unaccountable inevitability — to follow. The cause of the accident was the sharp jagged corner of a poorly sawn two by four, slid through the window by one of the other carpenters, that caught him just as he was turning that way, and it neatly gouged his right eye out and flung it across the unfinished boards of the floor, through sawdust and mud from his own boots, and Brother Bobby felt the most searing pain he had ever felt in his life. He did not know at first that his eye was out, only that he had been hit and his head jarred so that his neck and his shoulders spasmed and caused him to buck back against the unpainted wall board. He was momentarily blinded and he bit his tongue so hard that blood flowed from both corners of his mouth and mingled with the blood from his empty eye socket, which looked, to the men who got to him first, deep and empty and black. As though there was nothing in there but darkness and pooling blood.

By then he had passed out and slid to the floor, and they managed to find his eye and put it in an empty ziplock bag that somebody had brought a sandwich in (they had to rinse off streaks of mayonnaise), so that when Bobby went to the hospital emergency room in Alabaster, his eye went with him. The damage to the socket and to the eye itself, the doctors said, was too severe to try to reattach it.

Brother Bobby's first appearance in the pulpit after the accident was marked by an eye patch, royal blue to match his suit, and it gave him a rakish, foreign look. His good eye was so fierce it glowed. He brought the eye that had been knocked out with him in a mason jar full of formaldehyde. He sat it on the lectern so that the blue iris was visible to the back of the church, and everybody there, wall to wall, some folks standing in the back, felt that both blue eyes — the one in the jar and the one still in Brother Bobby's head — were together focused directly on them. They shifted uneasily in their seats and shuffled their feet.

"His eye is on the least of these," Brother Bobby said, in his voice like a sawmill blade, and there was not a sound in the church, not even a cough or a clearing of a throat. Even the children seemed to know that something important was happening. Word had raced through Shortleaf about the accident and Brother Bobby's eye. Everybody all over town whispered that the other carpenters and the nurses in the emergency room had claimed that the eye had been still alive and looking at them. The doctors were going to put it in a red bag and burn it before Bonnie claimed it.

"It's my husband's body," Bonnie had said. "It's the window of a temple."

"It's nothing but tissue now," a doctor, a young man, said. "Nothing but a cluster of cells."

"It's got a shred of his soul in it," Bonnie said.

"Nonsense," said the doctor.

"We're gonna bury it," she said. "Because truth is truth. Bless you."

So they had a grave side service and they buried the eye in the ground behind the church. Brother Bobby preached his own partial burial. The eye sat in its jar on a plank over a freshly dug hole. "Ashes to Ashes," Brother Bobby said, "and dust to dust." He looked around at the gathered crowd. Most of the members of the church had come. It was a Saturday and they were in their work clothes, overalls and jumpers, though some had dressed up in Sunday clothes. "Value your toe or your tongue, your knee or your heart," he said, "because you never know what part of you the Lord will call home, what part he needs. You don't know what part of you is so full of sin that it needs reckoning with the Lord!" His blue eye patch was stiff from washing and ironing. His hair was shining in the sun and Sister Bonnie watched him with feverish eyes. It was as though she alone knew what was happening to him.

"My eye itches," he had said to her last night, after supper.

"Scratch it then," she had replied.

"My eye yonder, in the jar," he said, pointing. The eye jar sat on the kitchen table, awaiting its journey to the graveyard.

"You mean your socket," she said. "I've heard about that. About an arm or a finger, keeps on itchin or hurtin after it's gone."

"No," he said. His good eye seemed glazed over. "That ain't what I mean. I can see through it, through that very eye over yonder. Cloudy, like through the liquid. Through a glass darkly."

The look in his good eye made her shiver. "Don't be woofin me, Bobby," she said.

"As Jesus is my witness," Brother Bobby had said. "I put away from me that which is unclean. The Lord meant for it to be that way. The Lord took my eye. The Lord means for me to put it away from me, to let it go on with Him."

BROTHER BOBBY STOOD beside the grave; he gripped his worn Bible so tightly that his knuckles turned white. "I commend a part of my soul back to the earth," he said. His voice trembled. A cloud was coming up and there was a roll of distant thunder. Everybody in the crowd shivered, at once. He saw Sister Bonnie turn away from the steady level stare of the eye in the jar.

Bonnie had been a majorette at Shortleaf High School ten years ago. She was popular and had been working in the office of the local Piggly Wiggly for several years when Bobby Loomis spotted her for the first time, at a Fourth of July picnic in Orr Park. Somebody, he didn't remember who, had introduced them, and Bobby had held her hand in a warm grip, her hand slightly damp from the heat. Bobby felt his eyes glowing like hot charcoal briquets, and he had said to her, "Praise the Lord!" He had come to town with the construction crew for the new Westinghouse plant over at Calcis.

"Let's break bread together," he had said to her. She had on a WWJD bracelet, and he had on a Promise Keepers T shirt.

"Are you married?" she asked. She pointed to the front of the T shirt.

"I was married," he said. "My ex-wife ran off with the devil. It was a mistake for me." He squeezed her hand. He could see her going limp. "Thank the good Lord she did it," he said. Two weeks later they were married.

"I ain't like her," she said, "for me it's forever."

"Amen," Brother Bobby said.

Brother Bobby had never been so happy and content. Bonnie was like an angel sent to him from Heaven. She was nothing like the first wife who had whored on him. Sometimes Bobby thought that everybody he'd ever loved had betrayed him. His father was but a vague memory who had left home when he was not yet two, and his mother abandoned him to his old grandmother when he was six. The dried up old woman had rarely spoken to him at all, only providing him a cold roof and a sparse table until he was sixteen and able to get away on his on. Bonnie was as pure as spring rain out in the countryside. She was sweeter than the icing on a three day coconut cake. Life with her was bliss.

Until Brother Bobby lost his eye. She changed then. He thought he should never have told her that he could still see out of it, that even after it was there in the ground he could still see through it and he never knew what it was going to focus on next. He would catch her looking at him sideways, the way she might look at a freak in a show. She wouldn't look him directly in his good eye. She wouldn't talk to him. He thought she had become selfish, self centered. He studied on it, tried to figure her out, and he decided she was not really interested in him as a man any longer, because he was maimed, but only as a preacher who could save her soul. She took to gossiping and backbiting. She spat hurtful things as quick as a cat. He thought that having children might save her, might save them both. He loved her so deeply he could not bear the thought of losing her to sin.

"There's somethin vile about you," he said to her when she failed to conceive and the doctors told them it would be difficult for her. He had had to go and give them a sperm sample. He had been irate about spilling his seed on the ground. He saw himself doing that, out of his buried eye, like a dirty picture show, and he hated it.

It had turned out to be something wrong with her tubes. They were twisted and kinked. "Somethin vile that displeases the Lord," he said. He was hurt and disappointed. It was time for him to have a child. A son. He believed that that might set things back right.

"How you know there ain't somethin vile about you?"

"Because the doctor said so. Because I asked the Lord."

"And what did He say?"

"Don't be cheeky with me, woman!" His voice squeaked like an old man. He lost his temper. He slapped her across the face.

"Forgive me, Lord," he said on his knees, tears running down his cheeks.

Brother Bobby tried to get accustomed to not being able to close his other eye, the one in the ground in the cemetery. He prayed for the strength to live with it. Light filled his head day and night. He saw little children turned into pink angels before they had a chance to become people. He saw Jesus often, and heavenly choirs, streams of people moving toward the bright light of heaven. He saw crowds of the lame and the blind, the afflicted, moving lost in desert places. He saw the seven angels carrying the seven bowls full of the seven last plagues, and he heard a voice say, "Behold, I make all things new."

People came from far and wide to see the preacher who had buried his eye. The inside of the church would be stifling with so many people, and Brother Bobby's hair would mat to his head with sweat. Sister Bonnie would sit in the second row. Sometimes she had marks on her face, as though she had been struck by something, and her eyes were red from crying. "I see a sinful world," Brother Bobby squealed, his good eye closed tight. "I see —" And he stopped. The church was quiet, only the rustle of fans. He could not go on. Because what he saw clearly through the eye in the ground was Bonnie, naked in the arms of another man, and he squinted hard enough to see that it was Brent Eversol, one of the other workers on the Wayne construction crew, naked, too, and on top of her. Her face was thrown back, a look of ecstasy in her eyes that were focused right on him.

He opened his good eye and stared at her, there in the second row. She was wearing a white cotton dress. As virginal as Mary. Her face was full of a mute innocence. He could tell by her eyes that her mind was far away, that she was thinking or dreaming of something else, and he knew what it was. And he knew in that moment why she was barren. His heart sank to the bottom of his chest, like a deflated balloon. He raised his arm and pointed to her. "You are a harlot," he said, "as crimson as blood on the snow!" His voice trembled. The fans shushed. "Get thee from me, woman, until you are washed of your sin!"

Bonnie stood up. She walked slowly to the back of the church, looking back at him once, and then went out the door, her shoulders stooped. Nobody moved or said a word. Brother Bobby's body began to shake. He could still see her, now kneeling in front of Brent Eversol, in bright color. His eye socket burned like acid, and now, with his good eye squint shut, he could see them all, the people in his congregation, some of them sitting bone thin on toilets and others doing the most depraved things he had ever seen. He had known they were dirty and sinners, but this was beyond his wildest suspicions. It was an orgy of depravity. Their faces were twisted grotesquely and their naked bodies were pale, some fleshy, some little more than skeletons. It was so awful that not even he could bear it. Without a word he walked down from the pulpit and slowly followed his wife's path up the aisle and out the front door of the church. The people watched him in silence.

Outside the sun split his head in two. He spat on the ground, almost wretching. He shaded his eye and searched the parking lot, but Bonnie was nowhere to be seen. He closed his eye and saw her sitting at home, at the kitchen table, crying.

She began to fade away, to disappear, before his sight. She lost a third of her weight and was so weak she could hardly hold her head up. The doctor gave her all kinds of tests and then sent her to a specialist in Birmingham. Nobody there could identify the condition, and they sent her to the National Institute of Medicine in Bethesda, Maryland, where she stayed two weeks and then came home. Not even the doctors up there could find out what was wrong with her. Brother Bobby knew it was demons. The devil. When he looked at her his mouth was dry. His heart would ache, and tears would spring into his eye. He had loved her and she was not a whole woman — as he was not a whole man — and she was a whore. And God had sent a plague on her.

"Please," she said to him, her eyes like dark pools.

"It ain't me," he said. "You done it to yourself. You done it, not me."

She just sat quietly in a rocking chair for hours, like an old woman. Soon there would be very little she could do for herself. Her eyes pleaded with him.

He brought her into the church, sat her up on the podium with him. "Look," he said, "come up here one by one and look, and see the presence of the devil on this earth!" And they filed by, one by one, old and young, and they looked at her sitting there and crying, the big tears rolling slowly down her raw cheeks. There was nothing anyone could do for her because the devil was in her. The crowds were bigger now, and Bobby had to schedule four services every Sunday. They came from as far away as Atlanta and New Orleans to see Sister Bonnie. "Look and take Jesus into your heart and go and sin no more," he said, "throw the devil out of your heart! Look at what sin can do to you! Look and repent! Look with both your eyes, and see!"

Months passed, and Sister Bonnie sat now with a hollow stare in her wasted eyes. She was as thin as a skeleton. Brother Bobby's heart pained him in the hollow of his chest. He cried when he looked at her.

The women of the church took turns bathing her and feeding her and changing her clothes for her. She sat in the living room of their little house, never speaking, looking at the wall. The women walked lightly, treading softly, preparing meals for Brother Bobby, food that he didn't eat. He had lost weight, too. He had quit his job with the construction company and now held revival meetings at the church several nights a week. He baptized hundreds and hundreds.

Brother Bobby could not sleep. He tossed on the clammy sheets all night long. He continued to see clearly out of the eye, maddening things like the scenery passing by as though he were driving when he was lying dark still in his bed, listening to the soft weeping of his wife in the other room. Or he would see plants in another season, flowering azaleas in the dead of winter, in the snow, or daffodils in the fall. Or the daytime sky, with high puffy clouds drifting across. Or he would see old Mrs. Shaw, who lived across the street, washing her dentures. Mr. Shaw putting up drapes. The inside of a strange house somewhere bursting into flames that roared and darted at him like fingers, or the mangled inside of a car, bloody steel and plastic, still noisy and hot with the collision, dust and vapor floating everywhere. He would smell the acrid smoke, feel the shocks to his body.

Sometimes it was as though the buried eye were looking into a mirror at his own face, searching the emaciation of his cheeks and the emptiness of his good eye. And he continued to see all the sins of his congregation, like some vast writhing image of hell, exhausted and insane. Night after night and all day Sundays he glared at them, shouted at them. "You are full of the vilest sin," he would yell, waving his arms, "unwashed, unclean, dirty with the devil's doings! I see you every one! You have no secrets from me! I know! Repent and repent now! Or you will be lost for eternity! You will burn in hell for all time!"

"Please," Sister Bonnie said to him. That's all she said anymore. That one word. Brother Bobby had stopped eating altogether now, because he saw himself starving to death along with her. Is that it? He thought. Am I seeing into the future?

"You did it," he said to her, "you did it with him, didn't you. Brent. You did, didn't you? Tell me I'm right, that it's true."

"Please," was all she said.

"Of course you did it. You sinned with him. I know that. God is punishing you, and punishing me." He sobbed aloud, his whole body shuddering.

He saw himself dead, in the rain, mud streaked on his face. He saw his dead grandmother sitting looking at him, the rain splattering on her thin gray hair. He went into the bathroom and pulled up the eye patch and looked as deeply as he could into the socket. The skin was stretched, and he could still see the scars left from the stitches, but the socket seemed to go deeply into his head, like the old well behind his grandmother's back porch when he was a child, disappearing down into murky darkness. He had known as a child that that was where hell was. He could see two images. The one in the mirror, and a clear image of himself peering into the mirror, from outside and above, as though his dead eye were not in the grave at all now but drifting about in the corner of the ceiling like a soul before it departs.

APRIL IS A TORNADO MONTH in central Alabama. They form out of vast dark thunderheads that come up out of the west, creeping and spurting eastward, flinging hail sometimes as large as softballs toward the ground, shattering windshields and battering roofs and ripping through trees just leafing out with their incipient springing. The clouds are coal black, as ominous and oppressive as fate itself, and the lightening against the darkness is golden and spectacular. They turn a noon to midnight, a dusk to the dark of the middle earth. When the storms would come, Brother Bobby would never cease to think, "And God shall show forth his handiwork!" The very ground would tremble with the power and majesty of the storms.

It was Palm Sunday morning, and a cluster of thunderstorms formed along a line between Tupelo and Starkville in Mississippi and moved steadily into Alabama, pointed directly toward the center of the state. Tornadoes began to touch down in Fayette County, then in Cullman County, just northwest of Shortleaf. The churches all over were packed, Brother Bobby's Shortleaf Church of God being no exception. They crowded the benches and stood against the walls. The heavens rumbled and the rain began to thunder on the metal roof.

"PRAISE GOD!" Brother Bobby shouted. The PA system crackled with lightening and bounced his voice off the metal walls, which shook against the rain and the hail coming now in almost horizontal sheets. The lights flickered. The windows darkened. Brother Bobby raised his arms to the ceiling. "LORD JESUS!" his voice boomed out. "He will come on the whirlwind! He will come bearing a sword!" The people huddled on the benches, looking around, their eyes beginning to panic. They surged together in groups, as in his vision of them naked and writhing. Miss Willodelle Summers began to pound on the piano keys and ragged voices began to sing along with Brother Bobby, who held the microphone in front of his face. "There's a land that is fairer than day," they sang against the whirling of the wind and the pounding of the rain, "and by faith you can see it afar! Where the master waits over the way . . .to prepare us a dwelling place there!" The building shook. There was a great roar all around them. "In the sweet by and by," they sang, "we will meet on that beautiful shore . . ."

The tornado touched down on the outskirts of Shortleaf and chewed its way up Middle Street, bending trees flat to the ground and exploding houses and sending mobile homes tumbling about like toys. It made the most God-awful sound anyone there had ever heard. It ripped through the row of warehouses along the road toward the Shortleaf Church of God, propelling huge sheets of metal through the air like frisbies, twisting and snapping thick iron beams like matchsticks. It moved itself on north of town, leaving the elementary school a pile of bricks, flattening an area a mile wide and six miles long. Several full churches were totally wiped away, the worshipers — men and women, children and babies — hurled about like bundles of rags. The raging, angry tornado destroyed everything and everyone in its path.

Except the Shortleaf Church of God and all those inside. Just at the end of the hymn the winds began to lessen, the pounding began to cease, and they all looked up in wonder. The storm had passed them over. Brother Bobby stood before them, his arms still extended skyward. Soon outside there was only a spring thunderstorm, rain brushing the roof, the rumbling way in the distance now, and they surged toward the door, crying out, laughing, glancing tentatively at each other in disbelief.

Outside the devastation was total. Everything in every direction was leveled. Except their church. They milled about in the muddy yard, touching each other to make sure, praying and crying because they knew their homes were gone, everything, cars turned over in the parking lot and twisted together like a pile of pretzels. But they were alive. They had been spared. The rain pattered against their upturned faces.

Brother Bobby stood alone on the raised pulpit, his good eye closed tight. His suit sagged on his gaunt body. He saw every house in town, one by one, shaking and imploding as though they had been swept away by a giant hand. He heard the townspeople's cries, felt their pain like sharp shards of glass in his skin. His head pounded. His socket burned like fire. He clearly saw Bonnie, at home, sitting helplessly in her chair, her face cocked to the storm, sitting, waiting, and he saw her dashed against the wall and through it, her body crushed and her head battered into oblivion.

Brother Bobby went out the back door of the church and out to the graveyard. Falling on his knees he began to claw at the ground where his eye was buried. The dirt was still loose and it was soaked and softened, and he pulled away at it until he reached the jar. He pulled it out, letting the rain wash the mud away from the outside. He saw the eye. The eye stared back at him. He shivered. The rain fell steadily on his head.

He looked upward at the roiling clouds overhead, purple now and bruised. He opened the jar and poured the eye out on the ground. Standing, he crushed it beneath the heel of his shoe. A blinding whiteness raged through him, so sudden and powerful that it knocked him to his knees again. He could not see. He was completely blind, and he felt the storm again, heard it raging again. Gradually, then, everything seemed to ebb from his mind and there was only silence around him. He opened his eye.

Bonnie stood before him. She was whole again. She wore the white dress, and she opened her arms out to him, as though to embrace him. She smiled. She turned and walked away from him, moving between the tombstones, almost floating.

Brother Bobby knelt on the wet ground, the rain all around him fading into a fine drizzle. His hands and his suit were smeared with mud, were stained with the dark red earth of his own burying place. He could just barely see Bonnie's white form drifting away, wafting away among the pale monuments. He squinted and strained, leaning forward toward her, trying to follow her with his one good eye. He watched her dissolve and vanish into the gray and gathering mist.

Passin' Side / Suicide

Glory Sanders is a friend of mine. She's a drunk like me, only she calls herself a "grateful recovering alcoholic." She hauls me to the AA meeting in the basement of the Episcopal church over in Talladega every Thursday night, and when she gets up to talk that's what she calls herself. Glory runs the Waters Edge Bait Shop on county road 20. Glory has been around the bases a few times. She's been there and back, as they say.

I'm sittin in the little back room cafe at the Water's Edge, that looks out over the lake. I'm drinking coffee and she's behind the counter, leaning on it, smoking a cigarette. Glory's always telling me to get a job. That's what everybody says to me, get a job. "You need to get a job," she says, "you need to go to a meetin every day, ninety meetins in ninety days." I tell her I ain't the meeting type. They made me swear when I was leaving the treatment center that I'd go to at least three meetings a week. I raised my right hand up and swore to God, knowing right then I wasn't going to do it. No way. But I figured they wouldn't let me out if I didn't say it.

"When you going to — " Glory begins. She's leaning on the counter.

"Don't start," I say.

"Jesus, Robert," she says, "I'm just tryin to . . ."

She don't finish. She calls me Robert. She knows I don't like for people to call me Bob, but she always used to call me Bob before I went to treatment. Now she calls me Robert. Glory was there the night the cops took me in, after that fight at the Silver Moon Cafe. She goes around with the cops on Saturday nights, looking for drunks she can save.

"I'm a honorary deputy," she says, "on a mission of mercy." They put me in the county jail and then took me to a psycho ward on the top floor of Brookwood Hospital in the city. The windows had bars on them. After a few days they gave me a choice: thirty days in jail or thirty days at a treatment center out in Warrior. I thought it was a no-brainer.

Glory was waiting for me when I got out. "I'm your sponsor," she said.

"Like hell you are," I said.

There's a television in the café. Me and Glory are watching So You Want to be a Millionaire. Half way through the program she says, "These people are dumb."

"Dumb as a post," I say.

Glory is looking at me funny. "What are you, forty- four? Forty-five? What?"

"You got it right," I say.

"What?"

"Both."

She looks at me like that explains something to her. She turns back to the TV set. I have two birth certificates. I guess I'm two different people. One of them says I was born on April 9, 1956. On that one my mother's name is Annabelle Pleasants, and the father is listed as "unknown." I am Robert Pleasants. On the other one, dated April 6, 1955, my mother's name is Annabelle P. Fosque, and the father is Ralph Foscue. On that one my name is listed as Robert Foscue. "We was never married," my mother told me. "It was the fifties, you had to do that." "Do what?" I asked. I was about ten years old at the time she talked to me about it. "You know," she said. I didn't know. But I didn't say anything. "He was a real bastard," she said, "you're better off not ever knowing him."

"I don't give a shit," I said, and lit up a Camel. I kept them rolled in the sleeve of my white T shirt.

I have always gone by the name of Robert Pleasants. It has never made two hoots in hell to me that I've got two birth certificates, two names.

"Shit," Glory says, her eyes on the screen, "the next time I see forty-five it'll be a hunnert and forty-five!"

If you ain't a drunk, you don't know what the Big Book is. Unless you're married to a drunk, I guess, or living with one. It tells you all you need to know about recovery. It's the AA Bible. It lays out the twelve steps for you, right there. Glory keeps after me, and I'm on step nine. Sometimes I do them half-ass, but I try to do them. "Seek out those people you've hurt with your drinking and make amends to em," Glory says. "Just one'll do. It'd take you the rest of your life to find em all. Just one. Find em and . . ."

". . . and what?"

"Say you're sorry. Ask em to forgive you," she says. "It ain't easy."

"Shit," I say.

I think about Jolene. She would have to be the one, I guess. She was too young for me from the start, but she was something wonderful I just couldn't let alone. I could tell her mother thought I was trash. She didn't like me from go. They lived in a little white-washed frame house over on the other side of Pachuta, near Bay Springs. Jolene worked at the Ritz Twin Theater in Pachuta, selling tickets. I thought I might like to spend the rest of my life with Jolene, and when I thought that it scared the hell out of me. She would get off at eleven and we'd drive out to the quarry in my pickup and spread a quilt and make love under the moon. She was sweet as the inside of a ripe pineapple. Salty and juicy as a plum in June. She was not even yet twenty, but she was wise. She knew what she was doing.

"Why you come sniffin round me, old man?" she would say, running her fingers over my bald head, giggling. I'd root like an old hog, and she'd squeal like a piglet. Lordy. I get horny just thinking about it.

"We thought you was in jail," Jolene's mother says, when she finally gets to the door. The front yard has old tires painted white half buried in the dirt on both sides of the front walkway. There's one of these old bottle trees in the front yard. I knock and knock. When she opens the door she just stands there looking at me. Her name is Sheila. Her expression don't change at all. Her eyes droop like wilted blossoms. She's got on a pair of red shorts and a T shirt that says SHUT UP AND PITCH. She props herself against the door jam with one arm. She's got her other hand on her hip, the fingers of that hand holding a long thin cigarette with a little string of smoke rising straight up like the thing is hanging from the ceiling. Just stands there, like that, until all she says is, "We thought you was in jail."

"Nope," I say. "Jolene here?"

She don't say anything, but her lip curls down. She looks tired enough to've been digging ditches. She's skinny as a preacher bug but she's got this little belly, like half a soccer ball. It looks like it don't belong on her, like she borrowed it from some fat person. She's a lot closer to my age than Jolene is.

The living room smells like cigarette smoke and used up butane. It smells like cooking grease and dust. One great big old vinyl recliner. One of those console televisions that you don't ever see any more, that sits on the floor. There used to be a sofa with an old blanket thrown over it, but it's gone. I could smell coffee. These folks drink a lot of coffee, I remember.

"She ain't here," she says, after she's already motioned me in.

"Where's she at?"

"She's gone."

I look off out the side window. There are two lawn chairs out there, with the yellow and white webbing faded and broke and hanging down. There is a Snapper lawn mower and a charcoal grill, both gathering rust. I see clumps of crabgrass in the yard. I remember then how the grass smells when the sun's been on it a while. How the sun makes you smell the dirt, the earth. Ever since I got out of treatment I think about things like that.

"I ain't got no significant other," I told my counselor, when I was in the treatment center. His name is John Berry. He's a drunk, too, sixteen years sober. They want me to invite somebody to come for family week. They tell me I need to.

"You must have somebody," John says.

"No. You got the information right there." I point to this clipboard he's drumming his fingers on on his desk. It's the long form I filled out when they first admitted me. He holds a ball point pen in the fingers of his other hand. They are delicate and slim, like a woman's. He's all man, though, a wiry son-of-a-bitch. He don't let you get away with nothing. You can't shit him. I have tried, the whole time I've been here. "Mother dead. No sisters and brothers," I say.

"What about your father?"

I laugh. I have told them every story in the book about my father. I told them he was a black man, working in my mother's yard. I told them he was a Gypsy, passing through. That he was this rich doctor in Mountain Brook. That he played ball for the Yankees. I passed the time thinking up shit to tell them about my father. I told my therapy group my father was George Wallace. Half of them believed me. They had burned up so many brain cells they'd believe anything.

"Okay," he says. "But there must be somebody." I think of Jolene. It's been about a year then since I've seen her. I sit there seeing her in my mind's eye. She ain't what you'd call a knockout, but she's a pretty thing. Her mouth is too big. Her eyes are too close together. But she's got great hair, and legs. She's got legs so great they're prettier than eight miles of new road. You never saw better legs than Jolene's got. What got me, though, was how she always knew what I was thinking, and it made her laugh. She would look at me — she has these really black eyes, like marbles — and I would be thinking of something funny to say and she'd be already laughing. Like that.

"No," I say, "there ain't nobody. Period."

"Okay," he says.

"You got yourself a loner here, John-boy," I say. "I can take care of myself."

"Yeah," he says, "right."

Me and Jolene were easy together. We could just sit for a long time without even talking. "You're old enough to be her father," her mother said to me. "So?" I said, and Sheila cut her eyes at me. Her droop-tired eyes. Jolene's daddy is a welder, works at TCI in Birmingham. Him and me used to drink beer together. We'd smoke some weed, visit the craps game down at Zorba's corner. Named Sid, and he's restless as I am. He works all the time, ain't hardly ever at home. "I ain't never thought of myself as old," I said to her, "as old enough to be anything."

"Jolene wants a life, a family," she said.

"I ain't standin in her way, am I?" I said.

She told Jolene I'm a sorry one. Jolene laughs about it. She puts her hand on my arm and holds it there, leaves it there. She just looks at me. Her eyes smile at me.

I am at the Silver Moon Café, a few months before the night of the fight that got me sent up to treatment. They call it a café because you can get a hamburger or a platter of greasy fried catfish and hushpuppies, but it's mostly a night club and dance hall. It's got big plate glass windows overlooking the lake. It's got a long bar against one wall and a bandstand and a dance floor. Country bands play here, nobody you ever heard of, and it's always packed to the gills, specially on Friday and Saturday nights. These cowboys and their women come out from Birmingham, and good old boys from out in the county wearing their Caterpillar hats and great big silver BAMA belt buckles. College kids come out here sometimes, looking for trouble. Or for women. Same thing.

I'm flying high. Soaked to the ears. This woman, Jesse, is here. She's got eyes so green it sets your teeth on edge just to look at them, married to a mechanic at one of the shops over in Talladega. Her jeans been painted on and she wears cowboy boots and a little frilly white blouse. You can see her nipples from here. I've danced with her before. It seems like the whole world is loud and drunk and high and happy. The band tonight is called Naked as a Jaybird, and they play all these great old Eagles songs.

I sit and drink my beer and stare at Jesse, until she starts to stare back. I can see those green eyes glowing through the smoke. I don't see her husband. She's with these two women I've seen here before, both about forty, at least ten years older than she is. The three of them get up and dance together, and Jesse keeps looking over at me. I'm breathing smoke and beer vapor, and the band is whacking out on "Take it Easy." Overhead lights spin. Beer signs make these melting drops of colors on the wall across the room. It feels and looks good. Just right.

I'm glad I'm here. This is the one place I'm supposed to be, right now, in the whole world. I'm just about to go over when somebody grabs my arm from behind. I turn around and it's Jolene. She's smiling, happy. Laughing. She's got a long-neck Rolling Rock in her hand, waving it in time to the music.

I think: What are you doin? Checkin up on me! I say, "What the hell are you doin here?!" I'm thinking, She thinks she owns me. Just let a woman . . . just let a woman . . .

I say it real ugly like. "Well? You don't own me, woman," I say.

The grin just disappears from her face, falls away like a lightbulb blowing out.

"I'm sorry," I say, "I don't know you." I say it hard and nasty. "I was just fixin to dance with somebody," and I walk off and leave her standing there. As I walk over to Jesse, I can still see Jolene's eyes, the way they looked. They are like a little child's that you've disappointed, let down. Jesse sees me coming and stands up. Her body looks fluid, like I would drown in it. I look back and Jolene is gone.

That was the last time I saw her. I think about them eyes now, full of all that hurt, standing here in the living room with her mother. "Well," I say, "you gone tell me where she is, or what?"

"She don't want to see you," she says.

"Now how do you know that?"

"I just do," she says. She's tapping a filter tip cigarette against her thumbnail. "You want some coffee or somethin?"

"Black," I say. When she goes to get it I stand there smelling her cigarette smoke. I can taste it in my throat, scalding and spicy, the warm way it swells out your chest. I gave them up. When I got out I just threw my pack in the Coosa River. I figured without booze, I didn't want cigarettes. I want one now, but I won't ask her for one. I'm tense, tight like the skin of a drum.

Sheila brings me my coffee in a blue mug. There is a picture of Jolene on the table in the corner, in her high school cap and gown, that tassle thing hanging down beside her face. She is smiling her easy smile. It's as natural as a breeze, that smile. I realize I ain't seen Sid in months. The house has a feel like he ain't in it anymore. I don't ask.

"I want to tell her I'm sorry," I say. I blow on my coffee, sip it.

"Ha!" she says, "I already told her that." She don't look at me. She sits down in the vinyl recliner. When she brings her cigarette up to her lips I can see her hand trembling. She shakes her head. I can see where her hair is parted on the top, ragged, like when she combed it she was in a hurry. "Sorry is as sorry does," she says.

"I'm serious," I say.

"You think I ain't?" She looks up at me. She's got tears standing in her eyes, and I can see she's really pissed at me. She's really upset. She looks at me like she hates me. "You come in here . . . you come in here . . ." she mumbles. Her shoulders slump, just collapse and fall. "I have made my peace, and then you . . ." She drags on the cigarette and sucks the smoke deep, then blows it out like spitting.

"She's dead," she says then. I don't hear her for a moment. The word goes right by me. Then it comes back around and hits me in the back of the head. My knees go weak.

"What?" I say.

"You heard me," she says, her voice rising to a shriek, "she's dead! Dead! You want me to spell the word for you?" She stands up and turns her back on me. I can't move. I just stand there holding the mug, and I have forgot how to move my arms. I don't know what to say. I don't know what to feel. I think she must be lying to me. I can see the bones in her shoulders, under the thin cloth of the T shirt. I know she ain't lying to me. My mouth goes dry.

"What . . . what . . . ?" I manage to say. She don't answer. I find my voice, but it sounds hollow in my ears, like an echo. "A car wreck, or what?" I say.

"No," she says. "She was pregnant." She turns back around to face me. "She was pregnant, with your child, and she —"

"Wait a minute," I say, "wait a minute now —"

"With your goddam baby, and she wouldn't . . . she wouldn't . . ." It feels like the floor moves under my feet, like I'm gone fall, right there. "I tried to get her to have an abortion. I tried to talk to her, make her get rid of it, but no. No! She wouldn't listen to me. 'I'm gonna have it,' she says. 'I want this baby,' she says." She is just looking at me now, her eyes narrow slits. I can see tear tracks down her cheeks. She breathes real deep. I'm just hanging there, like in midair. I can't take it in. She looks like she wants to say something else. I can see her brain working behind her eyes. It's like I'm watching a television show or a movie. A long ash falls off her cigarette and she notices it and grinds the butt out in a glass ashtray that's already full. She starts tapping another on her thumbnail.

She takes another deep breath, then another. When she starts talking, her voice sounds calmer, but still tight and dry. "She was staying with my sister out in Center Point," she says. "She got a better job working at Rich's in Century Plaza Mall. Everything was fine, she said. She would come out here and I never saw her so happy. I kept tellin her she didn't know what she was gettin into. She didn't care. 'Don't worry Mama,' she'd say, 'I'm happy.' She said she wanted to be a single mother, was lookin forward to it. Then somethin happened. One day she started bleedin. She was eight months along, and they figured the baby was coming early, so they took her to the hospital. Took her to Medical Center East. Somethin was bad wrong. The doctors said the baby was dead. They had to operate on her to get it out."

She stops. I can feel my heart beating in my ears. "What happened?" I ask. My mouth has gone completely dry.

"Somethin went wrong with the anesthetic," she says. She opens her eyes wide. She looks at me like I'm pond scum. "She had a reaction to it. She had these convulsions. . . . She . . .went into a coma. She never woke up," she says. "And then she died. And I never got to say goodbye to my baby. You son-of-a-bitch. I didn't get to even say goodbye to her, and she was all I had, all I ever had."

I don't say anything. I don't think there is anything to say. There is nothing I can dredge up from inside me that would matter at all. She starts to cry, then, just stands there sobbing, and I can see her pale eyes go all opaque, like she's not seeing me any more at all, like she's totally all alone in the room, in the world.

I drive around. There is a lump of cold in my chest. I get on the expressway and drive all the way to the Georgia line, to Tallapoosa, then turn around and come back. Something is burning and smoldering in the back of my brain. I see five thousand billboards advertising whiskey and beer. Every one is like a mouth full that I can taste, and I swallow, and it's only air. I play the radio, but I don't hear it. It's like I keep dozing off from time to time, and I worry that I'll drive off a bridge.

Like I jerk back awake and I'm surprised that I'm driving down the road because I've been dreaming. I've been with Jolene, smelling her skin, smelling the soap she used to use. Shampoo that made her hair smell like fresh berries. Then I just feel her there next to me in the truck, sliding over, fitting herself around the gear shift lever, getting close. She's warm. Comfortable and quiet. I miss her now, something terrible.

It gets dark and I'm on the back roads, all the way up in St. Clair County, and I just keep driving. I can't think of anywhere I want to go. And I can't think of any reason to go home. Then I'm on County Road 20, and I can see lightening bugs twinkling like stars between me and the lake. I have shut the radio off long ago, and I pull off and shut the engine, and all I can hear are the crickets and the tree frogs, and off in the distance the deeper burping of bullfrogs at the edge of the water. There's no moon, and the night is dark as pitch.

I try to cry. Grief for Jolene burns the back of my eyes like acid. But the tears won't come. I feel dry as sand. Grief for that child. Our child. I remember the look in her eyes that night at the Silver Moon. That look is burned into my mind. I know I can't ever forget it. If I have Jolene in my memory, I have to have that look, too. Those eyes. And Sheila, too. I see the shiny tear paths on her face. I see the hatred in her eyes.

I don't know how long I sit there alongside the road. I start the truck and drive on. I feel drained of strength, like coming off a ten day binge. I see the neon sign for the Silver Moon up ahead. The clock on the dash says it's a little after midnight and the parking lot is full. I park half in the ditch and get out. I can hear the music, distant, the stomping of feet and laughter, and the bullfrogs, coming from somewhere a long way away from where I am.

I'm walking toward the front door. The crowded parking lot is dank-hot, smelling like sweat and tar and motor oil. Then I see them, these motorcycles, seven of them, pulled up in a row, gleaming black and silver in the dim neon light from the sign. There are four Harleys, two BMWs and a Triumph. It's a motorcycle gang from Woodlawn, in Birmingham. I've seen them before. They've been out here before, with their tough-mouth women and their tattoos and their leather pants. They wear curly beards. They're mean, real bad-asses. They carry knives.

In the pale light I'm looking at the first hog in the line. It must be the leader's. It's an expensive BMW that gleams like a freshly dug lump of coal. It's got silver side mirrors and rhinestone studs lining the seat. It's got these two little signs hanging on each side of the back fender, so anybody coming up from behind could read them. The one on the left says "PASSIN' SIDE." The one on the right says "SUICIDE." Cute. I stand there looking at the little signs.

I go back to my truck in the dark and find my sawed-off pool cue under the seat. Three feet of heavy, slick polished wood. A carved handle so you can grip it. I go back to where the hogs are parked. I swing my stick and knock the little signs off into the weeds. Then I start in on the first windshield. I swing as hard as I can and the glass is like iron. Then it smudges. Then it shatters some. I keep flailing away. I lose my breath, but I'm banging and chopping. My pool cue splinters in my hand, comes apart, and I fling it into the ditch and go back and get a tire iron from the toolbox behind the cab.

Then I really go to work on them bikes. Glass and metal flies. I move from windshield to windshield, knocking off mirrors, too. I hear someone say, "Hey," from the doorway of the café, "Hey, what the . . .?"

I'm like a maniac. I'm blind with my own sweat. I'm swinging away like crazy and the sound of the tire iron on glass and metal is like explosions in my ears. I can see the glass from the windshields spraying like bits of ice, and for some reason this strikes me as funny, and I start in to laughing. I can't help it, I'm laughing fit to kill, and all of a sudden I'm crying, too, and I don't know if these sounds I'm making, these gulps and sobs and carrying on, are laughing or crying or both or what. I'm flailing away and I must be making one hell of a racket, what with the tire iron on the bikes and these sounds coming out of me, and I can't catch my breath and I have to stop from time to time to heave and struggle and try to inhale. I keep on, my whole body getting numb and cramped.

And all the time I'm laughing and carrying on, howling like a crazy hyena. My arms are heavy under the numbness, but they keep moving, gripping the tire iron with both hands, and I'm ruining the hogs, really trashing them, and I see but never hear the old boys come boiling out of the door, all of them, all on me at the same time.

Walking Strawberry

HARRY'S BRUSHSTROKE IS strong, the paint clotting and thick, much bolder than it had been when he was a young man. His model's name is Annie. She is twenty five years old, and her face is as cold and precise as a stone angel's, and as enchanting. Her eyes, pale blue, are expressionless. Her naked body is like a burnished statue. He sees her exposed curves and angles and pores and flesh and hair and he sees through the parts, too, beyond them, and he lets his eyes caress her. He squints at her. He feels her in his fingers as he paints, warm and alive.

* * *

"IT WAS A terrible series," Harry says. He sits at the bar in the Grayton Beach Saloon, his gnarled fingers curled around his beer glass. The afternoon sun is muted by the dusty windows. The old mahogani of the bar, in the soft light from frosted globes behind it, glows as though lit from within. Duane, the young man keeping the bar, nods in agreement. He has a pony tail. He is heavyset, in his twenties. It's just after three o'clock on an October afternoon, still hot, and Duane wears a short sleeved white shirt. Harry is the only customer in the place.

"Not worth watchin," Duane says.

"You know when it completely turned? When it went down the tubes? When Maddox walked Strawberry, in the second inning of the second game. That was the end. After that, there was no way."

"Naw," Duane says.

"No, really. I was sittin there watchin, and when it happened I told Helen, 'that's it.'" There is green oil paint under Harry's fingernails. His fingers are long, his knuckles swollen and bony. Arthritis has changed the shape of his hands over the last few years. His hair is completely white, his beard still rust red and sprinkled with gray. His hair looks sleep matted, off center and mussed. He wears faded jeans and a dark blue Duck's Head work shirt, both speckled with paint, and he stares at his glass of beer for a long, silent moment. A bubble escapes the bottom and rises slowly to the top as he watches it, curious and concentrating, his brow furrowed. "'That's it,' is what I said," he says softly.

"Naw," Duane says again. "They coulda come back."

It is as though Harry does not hear him. Then he looks up. He blinks. He smiles. "The die was cast, so to speak," Harry says. "There is a moment when what you do—and maybe even more important what you don't do—when it changes everything. Just one little tiny moment. It changes everything that follows. You know it when it happens, and you know nothing will ever be the same after that. Greg Maddox knew it. Did you see him slap his glove on his thigh and whirl around and look into the outfield? He knew, in that one crystallized moment, that the Braves has lost the series, and it was forever, and the chance to change it would never come again."

"Naw," Duane says, "it ain't over till it's over."

The air in the bar is full of decades of cigarette smoke, exactly the way the imprisoned and suspended air in an old stone church cleaves to its ancient incense.

"I TOLD HER I hadn't seen my nipples in twenty years," he hears Helen say. She is talking on the phone to her best friend Mylene. They are talking about a mutual friend who has had a breast reduction and lift. Mylene is a novelist, now married to a fourth husband, this one seventeen years her junior. Years ago Mylene and Helen and Harry had lived together for several years. In their own minds they had been married. Helen refers to Mylene as "my ex-wife." They had all shared a bed and they had been young and uncomplicated. Mylene and Helen are both as dark and lean as gypsies. And as mysterious and elusive. He has been married to Helen for forty years. He knows everything about her. And he knows nothing about her.

Harry shuffles on through the house, out to his studio. Annie sits on a folding chair, looking out to the gulf.

"There were dolphins this morning," he says. She shrugs. She stands and begins to undress. She wears tight jeans and an Octowanna Junior College sweatshirt. She wears no bra and her small breasts swing free. He looks at her nipples. They are pink, the size of dimes. Her pubis is golden. She lives in Grayton Beach with her divorced mother. Her father is a shrimp boat captain in Destin.

"Turn a little sideways," he says when she is seated, stretched out. She is as pliable as clay. "Right," he says, "just like that." She knows what he wants, immediately and exactly. She picks up an orange on the low table in front of her, looks at it, replaces it. Her face settles into her familiar remoteness, and then she is still. He imagines that she daydreams when he paints. That she fantasizes. But he does not ask her.

He uses a big brush, its handle thick and comfortable in his hand. He uses a trowel as his palette knife. His canvas is large. It is heavy with paint.

Harry walks along the beach. The sand is blindingly white, even in the setting sun. The tide is coming in now, so Harry's bare feet are occasionally dashed with foam. His jeans are wet below the knees. The sound of the waves will be its loudest when the tide is high. They can hear it all night from their bedroom, through the screens, crashing and roiling and receding. "I couldn't sleep now without that," Helen says. Seven years now they have lived here. Harry never wants to leave. The light is pure here, as pure as in Provence. He has never seen colors quite like these.

He stands looking out over the water, at its changing shades of green and azure; it is emerald and pale lime. It is a blue so deep he cannot tell where the underlying black begins. Streaks of orange and yellow erupt from behind a low ridge of gray clouds near the horizon, and he can see the red sun behind them, pasted there like a hot wax seal against the bleached sky.

He stands for a long time gazing at the sunset. He is having a hard time finishing the painting. He has been sketching with charcoal. He has done at least fifty sketches, and Annie does not notice when he begins sketching instead of painting. She is absorbed in being what she is, the figure in the painting. She had said one morning, suddenly and with no preamble at all, no warning to Harry: "If I think on it hard enough, I can feel what it would be like to be the girl in the picture, hanging on the wall. In the museum or the gallery or whatever. With people looking at her. At me. I mean…I become her. I am her." She had smiled. One of her front teeth was slightly crooked. Her voice was clear and startling in the quiet of the studio. He stopped painting. He stood there motionless, his brush poised in midair. She resumed her pose, now oblivious to him again.

Something had changed. Something vague and unsettling, but as palpable as a sudden change in the temperature of the air. Since then he had been sketching in charcoal.

He could not finish the painting.

HELEN PREPARES HAMBURGS with thick slices of Vermont cheddar. It makes him think of their Vermont years, their house outside Bennington. He had known Pollock in the early years; he remembers the day of his death. Harry was a young teacher then, his studio on the edge of campus, near the sheer drop off the students called "The End of The World." He and Helen had known Frost and Kay Morrison in the early years. Later the Berrigans had sat around their fireplace with them and their friends, drinking their wine and smoking their dope, the heat of all their excited voices jumping and dancing like the flames on the logs. He recalls long Vermont August days that were cooler than northern Florida October days like these.

Helen sits across from him. He watches her chew and swallow, her eyes focused on the blue tile wall across from her. He can see that her mind is distant and he wonders what she is thinking of. She had designed the house herself and their kitchen is modeled on the kitchen in Monet's house in Giverny, full of sunlight and shades of blue and stark, clean whites, with an antique wood stove rebuilt for gas. She likes the bright kitchen, though she does not cook much any more. She sits in there and reads much of the day. Her face is like an abstract refinement of what it had been as a girl, when he had first known her. There are fine lines around the corners of her mouth and eyes, like the tiny cracks in good marble, and she still wears her hair long and parted in the middle though it is now dusted with gray.

Mylene had told her the style was too "kittenish" for her. For a woman her age.

"I don't care," she had said. "It's me. Besides, 'kittenish?' I'm not married to a child."

Mylene had laughed. Even the sound of her laughter was coarsened, like her voice, by years of cigarettes and whiskey.

Helen's eyes are dark, olive brown. They are sharp and alive, not at all the eyes of a woman approaching seventy. Her body is still slim. She has gained only a little weight, in the hips and breasts. He had observed her earlier that morning as she stepped from the shower. She had been his model once, long ago. Her breasts now sag just slightly, barely discernable bulges on the undersides. Her nipples are almost black, large and still ripe. She exaggerates to Mylene and to the woman who has had her breasts reduced. It is like Helen to be that self-deprecating.

She had come in response to his ad in The Village Voice, in New York. Almost a half century ago and he could still see her as clearly as now, bathed in sunlight, standing in the doorway of his walk-up on Bank Street, just off Hudson. She had worn a black turtle neck sweater, a long, wrinkled khaki skirt. She had been barefoot, a bracelet of colored beads around one ankle. Her hair was dirty. She had bathed in his old claw foot tub before posing, as lovely and innocent as a new flower.

Her body has mellowed, has grown worn and smooth with age. Their lovemaking is less frequent now, but it is still fiery and lustful. It is intense. It is open and free. Even more so, he thinks, than it has always been. There are just the two of them, together in the weathered house in the dunes. And Annie, the girl in the painting.

"How's the painting coming?" she asks him suddenly. "The big canvas of the girl?"

He looks up from his plate.

"Fine," he says, "great."

* * *

"Tell em your theory," Duane says. "Tell em why the Braves lost the series."

A couple, Ann and Nathan Palmer, sit at the bar. They are in their thirties and both teach English at the junior college. They are drinking gin and tonics.

"It was Maddox walking Strawberry in the second inning of game two," Harry says. Ann and Nathan look at him as though he has made some divine pronouncement, but Sam Mike Sullivan, the fourth person in the group of afternoon drinkers, says,

"Bullshit." He grins. The high sun is brilliant against the broad, freshly washed plate glass window at the front. Inside, the bar is dark and cool. The air feels damp to the skin.

Harry knows that both reactions have more to do with who he is than with what he has said. Everyone knows Harry Whitaker, the famous artist, on sight. Tourists point him out on the street. His paintings hang in museums and galleries all over the world. They hang everywhere, even in the White House. The Palmers are in awe of him, and so is Sullivan, but his way of responding is to challenge Harry, all the while winking and smiling. He pushes his light green golfing cap to the back of his head and tosses back a shot of Jack Daniels, then sips his beer. "Ahhhhh," he says. He pushes the empty shot glass toward Duane and nods.

"No, really," Duane says, "it makes sense."

"Come on," Sam Mike says. "You sayin that just one walk...come on."

"Yep," Harry says, "that walk was the sound of the fat lady singing." They all laugh. He sips his beer, his mind wandering to Annie, her thighs like butter. Her bare skin is warm to his touch. He wants the heat to enter his hand, wants it to be transferred to his brush. She sighs and her breathing quickens. "Maddox was trying to be too fine, and he knew it," he says to them. "He knew he should have grooved it. Of course Strawberry could have launched it into the seats. Or he could have flied out, popped up. Or struck out. Or hit into a double play. There were all those possibilities. Figure the odds. But ball four. That is irrevocable. No defense against that. Final. Kaput. Done."

"A lot of other things happened in that game," Sam Mike says. He is a retired stock broker. His face is red, and he is still sweating from being outside. He is still sweating from his morning golf game. He frowns.

"Of course," Harry says. "You are correct. But that was the defining moment. Maybe there were others. I don't think so, though." He slides his empty pilsner glass toward Duane, who deposits it into the sink behind the bar. He takes another glass from the freezer, frosty with a thin sheen of ice, and fills it slowly and carefully from the tap.

"I think you're right," Ann Palmer says, nodding. She turns to her husband. "I think he's right," she says.

"Thank you, mam," Harry says. He grins. His teeth, in his beard, are very white in the dimness of the saloon. "Think about it for a moment," he says. They all lean forward. "During that one split second, when ball four drifted outside, just think how many lives were changed. How many lives would never, ever, be the same again."

There is a long silence. There is the muffled sound of a car passing on the street. Harry says, his voice low and modulated, "You only have one chance in those moments." Harry sips his beer. The others sit quietly, staring at him.

"Well..." Sam Mike says. He scratches his gray widow's peak with his middle finger. He tries to laugh. He tries to smile, but what Harry has said forces his face down into a frown.

"That's the way it is. For all of us," Harry says.

Ann and Nathan Palmer nod in unison. Sam Mike Sullivan squints at his empty shot glass. Harry can see the tension in the man's neck, the rigid way his head is locked. He is angry. He will not look up, will not look at anybody. It is as though Harry has pronounced a death sentence over him.

She has a smell. A scent. It is there among the oils, the turpentine. The only sounds in the cluttered studio are the scratching of the charcoal on the rough paper and the distant murmur of the surf. She moves her legs. She looks up at the skylight. He sees her eyes swing upward, as though in some mysterious yearning. That's it, he thinks, that is the right expression. That is what I want. The light is wrong: the day is cloudy and gray, and there are stray drops of fine rain scattered on the glass of the skylight.

He smells her. He can taste her. He feels a youthful prickling, the beginnings of an erection. He puts down the sketch pad and picks up a brush. He squeezes several large tubes, one by one, then mixes on the palette using the brush. She stares off into the space beyond the skylight. She is gone. She is already the woman in his painting.

* * *

Helen looks up from her book. He stands in the doorway, saying nothing. Helen stares at him. He sees a soft accusation in her eyes, a question. Then he sees an acknowledgment, an acquiescence. Her eyes glow warmly, ignited and full. She nods. The novel is closed on her finger. The room is empty of sound. The surf is too far away to be heard back here.

"Did you finish it?" she asks. She smiles. She pulls her hand away and lets the book close. She rises.

He stands there for a long time looking at her. She wears a black T shirt and wrinkled khaki shorts.

"Yes," he answers, "Yes. I did."

photo: Loretta Cobb

William Cobb was for thirteen years Writer-in-Residence at The University of Montevallo before he retired to write full time. He has published six critically acclaimed novels: *Coming of Age at the Y, The Hermit King, A Walk Through Fire, Harry Reunited, A Spring of Souls, Wings of Morning*, and a collection of short stories, *Somewhere In All This Green,* which won the Alabama Library Association Fiction Book of the Year Award in 2000. Cobb has also written for the stage; three of his plays, *Sunday's Child, A Place of Springs,* and *Early Rains* were produced Off-Broadway in New York. He has held writing fellowships from The National Endowment for the Arts and the Alabama State Council on the Arts. He lives in Montevallo, Alabama, with his wife, Loretta, a short story writer.

Bert Hitchcock is a long-time faculty member at Auburn University, where he is now Hargis Professor of American Literature. With co-editor Margaret Kouidis he is presently at work on a new, eighth edition of *American Short Stories*, a Longman/Pearson anthology.